Praise for *Leaving Kent State*

"LEAVING KENT STATE does what excellent historical fiction is supposed to do--it breathes life into an era. Through the eyes of its young protagonist, this well-researched novel recreates the tensions in Kent, Ohio, during the Vietnam War years and the tragedy that resulted. Readers will love Sabrina Fedel's masterfully drawn characters, her compelling plot, and her rich prose. This is the debut novel of a sensitive and accomplished writer."

—Patricia Harrison Easton, author of Beverly Cleary
Children's Choice Award winner *Davey's Blue-Eyed Frog*

"A poignant and gripping tale of a young girl's love for a Vietnam Vet played out against state-side resistance to an immoral war. The ensuing violence on a college campus is conveyed with stunning historical accuracy."

—Pat Lowery Collins, acclaimed author
of *The Fattening Hut* and *Hidden Voices*

For Rita Tedesco Fedel for being my home

And for Flossey, Teo, and Aleks

for making me yours

Sabrina Fedel

Harvard Square Editions
New York
2016

ISBN 978-1-941861-24-0
Printed in the United States of America

Published in the United States by
Harvard Square Editions
www.harvardsquareeditions.org

THE OCTOBER SUN is never honest in Northeastern Ohio. Waiting on my front steps for Evan it felt warm enough, a splash of Indian summer roosting like a promise, hiding the winter that was barreling toward us. I scanned the corner for the sight of his dad's brown Chevy Impala. Yellow maple leaves fell from the sky like random pieces of rusty confetti, and Evan would laugh when I told him it was his own ticker tape parade. Somehwere down the street, a grill burned its husky charcoal smell.

I had pictured his homecoming so many times in my head. He'd smile in that way he had, as if he'd just been blessed by the God of the Stars. He'd jump out of the car and hug me and call me Rachel. He wouldn't call me Bug. Not after twenty-three months away. He wouldn't call me Bug anymore.

His crimson electric guitar sat in its case beside me, polished and in perfect condition. While he'd been gone I had learned to play his favorite Beatles' song, *Revolution*. Today was a revolution. Evan would know how to talk my dad into letting me go to Pratt.

Evan could talk my dad into anything. Maybe because my dad had always wanted a boy. Maybe because Evan had a way of talking so that you didn't even know he was asking for anything. Maybe because he was more like a member of our family than the boy next door. Evan would know how to make my dad see that having a parent who was a professor at Kent State didn't automatically make it my destiny, too. Evan would make my dad understand that I belonged at Pratt, and that I needed to go someplace where my art mattered.

KSU barely had an art department, something my dad was perfectly fine with, because he wasn't happy with me being an artist in the first place.

When we found out that Evan was being sent home, his mom had said that nothing was ever going to be the same, as if Evan wouldn't fit with us anymore now that he'd been gone so long. But she was wrong. I had reread every letter Evan sent me from Vietnam. Evan hadn't changed at all. He'd taken some shrapnel in his side so they were letting him come home a few months early. It was all part of the troop withdrawal President Nixon had promised. They were sending home the boys who weren't injured seriously and weren't going to replace them with new kids. Even Evan's brother, Robby, had said their mom was being melodramatic. Evan was one of the lucky ones.

The Impala came into view and drifted down the street before it lurched into their drive. I ran across our lawn, my heart beating faster than a sparrow's. Evan's dad clutched the wheel, staring at the driveway as if it were a runway and he had to land that enormous car precisely in the middle. Evan's mom sat rigid in the back seat, her face as pinched as always, like a suburban version of the American Gothic portrait. Evan was in the front seat watching me without his smile. His face was darkened by scabs on the left side and his neck was bandaged.

It's not that bad.

The car rolled to a stop. Evan turned and reached for the door handle, his eyes challenging mine. His left hand, bandaged to the elbow, had only small, empty rosebuds where three of his fingers should have been. I took a step back, my breath catching as he swung the door open.

"Hey, Bug. I'm home." His voice rang in my ears. The same voice that had played in my head like a record for the last twenty-three months, but off somehow as if it had been slowed or muffled. Inside me there was a vacuum, all the air sucked out of my lungs.

"Hey," I pushed out slowly.

Evan's dad was already opening the trunk, whistling to himself.

"I can get my sea bag, Dad," Evan told him. The crusty scabs on his face started near his mouth and pulled away toward the back of his head following the line he must have turned against the blast. His ear was streaked with lines of scabs. His old Rolling Stones t-shirt sleeve had been cut to go over the bandages on his arm, and he wore the same blue jeans he left with, his straight legged Levi's with the torn right knee. As if time had stopped somehow and yet managed to change everything, too.

"I've got it, son," Dr. Olesson said.

"It's okay Dad, I can get it," Evan replied, his voice tight.

He grabbed the big, green canvas tube and flung it onto his back, bending forward slightly to balance the weight against him. He wasn't quite as skinny as he used to be. He had filled out a little, gotten more muscular. I was just standing there stupidly staring at him, taking in every detail as if I were studying a Monet. His hair was longer than I thought it would be, short all around but not the severe buzz cut he left with. He hadn't shaved for a couple of days and it made his oval face seem even longer, his lips slightly thin but capable of curling into the most delicious smile. He caught me looking at him and stopped.

"You miss me, Bug?" he asked, a slight laugh dangling at the end of his words. I couldn't tell if he meant it or if he was just making fun of me. Maybe he realized. Maybe he'd always known. Maybe he thought it was funny, the blind devotion of the nerdy girl next door. I opened my mouth to say something, anything he would think was funny, but it was as empty as his hand.

He held out a small camouflaged canvas sack. "Here, carry my ditty bag for me, will ya?"

I reached for the bag but his mother's white-gloved hands were suddenly in front of me taking it from him. She was there between us, just like on the night before he left when he'd almost kissed me. He'd stood so close to me that there hadn't been enough room to breathe as he told me not to forget to write to him, that he'd miss how annoying I was. He'd been teasing me like always but in that moment there was something more, something almost, and then his mother had flicked on the porch lights like she was illuminating Cleveland Stadium and Evan had broken away from me and never looked back. Evan might have forgotten that moment but I hadn't. Maybe it had been nothing more than him being afraid of leaving home and going to Vietnam, but it still had been an almost.

"Rachel, dear," his mom said, "won't you come by after supper, after Evan's had a chance to rest a while?" She used her strict British tone. The one she would scatter the neighborhood kids with when we were younger. She never had to yell, but they would scamper home anyway.

"Yes, ma'am," I said, though I didn't usually call people ma'am, even Mrs. Olesson.

Evan blew a slight puff of air from his nose and gave me a half smile behind her back.

"Later, Bug," he said.

"Yeah, later," I echoed, not able to smile back, salvaging the words from some ocean floor inside of me.

Dr. Olesson nodded in an absent minded way that I guess was meant to acknowledge me somehow and then swept past me. I stood with my feet burning into the asphalt, watching the three of them go into the house. Evan walked differently than before he left. Before he walked in a swinging way as if he were hearing music in his head he didn't even notice was there. Now his walk was strange, more straight and guarded and taut, but maybe it was just the sea bag slung over his back. It reminded me of the broken hero walking into the sunset in an old western movie, away from the camera, out of your life. His mom walked behind him swaying on her heels as though she were practicing a new tightrope routine.

Look back, Evan. I haven't smiled.

Their door closed. I stared at the house, my chest tightening as if a ratchet were squeezing my heart. When I finally turned away the street whirled before me, the narrowly set homes folding in on me, crushing me.

I'd been an idiot, thinking they would send him home and he'd just be okay. I was such an idiot thinking he could ever love me. I was such an idiot believing I could ever leave my hometown. Kent was the kind of place that held you up so you could see the world beyond, but all the time it gripped your ankles and dragged you down like a slow moving river.

I crossed back to my house. Two Blue Jays shrieking cut through the conch like roar in my head with unrelenting precision. Evan's guitar case leaned against the wooden railing of the front porch. I sat down and rested my head against it, drawing Evan's face in my mind. When he didn't shave like that, you almost couldn't see the tiny scar on his right cheek from when he was ten and fell out of the tree house and we had to call the ambulance. Now he would be riddled with tiny scars, running along his face and hiding in his hair.

I pressed my hands against my eyes, the tiny squares of gauze crisp in my mind. His left hand. The last three fingers missing. One moment of destiny. *Why couldn't it have been his right?*

Ella Fitzgerald's voice floated through the living room window singing *Don't Get Around Much Anymore*. The sad, yearning notes splattered my skin like bacon grease.

The front door squeaked open.

"Rachel," my mom said. "How about you come and set the table for me?"

I couldn't turn around, but I let her words sink in knowing she'd wait. She must have seen from the window. She walked over and stroked my head, administering her soft blessing.

"Sure," I said, but I waited until her footsteps disappeared. I pressed my forehead against Evan's guitar case. It was a cardboard case with a gray scratchy pattern on it that reminded me of the television when it went to snow. The edges were made from a strong, black cotton binding. Evan had bought it when he was eleven, saving every penny from his paper route for two years, plus all of his Christmas and birthday money. The last five dollars he borrowed from me. He never paid me back, but he told me I owned five dollars worth of his guitar, so I never minded.

"Keep it for me, just in case, Bug," he'd said when he gave it to me.

"Just in case of what?" I'd asked stupidly.

"If I don't come back, you can have it, since you never mind hearing me try out a new song. And five dollars of it's yours anyway."

He was being serious about maybe not coming back, but all I could think about then was how he was trusting me with his guitar. I couldn't even think that maybe he was right and he'd never come home. So I'd laughed like it wasn't possible, like Evan was being ridiculous. Now I knew what a jerk I'd been. But that day it just didn't seem possible. Evan had seemed invincible.

I wiped my face with my thumb and got up.

Mrs. Olesson was right. Nothing was ever going to be the same. Evan had lost everything that mattered to him. The last thing he needed was to worry about helping me. The revolution I'd been waiting for was over before it even started. I was on my own if I was going to convince my dad to let me go to Pratt, and so far I had gotten nowhere with him.

And Evan still called me Bug.

2

THE COOL DISHES slipped between my fingers, the plates making a tolling sound when they landed on the solid walnut table. My mom was slicing carrots, her back to me.

"Why didn't Mrs. Olesson just tell us?" I asked when I was finally able to trust my voice.

"Oh, Rachel, you know how private Ellen can be. All she told me was what she told all of us. I suspected it was worse than you thought because she was so upset." My mom turned around, her tiny figure looking so much younger than she was. "I should have warned you that maybe it wasn't what we thought. But it could be so much worse! You have to remember that. I know people can be unkind, but he's here with us."

I nodded. Mrs. Olesson liked to think that everything in her life was perfect. And Evan wasn't perfect anymore. She would pretend like nothing had happened but all the while she would feel it. I placed the silverware correctly, the knife facing in toward the plate. The spoon on the outside of the knife. It always mattered to me that the order was right. Order is different from perfection.

"I know I have to be grateful that he's even alive. I just wish it had been his right hand. It should have been his right hand."

If I had known, I could have smiled. If I had known, I wouldn't have hoped for anything.

"All he ever wanted was to go to school for music and have his own band," I said. He hd been so disappointed when he didn't get into Berklee College of Music in Boston. "He was barely fourteen when he won that contest up in Cleveland for best guitarist. And he's left handed. How's he going to write? Or throw a ball?" I stopped. Another word and I would be sobbing.

My mom just nodded, because we both knew there weren't any words that were going to make it better.

Evan had lost more than a few fingers. I couldn't even imagine never being able to draw again, and that's what music was to Evan. It was the reason we were friends at all, my closest and best link to him because I had been his first and most loyal audience. Now his dreams were gone, and I had lost my only real chance to ever leave Kent. My dad had already let me know he had no intention of letting me go to Pratt when KSU was practically across the street just waiting for me. Evan's injury had robbed us both, and I couldn't even tell whose loss I felt more.

I went up to my room and set Evan's guitar in the corner across from my bed, just as it had been for the last twenty-three months, where no one would step on it or kick it. Where I could see it from my pillow. I took my blue cardigan out of the closet and dropped it over the main part of the case, so that only the neck stuck out, not sure if I were hiding it or protecting it. I lay on my bed and stared at the ceiling.

Why couldn't she have just told us?

"Nothing's ever going to be the same," Mrs. Olesson had said, her voice hard like January ice. Why couldn't she have just said "Evan lost three of his fingers?" I would've been able to smile when I saw him then. Now Evan would think I cared that he wasn't perfect according to his mom and the rest of the world. He would think I saw him like everyone else was going to do. That's what my mom meant. Everyone would look at him like he was a freak. Another Vietnam freak.

What if Evan never forgave me? What else had happened to him that I didn't know about? Maybe I'd never really know him again. Maybe he'd never understand why I hadn't smiled. The way his eyes had challenged me when he first saw me flickered in my mind. He had never done that before.

A soft knock peppered the open doorway of my room.

"Hey, Dad," I said, sitting up. "I didn't hear your car in the drive."

He pressed his lips together and nodded, walking over to sit beside me. The mattress sagged from his tall, heavy set body.

He looked around my room like he was seeing it for the first time in a long time. The cork board hanging over my desk covered with Peanuts' comic strips and pictures of me growing up, photos I had taken over the summer, and pieces of my artwork. My bursting bookshelves and desk with its art pencils, pens, and watercolor brushes arranged in little vases beside my stack of different kinds of paper. He glanced at my closet, open but otherwise neat, and finally at Evan's guitar shrouded in my favorite sweater.

"So our prodigal son has returned, eh?" His voice was husky.

"Yeah," I said, and we both sat there, the silence filling in all the words we couldn't bring ourselves to say. Then my dad sighed, as though our thoughts had walked down two parallel paths that had suddenly turned and intersected.

"Give him some time, Rachel," he said, tapping an unlit cigarette against his knee as though it were something he needed to concentrate on to be able to do. "I know patience isn't your strong suit, but he'll need time to adjust. Not just to losing his fingers, but to simply being home. To the television being on. To sleeping at night and waking up in the morning."

My head bobbed like a mechanical toy.

"He needs time to realize he's not listening to death stalking him anymore." My dad's voice was quiet and far away. He smoothed the hair down that he combed over his bald spot and stuck the unlit cigarette in his mouth. He never talked about his war, unless it was to tell some humorous story that had nothing to do with battle. Now his jaw was tight, his shoulders rigid, and the memories of World War II that he usually suppressed seemed to rise up inside of him as if they were locusts. He blew out a breath and patted my knee. He smelled of nicotine and coffee and my nose crinkled. "Give him time, Rachel."

"Okay," I said, my voice nothing more than a croak, wondering how I would ever manage to wait when every part of me wanted to run to Evan's house and beg him to be okay. My dad stood and shuffled from the room.

Time. I had spent plenty of time thinking about Evan in Vietnam, wondering what he was doing, when he would get to come home. His letters had been easy, funny even sometimes, and he'd always told me not to worry, that he was fine. I had always asked him if he needed anything, but he only ever wanted the OSU scores and Kodak film. I had just taken him at his word. I couldn't picture how he slept or what the jungle was really like. The newspaper and TV reports seemed different and unconnected from the photos Evan sent back. Crowded, dirty streets in Chu Lai. Shoeless children laughing and holding candy the Marines had given them. Evan's friends, sitting around, smiling and relaxed in front of little thatched houses or on dirt mounds with concrete blocks beside them, smoking and eating their c-rations, flashing peace signs with their hands.

I closed my eyes. My dad and mom were talking in low tones. She had sent him up to try to make me understand and he was giving his report. But understanding was the least of my problems. My heart had already told me that, whatever Evan had lost, I had lost, too. And my heart had already let me know that it would never stop loving Evan, no matter how much he had changed.

3

WALTER CRONKITE WAS SAYING something about more college protests fueled by bad news from the war zone when I came down for dinner. My dad turned off the little black and white TV on the kitchen island as though he didn't usually watch the news during dinner time. I went along pretending not to notice and mixed two glasses of strawberry Kool-Aid. I set them down where my little sister, Willa, and I always sat. Then I went to help my mom in her mad scramble to get everything to the table while it was still hot.

I scooped mashed potatoes into a serving bowl and grabbed a spoon from the drawer. My mom brought the lamb chops from under the broiler and handed me the green beans. A ketchup bottle sat on the table since I wouldn't eat gravy. A large bowl of salad rested on the island waiting for the end of the meal since both of my parents were first generation Americans from Italian immigrants.

Willa bounced into the room and slipped into her seat, looking at me as though she were ready to burst. "Oooohhh! Evan's finally home!" she announced. Then she looked at me and started dancing in her seat and singing, "in my midnight confessions—"

"Willa!" my dad said. "That's enough."

Willa stopped. She looked at each of us in turn, asking with her big gray eyes what she had done wrong. They could have at least told her already.

"Willa," my mom said finally, "Evan came home injured. Honey, Evan isn't quite the same."

"Of course he's the same," I said even though I already knew it wasn't true.

My mom pulled her head back in a defensive way that was more instinctive than calculated and I bit my lip. I shouldn't have snapped at her. But I couldn't say I was sorry, either.

"What's shaking?" Willa asked.

"What's *shaking*," I said, pronouncing the word as if it carried some disgusting disease with it, "is that Evan's lost three of his fingers. On his left hand."

"Wow," Willa said. "That's a bummer. But I'm so glad he's home. I missed him so much!"

"I'm not hungry," I said and pushed my meal away.

It was as if they didn't even remember him. I got up and carried my plate and glass to the sink as my older sister, Portia, walked in.

"Sorry I'm late," she said falling into her chair. "Bug, will you get me a glass of Kool-Aid since you're up? So, is Romeo home?"

I hated it when she made fun of how much I loved him.

"Portia," my mom said, shaking her head in warning.

I couldn't bear to hear them go through it again. I took the stairs two at a time and banged my door shut.

I turned on my alarm clock radio to cover the raging noise in my head. Diana Ross and the Supremes' latest song slipped into my room. *Someday, We'll Be Together*. I shook my head and sat on the floor, pulling the shoebox I had decorated with a collage of guitar pictures from under my bed. The bundle of Evan's letters fell softly into my hands as I untied the yellow ribbon holding them together.

I read them again, knowing now how it would all end as the light faded from my room and finally it was dark. "Don't worry, don't worry, don't worry," echoed through every one. And I had listened willingly enough. I welcomed the shadows, sitting there, the radio playing, the paper like wafers between my fingers, holding onto the before Vietnam Evan.

A soft knock on the door startled me.

"Rachel, we're going over to see Evan now." My mom's voice slipped under the door and found its way to me through the darkness. She waited in the silence.

"Don't you want to come?" she asked at last.

"I'll be down in a minute," I said, forcing the words out.

"Okay."

I stood and turned on the light, squinting from the brightness. The mirror reflected my makeup streaked from tears, and I tried to fix it. I brushed my hair and pulled the Abbey Road album that I had bought for Evan in September from my bookshelves and went downstairs.

My family openly stared at me as I came into the kitchen. My mom handed me the apple pie she had made for Evan. His favorite. His letters talked about it all the time, how he couldn't wait to get home and sit in our kitchen and have some of my mom's apple pie and drink Nestlé's Quick. I pinned the album against me with my elbow.

We tumbled out the back door and across the yard toward Evan's house. The leaves on the ground crackled under our shoes, though the grass was damp from the cool night air. The pie dish was still warm in my hands and I pulled it closer to me as I followed everyone else, Willa skipping with the light heart of a twelve-year-old. The moon was almost full, making the trip across the yard deceptively easy.

Robby answered the back door. Most people considered him the good looking one, with his sea blue eyes and curly, blonde hair, and a full inch on Evan's six foot two frame. But I never liked curly, blonde hair and his eyes never had Evan's

Fourth of July heat to them. We bustled in from the chill in a pack and followed Robby toward the living room.

"Is that pie for me, Bug?" Robby asked even though he knew it was for Evan. He was seventeen like me, but he was still a junior, since I had gone to kindergarten early.

"Don't call me 'Bug,'" I told him for the billionth time. That was Evan's nickname for me. He'd been calling me 'Bug' since the day they moved into their house when I was six and had stood there staring at him and Robby. "What are you looking at, you little Bug?" Evan had said, but the smile on his face had told me he was just teasing. He had never once called me Rachel.

Evan and his parents were in the living room watching *That Girl*, though Evan had a look on his face like he was watching some completely different show that was playing in his head. He jumped up, nervous and fidgety. My mom and sisters hugged him. Even my dad gave him a hug, the kind a grown man gives his dad, with lots of hand shaking and patting on the back. Evan looked around and found me in the doorway.

"Is that pie for me?"

I smiled and said "Yes," my answer lost in the chorus that erupted from my mom and Willa and Portia.

"It smells delicious," Mrs. Olesson said, taking it from me. "I'll cut some, everyone, sit down. Rachel, help me, dear, won't you?"

"I'll be right there," I told her. I handed the album to Evan.

"Thanks, Bug," he said, holding it with his right hand and running his left index finger over the picture on the cover, as though he were looking at an old photograph from the past, something he had forgotten about.

"Just a welcome home present," I said, pulling myself away even though I knew he was starting to look up from the cover to me, afraid of what might not be there.

I helped Mrs. Olesson serve the pie and coffee and Cokes. *That Girl* ended and *Bewitched* began, but Dr. Olesson had gotten up and turned the sound down on the big console TV. Everyone said stupid things trying to not say the wrong thing. Dr. Olesson and my dad smoked the room hazy with their Camels. Evan was struggling to hold his fork in his left hand and after a while he switched to his right, his movements awkward and stilted. But in my mind we were alone, and his hand didn't matter. He was telling me how much he had missed me and how my letters had gotten him through, in between kissing me with those perfect lips that were always playing at breaking into a smile.

"Evan, have another piece of pie," my mom said. "Rachel will get it for you, won't you, Rachel?"

I jumped up as if my mom had jabbed me with knitting needles and took the plate from Evan. My fingers brushed his bandages. As close to a hug as I would get. He looked up at me, his face serious, my earlier betrayal reflected in the glint of his eyes.

When I brought him the pie, he forced a short smile. "Did you leave me any for breakfast?" The piece was ridiculously big, but it was as close to the words I wanted as I could come.

I just looked at him. All the things I wanted to say were completely stupid, like "I love you," or, "I'll give up art school and become a pastry chef if you'll just love me back," or, "if you don't stand up and forgive me right now, my heart's going to burst." So I shrugged and went back to sitting in the corner nursing my Coke. Evan seemed to get lost in his own world again, staring at the cover of Abbey Road as if it were an oracle that might speak at any moment.

A few minutes later my dad put out his third or fourth cigarette in the ashtray on the coffee table and stood up. I stood next, eager to leave before I started crying. Every passing minute was growing more painful with Evan so close but moving further away all the time. He looked at me when I stood.

"Your hair's longer, Bug."

My hand flew instinctively to my hair, and I pushed it back behind my ear. Evan never made comments like that.

"I forgot how dark it is," he said. Or did I just think he said that? Everyone was standing, moving, grabbing jackets and taking plates and cups into the kitchen.

"See you," I said, suddenly not sure of anything.

"Yeah," he replied, sinking back on the sofa like he was really tired. "See ya."

I forced myself to turn and say goodnight to Robby and his parents. We crossed the yard, Willa hanging on my arm, my parents quiet. Even Portia didn't have anything to say.

As soon as we reached our kitchen I threw out my "Goodnight," before anyone could start dissecting how well Evan looked, considering, and how everything was going to be fine. I ran upstairs and brushed my teeth efore going to my room. I had forgotten to turn the radio off. Friend and Lover's *Reach Out of the Darkness* was playing and I pressed the door closed without turning on the light. I got undressed and slipped my night gown over my head. Moonlight filled my room as I padded over to the shoe box of Evan's letters, placing them all carefully back inside and putting the lid on. I lay down on my bed and held the box close, letting the radio fill my aching heart with anything and everything until I fell asleep.

4

THE NEXT DAY when I dragged myself to school, my best friend was waiting for me at my locker, a big smile on her face.

I bit my lip to keep my eyes from burning.

Her smile crinkled and ashed like burnt paper. "Do you want to talk about it?"

I shook my head but the words poured out anyway. "Evan lost three of his fingers. On his left hand."

Michelle stared at me, her mouth a round "O" of surprise.

"He's lost everything. Everything he was going to do when he came home. His guitar, his band, going to college for music. And since Mrs. Olesson didn't warn us about how bad it was, I had no idea what to say when I saw him. I acted like such an idiot, standing there just staring at him. Now he thinks that I think he's a freak. You should see him. His body's in Kent but his mind is still in some jungle half way round the world, and it's like he isn't really home at all. How's that for a happy homecoming?"

"Oh man, I'm sorry."

"Yeah me too." I leaned my head against the edge of my locker door, pushing back tears. "He's not a freak."

Michelle squeezed my arm. "So, show him the truth."

"I don't even know how."

"Well, if I know Rachel, she'll find a way. Just give it time."

Just give it time. I was in trouble if Michelle and my dad were giving the same advice. I had no idea how to give it time. I just wanted to fix it. All of it. Right that minute.

"It's not just Evan's dreams that are gone. He was the only chance I had to convince my dad I can't go to KSU. Just the thought of ending up there makes me feel like I'm in a cage."

"It's not *that* bad," Michelle said. She was headed there in the fall for nursing.

"Sorry," I said, scrunching my nose. "It's different for me. No one takes art seriously at KSU."

"I know," she said, forgiving me, "but I'm sure Evan doesn't believe you think he's a freak. He just needs a chance to get used to being home."

I laughed a little. "You sound like Dear Abby."

"It's a gift," she said with a small smile.

The day dragged by, every class another hour to think about Evan and how far gone everything was. By fifth period, it felt like days since he'd come home and I was pretty sure that giving it time was going to be the hardest thing I'd ever do in my life. I was sitting in trigonometry trying to concentrate when Mr. Miller opened the door and stepped into class, a soft sheen of sweat covering his forehead.

Miss Tate looked up from the equation she was copying onto the blackboard and dropped her chalk as if he had jumped out at her from behind the door and yelled boo.

Mr. Miller cleared his throat. "I'm sorry to interrupt your class, Miss Tate," he said, "but the Principal needs to speak with you."

Jim Harrington, sitting in the front row, said "Ooooohhhhhh, Miss Tate, you must be in trouble." Some of the kids snickered but she never took her eyes off of Mr. Miller. She looked like the star of an Alfred Hitchcock movie, standing there with her perfectly coiffed hair and plaid dress against the backdrop of the dull blackboard, a look of terror on her face.

Mr. Miller scowled at Jim and then scanned the class until his gaze rested on me. The responsible one. Teachers have radar for kids like me.

"Rachel, would you come out in the hall a moment?" he asked.

I got up, every pair of eyes in the room watching me walk out the door with Mr. Miller and Miss Tate. I could hear the frantic whispers of my classmates trying to figure out what was going on through the open door.

"Rachel, would you please go with Miss Tate to the office?" Mr. Miller asked, quietly enough that no one in the classroom would hear.

"Of course," I answered, though I didn't understand why. "Mr. Miller, I'm sure whatever this is, it's just a misunderstanding. Miss Tate hasn't done anything wrong." She had only been teaching for a couple of years, but I liked Miss Tate. She always took extra time with the students who needed it, including me sometimes.

"No, no, of course not," Mr. Miller said to me. He turned to Miss Tate. "Don't worry about your class. I'll finish the lesson today."

Miss Tate nodded vaguely and Mr. Miller looked at me and ticked his head toward the principal's office down the hall. I turned and began to walk and Miss Tate followed me mechanically. Mr. Miller slipped back into the classroom and the hall was weirdly silent except for our footsteps.

I glanced at the slender girl beside me, hardly much older than Portia. Her face was drained of color and her hands were shaking.

"Are you okay, Miss Tate?"

She replied with a little gasp and I grabbed her arm and led her to the stairs so she could sit down. She leaned her head against the banister, her breath coming hard.

"I'm sure it's nothing, Miss Tate."

She looked up and me and seemed to see me for the first time since Mr. Miller had asked me to go with her. "You don't understand, Rachel," she whispered. She took a deep breath and then stood up. I took her arm as we walked to the principal's office where the secretary waived me off as she grabbed Miss Tate around the shoulders.

When I got back to class, everyone stared openly at me. "Thank you, Rachel," Mr. Miller said and gestured to my seat.

"What is it?" Michelle whispered as I walked past her, but I just shook my head helplessly.

After class, I waited for everyone to leave, even Michelle who had to get to band practice.

"Mr. Miller," I said, standing on the other side of Miss Tate's desk as he wiped the chalk board clean. "Is Miss Tate in some kind of trouble?"

Mr. Miller kept the eraser pressed against the chalkboard a moment before he turned around. "You may as well know," he said, "as it will be common knowledge soon enough. I hope, Rachel that you will be responsible enough not to turn this into something to gossip about."

I nodded.

"Miss Tate's fiancé was killed in Vietnam. He was from Michigan and his parents called the school asking us to let her know. I think she knew as soon as I interrupted her class that it was the news she was most afraid of hearing."

Chills rolled down my arms in short waves. If anyone should have figured out what was wrong it was me. I'd lived with Vietnam for two years, but I'd been too naïve to fear it the way Miss Tate had. "I see," I said, gripping my books a little tighter.

I headed to my locker and crammed things into my backpack before I pushed out of the building like it would suffocate me to stay any longer. Evan came home alive, and what happened to Miss Tate's fiancé should have put that into perspective, but somehow it just multiplied the losses of Vietnam in a kaleidoscopic way as I thought of her in the principal's office with no escape from the news that her fiancé had been killed.

I took the long way home, through the Kent State campus. I knew every inch of it. My dad had been a professor in the English department since before I was born.

On the commons and Blanket Hill, kids were sitting on the grass near the Victory Bell, studying or just hanging out. The weather was even warmer than the day before. Everyone seemed happy it was Friday. Tonight they'd be hanging out at the bars on Water Street. But for now they were enjoying the mild afternoon, some of them probably skipping class to do it since it was Friday. Evan should have been doing the same thing on the campus at Berklee College of Music. He'd have been a sophomore. But he'd messed up his audition and they'd told him to try again the next year. Instead of applying to another school the way his dad told him to, he'd screwed around. First born son with no deferment. It hadn't taken two months for him to get drafted.

The football team was on the practice field down below Taylor Hall, whistles blaring, coaches yelling. My dad never missed the games, and when they played away he listened on the radio. I watched for a few minutes, pretending that football was still important. I tried to picture myself as a freshman instead of just standing there as I was, but the big girl feeling I'd had when I was little and would walk the campus was long gone, replaced with the feeling of being trapped. KSU wasn't a school for artists. It was a school for teachers and nurses and kids who didn't know what they wanted to be when they grew up. It was a small town school with a small town mindset and it wasn't ever going to change. And art needs change to grow.

I headed north toward home. Normally, I would've stopped by my dad's office to say hello but I didn't want to talk to anyone, especially not my dad. Cutting past the Music and Speech building, I crossed East Main into my neighborhood.

I came in the front door. My mom was in the basement banging the dryer closed.

"I'm home," I called down the steps. "Going upstairs to study."

She made a muffled reply and I grabbed some cookies and a glass of Kool-Aid. Willa was in the living room watching a black and white rerun of Gilligan's Island. Portia was probably still at school. Maybe I just missed her on Blanket Hill. She was a senior and pretty sure she owned the place. But she kept her grades up and my parents happy. My dad wanted her to go to law school and she had applied to Case Western. If she were a boy, she wouldn't have had any trouble getting in, but my dad was working his connections to make sure that being a girl didn't count against her too much. He was so proud of her.

I closed my door and dropped my backpack on the floor. Why did my physics teacher have to pick this Monday to schedule a quiz? All I really wanted to do was draw, to take all the frustration I had inside of me and force it onto paper, and I was already struggling in physics. I turned on the radio and walked to the window, staring out over the back yard. Blue jays and black squirrels darted around knowing it wouldn't stay this warm much longer. I looked into Evan's yard like I always did ready to stare at the empty hammock that hung between two Maple trees. Evan was sitting across the hammock waving to me to come down.

I smiled and shook my head "no," then waited for him to smile back. For just a moment, it was like nothing had changed. Evan knew that I'd come. It was a game we'd played since we were little. I had looked at that hammock a million times this summer wishing Evan were there and asking me to come down. I shrugged to him like it didn't matter and turned, checking myself in the mirror to make sure I didn't have Oreo crumbs on my lips before running downstairs.

"What took you so long, Bug?" he asked as I walked over.

"I came straight down." Before Vietnam, I would have just jumped on with him, but now I hesitated.

He was sitting in the hammock perpendicular to how you lie in it, and he rolled a little to make room for me.

"I mean from school. It's after four."

"Oh," I said, sinking into the nylon fabric, wondering if he could have been waiting for me, if he had missed sitting in the hammock together as much as I had. "I went by campus first."

In the corner of my eye, Evan nodded. His legs pushed the hammock back and forth. Mine dangled beside, not long enough to reach the ground. The touch of his arm against mine seeped into me, filling the empty crevices like water overflowing the banks of a stream. I was eight the first time we ever sat like this, my right side resting against his left from the incline of the hammock. That was the first time I knew that Evan was essential to my happiness.

"You think my old man will make me rake leaves with my bum hand?" he asked, holding his bandaged stump up and studying it like it was something he couldn't recognize. I smiled, knowing he was trying to find something funny about his life being blown apart along with his hand.

"Probably," I said. "But at least you'll be off the hook for that whole maxillofacial surgeon thing."

Evan laughed. His dad always told him how much he regretted just being a dentist and not going on for four more years to be a maxillofacial surgeon, and how that was what Evan should do.

"He asked me to fold the hammock up for the winter, but I've just been sitting here. I love this cool, dry weather. All it ever was over there was hot and wet. You've never seen rain like that, Bug. Monsoon rain. We used to take showers in it. Hot and wet. I don't ever want to be hot and wet again. And then I started waiting for you to come home from school. I was beginning to think you wouldn't come. I can't wait 'til it snows."

He'd been waiting for me to come home, like it mattered. There was a soft, cool breeze coming and going with the clouds overhead. The smell of decaying leaves was thick and pungent, reminding me of the sweetness of rotting apples and wet earth.

"Next Friday is Halloween," I said. "I promised Willa that I'd take her and her friends around the neighborhood. Do you want to come?"

"Maybe," he said, which in Evan's world meant "no." *Give him time.* My dad's words swelled in my head. Evan swung the hammock with his feet and I tried to bask in the happiness of having him home, next to me, and the way the sky tried so hard to mimic the color of his eyes.

"It was frickin crazy, Bug," he said, almost in a whisper.

"What?" I asked, just before I realized. He meant Vietnam. He wanted to tell me about Vietnam.

"Nothing," he said at the same time that I said "Oh, you mean Nam."

I had totally screwed up. He was going to talk to me about the war, and I had made him think I couldn't understand. Why was I such an idiot around him since he'd come home?

"Yeah," he said, but that was all. The moment was gone. We swung for a couple of minutes in silence.

"So what's with these bell bottom pants?" he asked finally.

I shook my head. "Everyone wears them now. You probably couldn't find straight legged jeans if you tried."

"They look okay on girls, but don't you think men look stupid in them?"

"Yeah, I do. I can't picture you in them."

"What?" he asked, turning his head to look at me. "I don't hear so well in this ear anymore."

I swallowed before answering. "I said 'yeah, I guess so.'" My voice sounded too loud but he just kept staring at me.

"Would you be embarrassed to be seen with me, in jeans like that, Bug?" he asked a sarcastic kind of smile on his face. We both knew he wasn't asking me about bell bottom jeans.

"No," I said, shaking my head. "I wouldn't be embarrassed." He nodded and looked up at the sky. He rocked us back and forth and stared at the blue above us. For a moment it was like touching the past, but incomplete so that my chest ached. *Maybe I could ask him.*

"I need a plan, Evan," I said, a little bit louder than usual to make sure he heard.

He rolled his head toward me. His eyes were so large. So unwaveringly blue. So remote. "What kind of plan?"

"You know, for Pratt."

"Oh that," he said. "Your dad's never gonna let you go to New York, Bug."

I sat up, my stomach tightening as if someone had just thrown a dodge ball smack into it. My dad didn't believe in doing things that were difficult to make a living at, like being a writer, or an artist, or an academic like he was with all the political junk that went on at a university. But with an education from the best art school in the country, I was sure I could prove him wrong. I'd never be as well off as Portia when she was a lawyer, but I didn't care. All I needed to do was to make a living at it, and Pratt would make that possible. I needed to go out into the world and prove to my dad that I could be part of it, that I didn't need to live my whole life like a mole in Kent.

But to prove that to my dad, I needed Evan to be on my side, even if he didn't believe in me himself. I just needed him to convince my dad. I just needed him to be willing to try for me.

He stopped swinging the hammock. My eyes began to sting. I jumped off, but Evan sat up and caught my forearm with his hand. The soft gauze scratched against my skin. His finger and thumb were warm and callused, and it was his touch that stopped me rather than the strength of his grip, or what was left of it.

"I'll think of something," he said trying to pacify me, just like all the times growing up when he'd told me Portia hadn't been making fun of me when we both knew she had. I looked away.

"Yeah, thanks," I said as he let go of my arm. I stood there a moment, watching the balloon I'd held onto for so long float off into the universe. If I wanted to go to Pratt, I really was completely on my own. I turned and walked back to my house, wondering as I walked if he even watched me go.

5

ON HALLOWEEN NIGHT, I had Willa and four of her friends to take around the neighborhood and we started at the Olessons'. When I still dressed up, Willa's costume had always had something to do with mine, like the year I went dressed as Snoopy and she was Woodstock. Or when I was a witch and she was my black cat. The year I turned thirteen and stopped trick-or-treating, I walked her around the neighborhood for my parents. My mom talked Michelle into going too, because "there's safety in numbers." Not that our neighborhood's dangerous, but my mom was raised in the city so she never believed in taking chances.

This year, Michelle was going to a party at our friend Lion's house. "If Evan comes trick-or-treating," she told me with a grin, "you two will want to be alone."

"We can't be alone with five twelve year olds," I had told her. "And besides, even if I want to be alone with Evan, he doesn't want to be alone with me."

"You don't know that," she had said, nudging me with her shoulder. But I was pretty sure I did know that.

Still, on Halloween night, I couldn't help wishing that maybe I was the one who was wrong.

Mrs. Olesson stood in the doorway with a tray of little bags filled with penny candy. The girls yelled "trick or treat" in unison. Evan came down the steps behind her like a halo rising.

"Hey, Willa," he said, checking out her costume. She twirled herself around and cackled her best witch laugh.

"Do you want to come with us? Rachel is coming."

"Maybe I'll catch you later," Evan said with a plastic smile.

The before Evan would have come with us, would have never told Willa no.

"You should go dear," Mrs. Olesson said to him. "It would do you good to get out for a while." Her left eye twitched.

"Maybe I'll catch up," Evan repeated.

I turned before he could see the disappointment on my face.

It was almost nine o'clock when we finally made our way back up the street to our house. The girls were dragging along, complaining that it was cold and they were tired and they wanted to see what they had gotten. They were already talking about swapping like they had jewels in their bags. We were just passing Evan's house when he came walking up the drive toward the street. I let the girls run on to our house and waited.

"Hey," I said, my teeth chattering from the chill.

"Hey," Evan said. "How was it? Did they get a lot of loot?"

I stuck my hands into my jacket pockets. "Yeah, they did pretty well."

He hesitated a moment. Maybe he had been waiting for me.

"Do you want to come over?" I asked, at the same time he started to talk.

"Well, I'm going to cut out to Water Street and see who's around," he said, looking down the block as though he couldn't wait to get away. I guess he had decided his mom was right and he should get out a little. I bit my lip at the irony of it being Water Street. I couldn't have gone if I'd wanted to since

I wasn't 18 yet. And even if I managed not to get carded, my parents would never have let me go.

When I saw him walking up the driveway toward me, I had thought, just maybe, he was sorry he hadn't gone trick or treating with us and was going to come back to our house for a while. But all he wanted to do was go to the Kove or Big Daddy's or Ron-de-vou and meet girls his age who could go to all the places I couldn't. And who wouldn't say dumb things about Vietnam.

"Yeah, okay," I said. "Have fun." Fun was the last thing I wanted him to have.

"Yeah. Okay. Thanks. See ya." He turned and started down the street toward town.

"Yeah, see ya," I said to his back, determined to control my voice so he wouldn't hear my heart spiraling down like a propeller from a Maple tree. He disappeared into the dark while I stood there loving the way he sauntered just a little bit, even now.

Some time after one o'clock a soft, sad whistling floated through the glass as I sat in my window seat and watched the stars, wishing they could take away enough of the pain to let me sleep. I had to cock my head to see the Olessons' driveway, but Evan was there, walking home alone. *At least he didn't go back with some girl and sneak into her dorm room.* From the way he was walking, he wasn't very sober. Mrs. Olesson was going to have a fit when she found out.

He stopped and looked up at our house when he got to the end of the drive. I couldn't tell in the dim light if he was looking at my window, or if he could see me. He just stood and stared. There were misty clouds around the moon holding us in their veiled darkness, making me imagine the details of his face. I pressed my fingertips against the cold pane.

A dog barked somewhere down the street and Evan suddenly recoiled like a frightened cat, pulling his jacket collar up around his neck. H swayed just a moment, then swung around toward his back porch and the light that had been left on for him.

6

I SPENT MOST OF NOVEMBER trying to "just give it time." Sometimes late at night when I couldn't sleep, I'd see Evan dressed in his camouflage jacket going to the hammock. He'd lay there watching the stars and the fog of his own breath, the hammock as still as silence. But I never turned my light on, and he never motioned me to come down if he knew I was sitting there.

I wanted to run next door and somehow make everything all right, back to the way it was before Vietnam, before our friendship was tenuous and elusive. The only thing that stopped me was the idea of Mrs. Olesson acting as sentry, letting me know that Evan didn't want to see me. There was something about that possibility I just couldn't bear.

I played Evan's guitar, my guitar, every day. I drew the pictures in my head. I did my homework.

President Nixon came on the television and asked us to support his war, telling us we were the "silent majority." There were lots of anti-war people, but I didn't know who the silent majority was. It didn't seem to be anyone I knew.

I worked on my application to Pratt. Michelle helped me pick out the pieces I should send for my portfolio. She said my pictures of Evan were the best, but that I shouldn't send more than two or three with the same person. She was right, so I worked a little harder, imagining him in drawings that I never put him into. An invisible muse was still a muse.

Near the middle of November, more than 250,000 people marched in the biggest anti-war Moratorium yet in Washington. Groups like the Students for a Democratic Society, or the SDS as most kids called them, and the National Mobilization

Committee to End the War in Vietnam, nicknamed the Mobe organized it. But except for Vice President Agnew, the silent majority stayed silent. The President told us he hadn't noticed a quarter of a million people marching against his foreign policy in his backyard because he'd been busy watching the Redskins play. "Must've been one hell of a game," my dad said. Students across the country had marched, too, even in Kent. Then the newspapers started talking about some attack by Americans on a little village called My Lai. They said that American soldiers had purposely killed women and children. They called it a massacre.

There were more reports every day, but no one really believed them, except maybe the radical anti-war people. But then the week before Thanksgiving the Cleveland Plain Dealer published pictures. Spread out on the pages of our local paper were piles of dead women and children and old people, clumped in ditches or in front of little grass huts, as though the tiny village of My Lai had invaded our kitchens to prove that Vietnam was real. I read the words of the army photographer who had taken the pictures and the hair on my arms bristled. How had he been able to hold his camera steady as soldiers used their rifles to pick apart the bodies of these people while they begged for their lives? He said he'd never seen American soldiers act this way before as he described the soldiers storming through the village and systematically executing anyone they could find. I read the article through twice and still it didn't make sense. Americans were the good guys. We were supposed to be there to help people. But Ron Haeberle's words and pictures proved something completely opposite.

My dad came into the kitchen. "We shouldn't be there," was all he said as he sat down and lit a cigarette.

"Evan would never do something like this," I replied, looking at my dad as though he had accused Evan of being named in the article. Evan hadn't even been in Vietnam in March of '68.

"Men do things in war that they regret. They do things in war they would never normally do."

"Evan would never do anything like this."

My dad nodded slowly.

It wasn't as much agreement as I wanted, but it was something.

At school everyone was talking about Mai Lai, but the more I thought about it, the more my stomach churned. I was glad when the day was finally over. I went home and sequestered myself in my room, but I spent more time drawing than doing homework. After dinner, Willa wanted to play twister, but I just went back to my room until my mom called me down for dessert.

"Would you go ask your dad and Evan if they want pie?" she asked when I walked into the kitchen. She stood on her tiptoes to put a bowl away in an overhead cupboard.

"Evan's here?"

"He came by about a half hour ago, wanting to talk to your dad. They went out front. Go check on them, please."

I walked through the hall leading to the front of the house, the wide cherry floors smooth under my socks. The lamp on the drop-leaf table was on, casting a warm glow through the hall, making everything feel snug and safe in the coolness of a November night. The front door was slightly open, rustling leaves blowing across the lawn.

They were standing on the porch with their backs at an angle to me, the glow of my dad's cigarette moving back and forth from his mouth like a strange winter firefly, orange and flickering. Their breath fogged in the night air. It had finally turned cold, and this time I was pretty sure it was going to last.

"… sent us out with a German Shepherd scout dog and a bunch of Vietnamese soldiers to get information from this village that was sympathizing with the VC," Evan was saying, leaning against the railing and looking into the darkness. "We walked through there and it was like a ghost town, but you knew they were watching you, waiting for us to leave so they could snipe at us some more. And then one of our guys found this little girl, maybe six or seven, and he brings her to our lieutenant. The Vietnamese jumped all over this kid, screaming at her and shaking her, asking her questions, and she started to cry but she wouldn't say anything. So they told the dog handler to scare her, and he has the dog lunge at the kid, snarling and barking, dripping saliva. And I thought, *what the hell are we doing*, you know? And then some girl, barely old enough to be the kid's mother, comes running out of her hiding place begging for her. You didn't need an interpreter for that. So the Vietnamese guys start roughing her up, telling us she's the wife of a VC, and our lieutenant is trying to get them to calm down, and then she spits in the face of one of the Vietnamese guys who hit her, and he throws her to the ground and rips her pants off. And then he and a couple others start undoing their belts. Right there, in front of all of us, in front of her little girl. And we're not supposed to interfere with the Vietnamese guys, but my buddy, Tom Foley, and I are looking at each other like what the hell are we gonna do, and then Tom shoots a couple rounds in the air and everybody stops and looks at him. And the lieutenant says to him 'what the hell are you doing?' and he says 'this is wrong, Sir!' and the lieutenant looks at all of us, and we're all looking at him, waiting for him to stop it. So he turns to the Vietnamese squad leader and says 'we're done here, let her go.' So Tom and I jumped forward and pulled her up, and Tom's handing her pants to her, but she's just glaring at him. And her daughter is screaming and crying, her arms wrapped around her mom's leg, and the dog is going crazy barking and snarling, and the senior Vietnamese squad leader yells at our lieutenant about how they're going report us and how when we get shot up that night it'll be our own fault. And the lieutenant tells him, 'I don't give a damn what you report. We're done.' Then he looks around at us and calls 'move out!' and we left, the Vietnamese guys growling the whole way back to camp."

I leaned my head against the door and stared at Evan, seeing him for the first time since he got home, his shoulders heavy with the weight of the war. My dad took a long drag of his cigarette before flicking the stub over the railing.

"We had a guy like that in our unit," he said. "Paul Whitmere. He kept us all straight in the head. He was older than the rest of us, maybe twenty-five. We called him 'the Governor.' One day we were climbing up a hill, and this Jap's body was lying in the path, decayed and rotting. Must've been there a while." He stopped and lit another cigarette. My hand was on the door, but the words to call them in were stuck in my head, unable to shatter the something they held between them.

"So we all step over him and then this one guy in our platoon, this real angry S.O.B. from out west somewhere, he shoves his boot right through the Jap's chest, splattering it everywhere. Well, Whit was all over the guy. Locked him up against a tree and started screaming at him about how you never desecrate the dead no matter what. But the thing was, Whit wasn't protecting the Japs. He was protecting us. He knew that every bit of humanity we dropped in that jungle was going to sink into that ground forever."

They stood there quietly a moment, my dad rhythmically moving the cigarette to and from his mouth. When Evan spoke again, his voice was so strained I hardly recognized it.

"Two weeks later, Tom was our point man crossing a rice paddy. We took small arms fire and I watched him snap back. It took us maybe twenty minutes to clear the area and I managed to get to him. He laughed, told me he was going home now, but by the time I carried him back across the paddy to the trees he was dead."

I tried to force the words out of me to tell them to come inside, but they caught somewhere deep and it was like trying to form a complete sentence in another language when you don't really understand it, none of the words within my grasp.

"Art, I don't know what I would've done if Tom hadn't thought to fire those rounds," Evan said, his hands pressed against his face.

My dad rested his hand on the back of Evan's neck. "But he did."

"I wanted to shoot those guys so badly. My finger was on the trigger. Tom saved me from going to prison. He saved me from getting a dishonorable discharge. I would've had no future with that on my record. Maybe I would've let them—"

Evan hurt so much it made something inside me crack. "Hey you two," I said, with as much fake cheerfulness as I could muster, "Mom wants to know if you're ready for coffee and pie."

"Tell her we'll be right there," my dad said. Evan swept his face with his arm, and I turned away before he could see that I'd seen it.

I didn't follow them into the kitchen. If Evan had wanted to tell me this stuff, he would have. My dad must have known I'd overheard them, but he didn't seem to care. It was all so long ago, I guess. But for Evan it was different. Evan could only talk to my dad. I could wish it were me that he wanted to share his problems with, but it wasn't. He had tried that day in the hammock, and I'd been too stupid to understand. He needed my dad. His own dad had served in World War II, but as a supply officer at an air base in England. He hadn't seen any fighting. His only souvenir was an emotional popsicle of a war bride. It just wasn't the same as what my dad and Evan had been through. And now My Lai was bringing it all back to both of them.

I went to my room and took out the shoebox, reading through Evan's letters for the thousandth time. But in a way I read them for the first time that night, seeing for the first time his need to tell me over and over that things were okay, that he was okay. He hadn't been reassuring me. He'd been reassuring himself. I noticed the way his letters stopped talking about his friends as the months wore on and they had been sent home one way or another. Now I understood what he had meant when he wrote that Tom Foley had gone home on a first class ticket. How stupid was I not to have figured out what that meant? He talked less about what he wanted to do when he came home and more about the kinds of rations they were getting and the weather. He started to remind me to write, even though he knew I didn't need to be reminded. He even started talking about how short he was getting in his last few letters. He said once you got short enough, people didn't mess with you. They didn't ask you to walk point, or clear tunnels, or do anything too crazy or stupid. How had I missed all of the crazy, stupid stuff they had asked him to do? Why couldn't I find that in his letters? Had he been protecting me, or just underestimating me? If he had died over there, it would have died with him, pressing down on him forever.

The click of the lock in the sliding glass door popped from downstairs and then my dad's heavy footsteps came padding up the steps and along the hall.

"It's after 11, Rachel," he said as he passed my room. "You have school tomorrow."

"Okay," I replied, tucking the letters into the box and carefully putting the lid back on. "Dad," I said, waiting for him stop and turn back toward me.

"Yes?"

"Do you still think about it, every day?"

He took a slow breath in.

"Some things, Rachel, are so powerful, they become part of you. Whether you think about them or not." He looked down at his arm, holding it out in front of him and flexing his fingers. I was sure he was thinking about Evan not being able to do that anymore. "Can you understand that?"

I nodded, pushing the hair back from my face. There was an uneasy feeling in my stomach, a pulsing kind of unnamed regret. "Yeah," I said. "I'm beginning to think I can."

7

I STAYED AFTER SCHOOL on the following Wednesday, carefully typing information onto the Pratt application form, which I had carbon copied and handwritten the answers onto first.

"Are you almost done?" Michelle asked, appearing in the doorway of the typing classroom where every girl learned how to be a good secretary.

"Hey, yes, I'm almost done." I waved the huge envelope with my portfolio at her, already addressed, just waiting for the form.

She came in and set her oboe case on the floor and sat down next to me. Her bangle bracelets clinked against the desktop. She picked up the envelope, pulling out the artwork I had chosen to send. She flipped through them approvingly. "This is going to wow them. I'm glad you finally got it done."

"The application just says it's supposed to be in 'as soon as possible' after starting your senior year and I needed to make sure these were as good as I could make them."

"Well, they are," she said, pushing back her curly brown hair as it fell around her face in an unruly mass. "This one is the best thing you've ever done," she said, holding a drawing I had made of the picture Evan sent me of himself in Vietnam. He was shirtless and half smiling, standing with his rifle barely meaning anything to him, almost laughing at the camera. Except I had added two flag poles behind him, and the Vietnamese and American Flags were flapping against each other so that they bled into one.

"Thanks," I said. "Since tomorrow is Thanksgiving, I figure if I mail it today, the holiday might carry some weird karma kind of luck." I smiled and she laughed. My dad hadn't told me that I couldn't apply. He had only said "no point in applying to a school you aren't going to go to anyway." That meant "I'm not paying for another school when you've got a faculty scholarship and you're going to KSU." But maybe if I could get in, then maybe I could figure out how to change his mind. It was the only chance I had.

"Have you seen Evan?" Michelle asked.

"No, he's still hibernating. He used to spend more time at our house than his own. I'm just afraid it's because he's mad at me, about the way I reacted to his hand. He's so different now."

"He's been in a war, Rach. And he's lost a lot. I doubt if he's mad at you. He seems pretty wrapped up in his own problems."

I shrugged, feeling really stupid. I didn't know what I expected. I just needed it to all be okay. "I keep trying to remember what my dad said about him needing time to adjust to being home."

"Well, your dad would know," she said, although she sounded skeptical. "Come on," she added, brightening, "let's go mail this and it will be the first step to making good things happen."

"Okay," I said, forcing myself to be cheerful. "From here on out, I only think positive things."

We left school and headed down Mantua toward South Water Street and the post office. I bought a money order to cover the application fee, carefully counting out the bills from my savings. I hoped I wasn't wasting my money.

"Hello, Pratt!" Michelle said as the clerk stamped my envelope and I paid the postage. I started laughing. Just sending my application made me feel like spinning and dancing. I had to find a way to get my dad to let me go. The best art school in the country. It would be the chance of a lifetime if I got in.

"Let's go to the Hub and I'll buy you a milkshake for luck," I said.

"Karma would definitely approve of milkshakes. Let's beat feet."

The afternoon sun fought with the clouds as we walked up Lincoln in the brisk air. Campus was deserted for the holiday weekend and the Hub was nearly empty, but to us it was like a second home, and we had both outgrown it. But Michelle wasn't afraid of being stuck in Kent forever. Maybe because there was a part of her that seemed more like wind than flesh. We both kind of knew that, sooner or later, she would blow away. We got our shakes and sat by the window and Michelle was quiet. The frothy cold chocolate left my mouth almost numb.

"I know you don't really want me to go, but I need to," I said.

Michelle looked away and nodded. "I know. It should be me who wants to get away, I'm the wild one." She gave me a mischievous grin.

"You could come visit me in New York."

"I'll have to," she said, "it'll be the only time you get out and have any fun. Otherwise, you'll just waste New York by studying every weekend."

We both laughed. We finished our shakes and started for home.

"Besides," Michelle said as we crossed Main, "you might even change your mind once Pratt accepts you."

"What do you mean?"

"Sorry, Rach, but you're not a big city kind of girl. I just can't picture you in New York, alone. You're a total mamma's girl. But if you really want to go, then Pratt will be lucky to have you and I'll support you one hundred percent no matter what your dad thinks."

"Thanks," I said, with a face that let her know I hadn't glossed over her reiteration of my character flaws. I was a total mamma's girl, but I just needed someone to believe in me. Then maybe I could believe in myself.

We stopped on the corner where she turned off to go to her house and she gave me a hug. "I'll call you on Friday. Happy Thanksgiving!"

"Happy Thanksgiving." I looked past her to the setting sun that had finally beaten the clouds out. Maybe Karma would be happy with the weather and decide to smile on me. Maybe it would be cold enough to snow soon for Evan. And maybe this *give it time* thing would work out after all.

When I got home, my mom was making the rice for the turkey stuffing.

"You're home late," she said.

"Michelle and I went by the Hub and had milkshakes." I hesitated before leaving out the part about sending my application. I wanted to tell her. I wanted her to be excited at the possibility. But I knew she wouldn't be and she'd seen the application form on my desk. She knew I was applying, which meant my dad knew I was applying. But they'd ignored it as if it meant nothing. For weeks she'd been dropping not-so-subtle hints about how much she was worried about Portia being in Cleveland in the fall, and how much further New York would have been as if the option had been fully discussed and we'd all agreed that it just wasn't possible. I decided there was no point in mentioning Pratt again until I had a plan, and Evan's silence told me I was on my own for that. So far, I had come up as empty as a piggy bank in the third week of December.

I was in my room playing the guitar after dinner when a slight knock startled me. Evan stood in the doorway, which outlined his long, lean body like a picture frame.

"Your mom said it'd be okay to come up and say hi," he said awkwardly, even though he looked me in the eye. That was the thing about Evan. He always looked people straight in the eyes. The war hadn't changed that about him. He had on old straight legged jeans and a button down plaid shirt over a t-shirt. Neither was tucked in, adding to the flow of lines that was always him. The bandage on his hand looked almost like a glove with the missing fingers tucked into his palm. I dropped the guitar onto the bed and jumped up.

"Yeah, it's fine," I told him. Evan stepped into my room like the instrument meant nothing, while I shuffled and sat on the edge of the bed almost on top of the guitar but not willing to let him see me push it further away.

"I didn't know you were here," I said stupidly.

"Yeah, I just stopped over to see everyone." He walked over to my desk, looking at the *Peanuts* strips and the drawings I had made and photos I'd taken. There was a picture of the two of us taken right before he left, tucked up in the left hand corner, but he was the only one smiling in it. His delicious smile. In the middle, kept up by a push pin that didn't go through it but held it by the edge, was the picture Evan had sent me of himself in Vietnam. A flush slowly prickled over me. He ran his left index finger across the picture and turned to me.

"We were in Arizona then."

I furrowed my brow, confused about what he meant because I knew he'd never been to Arizona and he smiled. "It's just what we called this valley we fought in last summer. I liked it, relatively speaking. It didn't have any mines because both sides moved too many supplies through to chance it. And we got resupplied every other day. That was about as good as you could hope for over there. I was always scared we'd get trapped somewhere without enough ammo."

He pulled out my dog eared copy of *All Quiet on the Western Front* from my bookshelves. I first read it in seventh grade. It wasn't exactly normal reading for a seventh grader, but I was the daughter of an English professor who had grown up with World War II all around her. My dad fought in the Pacific. My Uncle John had been a German POW. My mom's brother was killed in Germany. My mom had always told me stories about what it was like during the war, and how, when they found out about my Uncle Bill, my grandmother started keening in Italian, rocking back and forth and crying "oh mio figlio, oh mio figlio." I had read all of my dad's letters to his mother. I knew what war was about. But Vietnam was different somehow.

"Did you keep all the pictures I sent you?" Evan asked, looking at the one of him again.

"Yes."

If he wanted to see them, I was going to have to pull out the shoebox I kept them in with his letters, and he was really going to think I was pathetic.

"Sometime—someday—you'll have to show them to me. But I don't want to see them now. Now, I just want to forget. I sent you all my pictures. I don't have any."

I nodded, trying to think of something to say that wouldn't sound stupid, and he turned back to my bulletin board. He pointed to some pictures of the Cleveland skyline and downtown that I had taken over the summer when Michelle and I had gone to a baseball game with some friends. "These are really nice. I forgot how pretty the lake can be."

"Thanks," I said. "I'm thinking maybe I should ask to major in photography."

"But you're so good at drawing."

"You think?" Evan had never complimented my artwork before.

"Yeah, definitely," he said with a shrug. Then he stared at the pictures again. "But these are good, too."

"It was just with my dad's old Brownie."

"Really?" He turned to look at me.

I couldn't hold his gaze. "Yeah. I've been reading a lot about taking photos, and I'm saving up for an SLR camera. The good ones are kind of pricey. I'm hoping after my birthday that I'll have enough. At least for the camera, I'll have to wait for a good lens." I looked up. Evan had turned back to my desk and picked up a pile of pictures I had taken of different things like Willa in the backyard, and Michelle playing her oboe, and my dad working on the lawn mower, a cigarette hanging from his mouth. He laid them out on my desk in neat lines and studied them.

"I got into Berklee," he said suddenly, without looking away from the pictures. His voice tasted like late cherries as it sunk into me.

"When did you have time to reapply? That's amazing!" My mind jumped to the idea that he could be in Boston in the fall while I might be only an hour or so away in New York.

"No, Bug," he said still staring at the pictures. His voice had turned the kind of quiet you use in a churchyard. "Before."

My mouth went dry and I stared at the back of his head, the short bristles of his light brown hair, his small, sweet ears, his long, thin neck, his lean shoulders. For just a second, I couldn't breathe. I was such an idiot. He couldn't play anymore. Berklee wouldn't want him anymore.

The silence crowded the room, pulling us together and pushing us apart at the same time, while he stared with determination at the rows of photographs, every line in him rigid. He was waiting for me.

"Why?" I whispered at last.

Evan shrugged, his head down. He seemed suspended, hesitant, unwilling. But then he turned to look at me. His eyes were quiet, and a chill snaked over me. "I guess I thought it wouldn't really happen. I guess I thought it would be an adventure if it did," he said. "I was scared of not being able to meet the expectations of Berklee. I mean, Berklee, Bug! I thought, if I waited a year, I could work on my music, make sure I wouldn't go in there and flop. I guess I had to tempt fate and see what it would do. Part of me wanted to be a hero, like your dad. I had no clue what Vietnam was about. I told myself that what was meant to be would happen, and I should just go with it.

"What a bunch of garbage, huh?" His gaze locked on mine and I couldn't say anything. There was a sarcastic smile playing on his lips, and it felt as though he wanted me to tell him how stupid he'd been. But there wasn't anything I could say that he hadn't said to himself already. And I wouldn't punish him when he had already been punished enough.

"Don't tell anyone, okay?"

"No," I practically whispered, not able to make my voice any louder. "I won't say anything."

Evan nodded his approval. "Are you having Thanksgiving here?"

"My Aunt Mary and Uncle Armand are coming just like always, and some stray grad student my dad is bringing home. He's from Colorado and didn't have the money to get home or something. I met him once at my dad's office. He looks like a frog."

Evan laughed a little. "I have to go to my Aunt Kate's. She asked the whole family. They'll all be there." He grimaced and looked at his hand. He wasn't ready to have them all gushing their condolences on him.

"I wish I could just stay here instead," he said.

Willa popped her head in the doorway. "Are you coming down for dessert or not? Mom wants to know."

Evan looked at me a second, judging me to make sure I had meant it when I said I wouldn't tell anyone about Berklee. Then he smiled.

"Absolutely," he said, straightening up and heading for the door. "You coming, Bug?"

I nodded and followed him and Willa out of the room, wondering which one of us wished he could just stay more.

8

THE MONDAY AFTER THANKSGIVING, everyone at school was talking about the draft lottery. President Nixon's new system was supposed to be fair because each day of the year would be assigned a number based on the order it was picked in the lottery. Boys would be drafted in the order their birthday was chosen in the random lottery drawing. The higher the number your birthday was assigned, the less likely you could get called. When the boys in my math class worked out the statistical probability of being drafted, figuring that if your birthday number was higher than 60 you were probably safe, Miss Tate told them she was glad to see them applying their math skills to real life. The hopeless smile on her face made me wonder if death were the only way people could lose their lives.

The lottery was being televised, and some of the teachers gave us reports every so often from a television in the teachers' lounge.

"This is so ratty," Dave Blakely said to his friends as I walked by their table at the end of lunch. "We can't even vote, but they can send us to war. I thought I was set up since my brother went, and then they go and change the rules."

"And now, it's not going to even matter if we get into college," Pat Holbrook said. "At least the guys before us got a deferment for school."

"Yeah, and who'd be stupid enough not to go to college?" Jim Harrington asked, his words following me out of the cafeteria, chasing me down the hall all the way to my locker.

Yeah, who'd be stupid enough not to go to college? My dad had kids who changed their majors if their grades slipped at all just to make sure they didn't lose their deferment. He called it the "deferment dating game."

But I didn't care as much as I should have. The lottery didn't mean much to me. Evan wasn't going back. The war was becoming a machine that would suck in the best and spit them out mangled and broken, and there wasn't anything I could do to change that. I was just a girl who wanted to be an artist. I couldn't even vote yet. I had no power to change anything.

By fifth period, everyone was talking about how Joey Turner had found Colin McElhenny sobbing in the boys' bathroom because he was already eighteen and his birthday had been drawn first in the lottery. Mr. Miller had to talk him out of the bathroom and then call his mom to come get him, but she was more hysterical than Colin. Joey Turner said Colin kept saying he'd kill himself before he'd go to Vietnam, but Pat Holbrook said that was stupid because all Colin had to do was shoot part of his foot off, and killing himself kind of defeated the whole purpose. Besides which, Pat argued, Colin should have already had a plan to go to Canada, because if anyone could come up short on a one in 365 chance, it was Colin, who had been nicknamed "Charlie Brown" since fourth grade.

Michelle came by my locker after school the way she always did on days she didn't have band practice. "Something else about Colin, huh?" she said. "I feel so sorry for him." Her words jarred against the flowered bell bottom corduroys and bright orange top she was wearing.

I nodded, tossing my backpack over my right shoulder. We walked out the front doors of Roosevelt High and down the sidewalk past the field where John Davis was standing on a milk crate at the edge of the track.

"We need to stop the oppression of the draft!" John yelled to the small crowd gathering around him. Michelle and I stopped.

"He's so cute," Michelle whispered with a smile. John wasn't my type, but I could kind of see why she thought he was cute. He pushed his brown curls out of his eyes and scanned the small crowd, as if he were waiting for someone to cheer. I followed Michelle over to where he was.

"We need to tell the Man 'hell no, we won't go!'" John shouted, mimicking the antiwar chants reported in the papers and on the news. It was cold out, but he was wearing a jean jacket over an unzipped sweatshirt, his Beatles' t-shirt underneath like a flag across his chest.

"You're just being a coward!" Phil Thomas called out from the crowd.

John looked stunned for a moment, but then tried to turn the attack to his advantage. "You're the coward, Phil," he yelled. "Everybody knows you only want to sign up for ROTC so you don't have to go to Vietnam!"

Everybody laughed. "Why don't you sign up for the real deal, if you're so brave?" John taunted him.

"I'm going ROTC while I go to college," Phil said, looking at the kids around him. "Then I'll go wherever they send me, including Vietnam!"

"Oh, so you'll get commissioned just in time for Nixon to pull the troops out?" John asked. "Why don't you enlist as soon as high school's over since you're not a coward like me?"

Everyone had turned and was looking at Phil. I don't think anyone really wanted him to enlist, but he was being a jerk. The only reason a guy joined the ROTC or the National Guard was to avoid Vietnam. I felt kind of sorry for him, since no one was going to be on his side, but it wasn't fair of him to call John a coward. What difference did bravery make anyway? Evan and Miss Tate's fiancé hadn't been cowards, for all the good it had done them.

"We're not old enough to vote, but we're old enough to get slaughtered in their war machine!" John cried. A bunch of kids started whooping and a girl I didn't recognize who was dressed in full hippie mode yelled "Amen" as if she were at a spiritual revival, which kind of made the whole scene ridiculous even though the war was as serious as you could get. I doubt if there was one of us there who didn't think we could change the world if only we could vote. But then a few of the boys who had brothers in Vietnam began edging their way toward John, staring at him.

"Hell no, we won't go!" John started repeating and pretty soon a bunch of other kids joined him. The chant began to take on a life of its own, as more kids straggled out of school and stopped to join the growing crowd. Some of us were just watching, but enough were yelling that the chant was like a rocket getting ready to launch. Michelle and I were being pressed closer in toward John as kids gathered behind us.

"Why don't you shut up," Matt Grayson called to John, moving in as though he were ready to push John off the crate, his fists clenched. His brother had joined the army last spring and was in Vietnam.

Then Danny Taylor, whose brother had come home with facial burns, stepped up and stood beside Matt and Phil, but some of the boys who didn't want to get drafted were gathering around John chanting and supporting him. Someone shoved Danny and fists started flying, and a boy in front of me was pushed into me. A punch coming in toward the boy headed in my direction instead and I ducked just in time to avoid it. I grabbed Michelle's arm and towed her away, shifting through the crowd as the gym doors flew open and Mr. Miller came running out, the lapels of his corduroy jacket flapping with the effort. The boys' basketball team had been practicing in the gym and now they tumbled out of the door after him. Robby laughed as he saw me stumble from the crowd, dragging Michelle behind me.

"That's enough!" Mr. Miller yelled as he pulled Danny off of the kid who had shoved him. "They'll be no anti-war protests on school property! And no swearing either!"

He looked up at John and ticked his head to the side. "Get down, John."

John threw his hands up and stepped off the crate as everyone began to scatter, mumbling about the establishment controlling our lives. Michelle and I melted into the flow of kids leaving and worked our way to Mantua Street.

"There's no way I'd go," Michelle said. "I'd totally be a draft dodger."

"I'm glad George is only fourteen," I replied, thinking about Michelle's brother. "The war has to be over by the time he's 18."

"I don't know," she said. "It's been going on for forever, already, and it just keeps getting worse. Sometimes I'm really scared for him. Everything would so be different if Bobby Kennedy had lived."

I nodded. If RFK hadn't been assassinated, he would've been our president instead of Nixon and he would have started bringing the troops home. I had cried with everyone else the night Bobby Kennedy died, but I didn't know then how much it might have changed my little world. "Maybe Evan would never have been drafted."

"Rachel," Michelle said, the tone of her voice telling me that I wasn't going to like what she had to say.

"What?"

"I know how much you love Evan, and no one wants you to be happier than I do, and I know I've encouraged you so far, but maybe you shouldn't keep waiting for him."

"I'm not waiting for him."

She pressed her lips together and gave me a 'get real' look. "I'm just saying he's been home for almost two months, and he hasn't given you the slightest reason to hope. I thought for sure once he got settled, he'd see how wonderful you are. But he's barely talked to you since before Halloween."

I stared at her, unable to say anything. She'd been more sure of Evan and I being possible than I ever had, and now she was telling me how hopeless it was.

"He's just got too much going on in his head," she said. "I think it's going to be a long time before he's ready to think about dating anyone."

She'd been over doing homework with me on Saturday and Evan had come by, but he'd sat there brooding and aloof for the few minutes he'd stayed. He'd barely even answered me when I asked him how Thanksgiving with his Aunt Kate had been.

"Besides," Michelle added "it's not like he would take you to winter formal or prom. The guy should be a sophomore in college now. And he's a vet."

"What's that supposed to mean?"

"Nothing," she said, "just that a war vet isn't going to think going to the prom is copacetic."

"Why would I even care about going to the prom?"

She shook her head as if she couldn't believe I had really just said that. "Well, I'm going to go if I get asked, and I think you should, too." There was something pleading in her face that made me forgive her labeling Evan a 'vet' like it was some diseased status. "This is high school, the best years of our lives, remember? And I'm afraid you're going to miss out on all the fun waiting around for him. It just seems like he's not very—" she hesitated as if she were searching for a word that wouldn't make me angry and then said "together anymore."

I turned away. "He needs some time, that's all."

"I just don't want you getting your hopes up when it doesn't seem like he feels the same way. He's got a lot of stuff to deal with, and maybe he isn't ever going to be, you know, okay. And you're going to miss the best part of being a senior. Unrequited love isn't all it's cracked up to be, Rachel."

"Thanks, you really know how to cheer a person up."

"I'm sorry," she said. "I'm just afraid you're setting yourself up to get hurt."

We walked without talking. I was way beyond set up and we both knew it. We were almost at her street and I quickened my pace a little.

She nudged me. "Maybe you'll meet some really cute architecture student at Pratt and fall head over heels and he'll make you forget all about Evan."

"Maybe" I said, trying to make her happy so she'd stop making Evan out to be crazy.

I guess she didn't like my answer, or the lack of conviction in my voice. "I'm just saying, you could at least try not to love him. So much." She looked at me skeptically but hopefully, too.

"Okay," I lied, deciding it was probably best if I didn't talk about Evan to her anymore. "I'll try to not love him. So much."

I didn't like lying to my best friend. But for now I took the easy way out because I knew that training my heart not to love Evan would have been like Evan playing the guitar again. It just wasn't going to happen.

9

THURSDAY AFTER SCHOOL, I made a batch of Pizzelles for Christmas. Evan walked in as I was standing at the big kitchen table, the iron plugged in with hot steam rising from it.

"I swear I could smell these from my house," he said.

I rolled a pizzelle off the iron with my fork. Evan picked up one of the cooled cookies lying on the table and started crunching.

"I loved it when you sent these," he said, staring at the cookie in his hand. "Even when they turned all soft as soon as I opened them. It was so stinking humid all the time. I only got one from the tin you sent at Easter, though. We were pulling out just as we got mail and I couldn't carry them. I left them for the guys who stayed behind. They didn't even wait for us to leave. We were walking down the road and they started yelling after me, begging for your address. One of them wanted to propose to you."

I laughed and scooped another lump of batter onto the iron and clicked it shut. Evan leaned his head over and closed his eyes as he sniffed the anise soaked steam.

He opened his eyelids suddenly, a flash of August sky and I winced at the thought of the look that must have been on my face, dream filled and pitiful. But he didn't seem to notice. He walked over to the fridge and got out the milk and poured himself a glass.

"Where's the Nestlés?" he asked, looking in the cupboard where my mom kept it before he left.

"Oh, she moved it over there," I said, pointing with the fork at a cupboard in the corner.

Evan frowned and nodded. He dumped four spoonfuls into the glass and stirred maniacally. Then he came back and picked up another Pizzelle.

"I'm not going to have any left for Christmas."

"Sorry," he said without regret. He smiled like he owned the world. "What are you doing Saturday?"

"Baking, I guess. Why?"

He kept grinning. He knew surprises drove me crazy.

"Come on," I said.

But Evan just shook his head, downed his chocolate milk, grabbed a couple of Pizzelles and started for the door. "Be ready by 10:00, okay?" he called as he stepped outside, not waiting for me to answer. He jumped off our back porch and was gone like a kid scrambling out of trouble.

Portia walked in and perused the selection for a perfectly colored cookie. "Why are you smiling like the Cheshire cat?"

"I'm not," I said, trying to stop.

"Evan must've been here." She made a moon face at me. "I thought I heard voices."

My mom slipped through the door from the basement with a basket of clean laundry.

"Mom," I said, "Saturday morning, Evan and I are going…."

"What? Did you forget already?" Portia asked when I faltered. She was still pretty even with a smirk on her face.

"No. It's just that, I don't know where we are going exactly." My mom pressed her lips together, but she didn't smile. "He has something he needs my help with, that's all," I said. "He probably needs me to help him pick out a Christmas present for his mom or something."

"Oh brother," Portia said, and I thought she would be much better suited to acting than law. "You didn't even ask him where he wants you to go? You'd follow him to the ends of the earth, wouldn't you? He probably has a crush on some girl and wants you to help him shop for her."

"Portia," my mom said.

I shrugged with as much bravado as I could summon. "It's no big deal." I started concentrating on the pizzelles with an energy that my physics homework could have used.

"Leave her alone, Portia," my mom warned as my sister opened her mouth to say something. Portia just shook her head instead.

I was up early on Saturday and ready by nine o'clock. My dad was in the kitchen having one of his rages, banging pots and pans around and yelling at my mom for not having any bacon. I should have been used to his tantrums, but they still set me on edge and made me hate him for upsetting my mom. She would defend herself blindly, as though she didn't know my dad had these irrational outbursts every other week or so that ended as abruptly as they started, without any semblance of recognition by my dad that they had even occurred.

"Why can't a man have some damn bacon in the house when he wants it is all I'm saying," he yelled as he slammed a cupboard door.

"I do my best, Art," my mom said, "but I don't always know what we're out of!"

I was in my room drawing, trying to shut out my dad's angry reply, when Willa came to the bottom of the steps to tell me Evan had come.

"Oh, that's right, I'll be down in a minute," I called as if I had forgotten, making sure I didn't rush down the stairs. My dad was still raging at full speed, scraping a fork over one of my mom's non-stick pans just to make her crazy as he cooked himself scrambled eggs.

"We won't be back until after lunch sometime," Evan was saying to my mom when I walked in. My dad stopped yelling. His face changed from anger to calm. In a few minutes, he would act as if nothing had even happened, and we would all follow along.

There was something scary about my dad when he was angry. He was the kind of guy who didn't need to hit you to make it sting.

"You ready?" Evan asked, without any apparent fear that I might really have forgotten.

I nodded and grabbed my navy wool pea coat, glad to escape into his dad's Impala. The seat was hard from the cold and I tucked my hands into my coat pockets.

"Sorry," Evan said. "I should have warmed it up first."

"That's okay."

"I guess it's a good day to get out of the house, huh?"

I twisted my face into ironic agreement which made him laugh.

I was determined not to ask where we were going. If we were shopping for some girl he liked, I didn't really want to know. He turned the radio and the heat on and backed out of the driveway, enough space between us on the bench seat to accommodate a baby hippo.

Evan drove down Crain and then picked up Mantua, heading north toward Cleveland. "So, you're not the least bit curious?"

I shook my head, trying to prove I could wait him out. He laughed. "You're too easy, Bug," he said. "We're going to buy me a new car. A Camaro to be exact."

I couldn't help the surprised look on my face. He didn't even have a job, how was he going to pay for a car?

"Thanks to Uncle Sam," he said, reading my mind with a sarcastic smile on his lips, "I get a paycheck for life now." He still wore bandages over the stumps of his fingers, but I was pretty sure he didn't need them anymore. Mrs. Olesson had told my mom that the VA doctors had "cleared" him.

"Right," I said, always able to come up with the wrong thing to say. I changed the radio station to cover how stupid I was. Chicago was on. I sat back and looked out the window, singing along quietly. I didn't like the idea of Evan having his own car. Somehow it made him seem so much older than me, so far removed from where I was. If he had a car, he might as well have a plane. He could fly away any time he wished.

"Why are you so quiet?" he asked after a while.

"I don't know," I replied. I tried to be happy for him. But why did he have to pick a Camaro? Just the week before, the guys at the end of our lunch table had gotten into a big debate about their dream car, finally agreeing that it had to be a Camaro because it was a "chick mobile."

"Maybe you should get a Mustang."

"You like those better?"

"Yeah, I guess so," I said. They looked pretty much the same to me, though, so I couldn't understand why a Mustang would be any less of a chick mobile than a Camaro. I decided to quiz the boys at our lunch table about that on Monday.

"Since when do you pay attention to cars?"

I shrugged and then smiled. I didn't really want to, but there was something about the way he was looking at me that made it impossible not to smile. "I guess a Camaro's good. But why couldn't you just buy it at Lyman's?"

"I want to do this on my own. Not have anyone calling my old man behind my back to see if it's okay with him."

"Fair." Everyone knew his dad, and half the town were his patients. If Evan had tried to buy a car at Lyman's the salesman would've been sure to call his dad first.

"Sometimes this town is just too small. They hate the University, but without it, we wouldn't rate a single stop light."

He was right. All of Kent was divided into two distinct camps, like the North and the South in the civil war. You were either part of the University or you blamed it for any and all of the town's problems. People who grew up in Kent complained endlessly about the "gowns" who crowded town and drank too much. The locals conveniently forgot about the commerce and tax revenue the University brought to Kent, not to mention the free flow of ideas, a commodity that was sorely needed. And everyone at the University looked down on people from Kent, calling them "townies" because they thought Kent was the center of the universe and that KSU existed only to orbit Main Street.

We pulled into a Chevy dealership a little before eleven. Evan headed straight for the Camaros. An eager salesman in his mid-forties came bounding over.

"Sweet, aren't they?" he asked, watching Evan like he was a stray dog that just needed to be handled the right way.

Evan shrugged with the hint of a smile on his lips.

"We could have you and the little lady driving off the lot in one of these babies in no time!" the salesman said.

Evan and I looked at each other, the surprise evident on his face that the guy thought we were a married couple. I guess I could've passed for eighteen.

"Oh, she's my neighbor," Evan said. I didn't even rate as a friend.

"Oh, well, that's fine, that's fine," the salesman said. He looked us over suspiciously, but seemed content enough with Evan's clean cut appearance. Evan was reading the sticker on the window of a red Camaro. He pulled his hand out of his pocket and ran his index finger along the list. The salesman's eyes widened.

"Are you sure you can drive okay, son?" he asked.

Evan stared at him.

"He can drive just fine," I said.

"Oh, of course he can, little lady. I just was surprised a little, that's all." The man was fingering his tie, looking apologetic and skeptical all at once.

"She's not your little lady," Evan said. "Come on, Bug." We side-stepped the salesman and headed back to the Impala. The salesman followed us the whole way, assuring Evan that he hadn't meant to offend him and that his dealership loved vets. Evan never stopped, never turned around. He opened the door for me and then walked around to the driver's side. As we drove away, I looked back at the salesman still standing on the sidewalk of the showroom as though we might not actually go.

Stevie Wonder's "Yester-me, yester-you, yesterday," came on the radio. Repeating fields with their resigned cows disappeared along the highway and I bit my lip to keep from crying for Evan. At the first chorus, he leaned forward and turned the dial.

"You like Stevie Wonder," I said.

"Not that song."

We drove east, stopping for lunch at a little roadside diner. We ordered cheeseburgers and French fries and cokes, and Evan got a large chocolate milkshake.

"You want some, Bug?" he said, sticking the straw in and sliding the frosted glass toward me.

"Just a taste. It's too cold for milkshakes today." The creamy chocolate was icy on my tongue. I shivered.

"I like the cold, now," he said, flashing an off-handed smile as he shoved Vietnam back in its box. Sometimes, it was like looking at the before Evan for just a second, as if he were inside somewhere hiding.

I pushed the milkshake across the table to him and he slipped his fingers over the base of the glass as I slid mine off. Portia was right. I'd have followed him to the ends of the earth.

"Did you send your application to Pratt?" he asked. I looked up. He hadn't said anything about Pratt since that day in the hammock.

"A couple of weeks ago," I said. I poured more ketchup on my plate, trying to ignore a little girl two tables away who gawked at Evan's hand.

"You really have your heart set, huh?"

"I can't go to KSU, you know that."

"New York's a pretty big place for a little Bug."

I pulled back in my seat. "What's that supposed to mean?"

"Don't get mad," he said, with a smile that told me he thought I was pretty entertaining.

Mad wasn't quite the word that came to my mind, though. Especially since a big part of me was scared of leaving home. It was like Evan knew I had an Achilles heel, as he sat there waiting for me to admit I was afraid. Or maybe it was just that not one single person really believed in me, so how was I supposed to believe in myself? Even Michelle was worried I'd be lost in New York. I understood what Evan had meant when he'd said he was intimidated by Berklee. I hadn't even been accepted to Pratt yet and I was already worried about not being good enough to make it. And even if I were a good enough to be at the best art school in the country, I wasn't sure I would survive the homesickness. As much as I needed to break free of Kent, I still loved my family. Why couldn't he, of all people, understand that?

"It's not like I'd be moving to New York and living in an apartment, trying to get a job," I said, trying to convince myself as much as Evan. "It's a school, with dorms and buildings and classes, just like KSU. Except it's in a big city and has an amazing art school. I'm sure the teachers there look out for the kids just like my dad does for his students. You should see the brochure. The campus is beautiful and historic, nestled in a quiet neighborhood. And the art school is this amazing building."

"It just seems pretty far."

"Berklee's farther."

I pushed my plate away. "I'm sorry," I whispered, looking across the room.

"No, you're right. Boston is farther than New York. And Vietnam is even farther. It's okay, Bug, I deserved that. If you want to go to Pratt, you should go. You shouldn't screw up like I did."

"That's not what I meant," I said, desperate to make him remember that he had wanted to go away, too. I wanted him to remember how much he had wanted Berklee—so much that when he'd gotten it he was too afraid to take the chance. Why couldn't he understand that being afraid wasn't a good enough reason not to go?

"Don't sweat it," he said, his gaze resting on me quietly.

Maybe that was how he'd felt about Vietnam. Being afraid wasn't a good enough reason not to go. But Vietnam wasn't Berklee.

The waitress brought the check over and dropped it in front of Evan. He pulled out his wallet and paid her and we went to the car without speaking.

Evan headed North, both of us quiet. Rolling hills turned into new suburbs, but Evan and I kept moving closer only to get further away from each other.

He pulled into a Chevy dealer on the outskirts of Cleveland. A young salesman near the showroom door made a dash for us.

"Good afternoon, folks," he said. "What can I interest you in today? A little family wagon?"

I shook my head as Evan said, "No, I'm looking for a Camaro."

Suddenly the man realized. That awkward movement of the eyes as he stared a moment too long, pity and disgust flashing across his face as he took in Evan's deformity, the sudden suspicion we weren't married but some kids looking for a sports car and free love. My face flushed even though I was angry at the man. This time, Evan let him show us the Camaro and we even sat in it. But I could tell from the way he barely answered the man's questions that he wasn't going to buy a car from him.

"So, shall we take it for a test drive?" the man asked. "Unless you want your lady friend to drive it?" He just couldn't help himself, giving Evan's hand a glance as he said it.

"No, thanks," Evan said, getting out. He held the door for me and we turned back to where the Impala was parked.

"But it drives like a dream," the salesman said, following us. "You have to drive it to believe it!"

"I'm sure you do," Evan replied as he opened my door.

We drove away, another salesman standing after us in the rear view mirror. I wasn't sure how far it would be until we found the next Chevy dealer, but Evan surprised me by pulling into a Ford dealership further down the boulevard.

We walked into the showroom and Evan went straight up to one of the older salesmen. The man shook his hand and Evan pulled his left hand from his pocket. "Do you have any problem with this?" he asked.

"Vietnam?" the salesman asked.

Evan nodded. The man nodded back. "Korea. Got three holes from shrapnel in my leg, here, here, and here," he said, pointing to different spots on his right thigh. Then he smiled, like he and Evan shared some inside joke. "You got the scratch, I got the car. Let's talk."

Evan laughed, but I didn't think being flippant about his disability pay was funny.

The salesman walked us out to a shiny row of Mustangs.

"Do you have any with a tape player?" Evan asked.

"They're pretty rare," he said, "but I got two, actually, being as we're close to Detroit. A red one and a blue one."

Evan looked at me.

"Blue," I said. *It has to be the blue one.*

"The lady says the blue one."

We took it for a test drive and I sat in the back as Evan and the salesman discussed the endlessly wonderful features of the amazing chick mobile. An hour later, Evan had signed the papers and the salesman gave him the keys.

Now I realized why he had asked me to come. Someone had to drive his dad's car back. I looked up at him as he handed me the keys to the Impala.

"I'm not going to be able to reach the pedals."

"I'll pull the seat up," he said, climbing in and pulling it forward until his knees surrounded the steering wheel. I didn't tell him it was still going to be too far. He got out and I climbed in. My toes dangled just out of reach of the pedals.

"You look pretty ridiculous. Like your mom's uncle from Pittsburgh, the one who drives that huge Lincoln even though he can't see over the steering wheel."

I glared up at him. "Okay, okay," he said, "you get to christen the Mustang." I tugged on the lever and used all of my weight to push the seat back so he could fit into the car. He handed me the Mustang keys.

"I don't like it being your new car."

"It's okay," he said. "Just *don't* scratch it. Or wreck it."

"Funny," I said, and he laughed. He put me in the Mustang, pulling the seat the full way forward so that I could reach the pedals and then fixed the mirrors for me.

"Don't be nervous," he said, leaning in the window until I thought my heart would stop. "This is just the most important thing to me in the whole world. But it's replaceable. In a different color." He grinned.

"Funny," I said again, his aftershave freezing my brain up. He looked happier than I'd seen him since before he left for Vietnam.

We drove straight back to Kent, Evan in the lead. A light snow started falling somewhere along the last ten miles or so, but the ground wasn't cold enough yet to make it accumulate. I pulled into the Olesson's driveway and parked behind the Impala, finally letting a full breath escape me. The lights were on at my house, and Portia was standing in the front window.

"Thanks, Bug," Evan said as I handed him the keys.

"You're welcome."

"How's it drive?"

Like a chick mobile.

"Fast," I said.

Evan smiled like a little boy seeing the store Santa for the first time. His dad came out of the house with Robby in tow. "So this was the big mystery," his dad said, "I should have known!"

"Oh, man, is this sweeeet!" Robby cried.

I slipped away as Evan showed them his new toy. The brass knob of our front door stung my hand with its cold and I closed the door softly behind me.

"There's a chick mobile if I ever saw one," Portia said.

I nodded and headed up the stairs to my room before dinner. Maybe she was right and the car would make Evan irresistible to every girl he met. Not that it mattered much, because as far as he was concerned, I was only a "little bug" who couldn't make it in the big, wide world anyway. Convincing Evan that I belonged at Pratt was going to be as hard as convincing my dad, and probably a lot more pointless. The only thing I knew for sure was that, if, by some elusive, wonderfully incredible miracle Evan ever did decide to love me, the first thing I was going to do was rub it in Portia's face.

10

EVAN'S CAR WAS GONE a lot the first couple of weeks he had it. The driveway would be empty when I came home from school, and sometimes it was late at night before the Mustang would be parked in the spot his dad had relegated to him. I figured he was hanging out in town in the bars, but I didn't ask him, too afraid I wouldn't like the answer. Instead, I spent a ridiculous amount of time thinking about what I should give him for Christmas. I found a Snoopy shaving mug at Thompson's drugstore and bought that for him. It was the kind of silly thing we'd always given to each other, something a brother and sister might exchange. But I wanted to give him something else, too, something more important. I finally decided on a drawing, hoping that would be right.

The Thursday before Christmas, Evan drove up as I was getting home from school. I was glad suddenly that Michelle left me two blocks earlier to turn to her house, but I felt a little like a traitor for thinking that. Evan pulled along the sidewalk and rolled the window down.

"You want to go for a ride, Bug?"

I leaned against the door and laughed. "You already have a car," I said, "what could you need me to help you buy now?"

He just laughed and my gaze fell on the odometer. Evan had put more than two thousand miles on the car in less than two weeks. His left hand rested on his jeans and the bandages were off. His skin was pink and tender and shiny. His knuckles seemed to be crushed inward. But there was no gauze, nothing left to separate him from the reality of himself.

I slipped around the front and climbed in, dropping my backpack and purse at my feet. Everything still smelled new. The car was warm after my cold walk home and I slid off my knit gloves and pressed my fingers to the vent. I stole another glance at Evan's hand as he drew it up to the steering wheel. His hands had always been so beautiful, his fingers strong from playing the guitar endlessly.

He pulled away from the curb but we didn't talk. We drove aimlessly, listening to the radio. It didn't really matter where we were going. Evan had been spending his time driving instead of in bars with alcohol and girls. I was glad to be wrong.

"How was school?" he asked after a while.

"Typical. Except we haven't done anything all week since tomorrow is the last day before break."

"Yeah, I remember that useless week before Christmas." The way he said it reminded me again how far away he was from me. Three years and a lifetime. I concentrated on the radio. He laughed as I bounced my head, singing *Along Comes Mary*, and did my best Mama Cass impression to *The Words of Love*.

"You know, Bug, you have a pretty voice. Too bad I won't have a band to put you in. Then again, it would have had to be a jazz or swing band. Your voice isn't strong enough for a rock band."

"I didn't know I was at a job interview or I would have sung louder."

"Stronger, not louder. There's a difference," he said. "An artist should understand that."

I smiled and shrugged but then Bobby Vee started singing *Come Back When You Grow Up, Girl*. Every word of that stupid song seemed like a wedge between Evan and me, my not-strong-enough voice silenced. Evan still thought I was living in a paper doll world, a tiny bug not capable of handling life, let alone love. I wanted to change the station, but I figured that would just make it seem true.

After a while, he drove us toward Twin Lakes and then pulled off the main street and followed the gravel road that circled West Lake. He stopped at a break in the trees and parked. A commercial for laundry detergent sang a sugary tune and he turned the radio off.

"It's pretty," he said, leaning forward and staring out the windshield.

"Even in winter." The trees were unashamedly bare, their branches and twigs rising in the air like the notes of a symphony. Misty ice was forming at the edges of the water. Most of the homes scattered along the lakes were summer places, hidden among the trees on the shore. The late afternoon sun spilled across the surface, catching the ripples only to release them. December silence penetrated the closed windows.

"I'm glad it's winter," he said. "I missed the cold. It was so freaking hot over there. But I miss the hammock."

"Me, too." The hammock was our special place. At least, that's how I thought of it. But at least he missed it. I snuggled down into my seat, the overcast sky a blanket above us. Michelle was right in a way. He just needed me to be there for him without me needing anything from him. She would have considered it a sacrifice on my part, but I couldn't regret it. I stayed as still as a listening deer. The cold began to fill me, slowly, from the tips of my toes and fingers.

Somewhere along the lake a dog barked. I couldn't tell how far away the muffled sound was. But Evan tensed and leaned forward for a better view. It reminded me of the night he had stood in the driveway after staggering home from Water Street. He turned and gave me a sheepish look.

"Over there, a dog meant movement. And movement was never a good thing." He paused, scanning the view slowly, like he was letting the memory in.

"We'd go into the villages in the day and before we ever got there, the dogs would start barking, letting us know the VC were going into hiding. They'd sleep in the villages at night and they always knew if we were coming, no matter how light we traveled. We'd get to the village and ask about them, and everyone would say 'No VC! No VC!' But we'd heard the dogs. They'd hide until we were gone, watching us, and then that night, or the next, they'd ambush us. My buddy, Tom Foley, he'd say 'there go the damn dogs, and there go the VC! We won't see them again til after dark.' Even after he was killed, I'd think of him saying that every time I heard a dog bark. Guess I still do."

"You never told me that in your letters," I said. My voice was so quiet, I wasn't sure if he'd even heard me.

Evan shook his head and a puff of air escaped him. "I thought about it every minute of every day. The last thing I wanted to do was write about it. Especially to you."

Especially to me. Bobby Vee popped into my head. *Grow Up Girl.*

"Besides, everything we said was censored. You had to be careful what you wrote."

It had never occurred to me that they hadn't let them write whatever they wanted to say. I knew my dad's letters had been censored. I guess I had figured that in Vietnam it just didn't matter, since the news cameras were following them around anyway.

"His widow lives in Bloomington. I've been thinking of going to see her, now that I have wheels. And visit his grave." He turned suddenly and looked at me. "What do you think?" he asked as though he needed permission. It took me a moment to realize he was talking about Mrs. Foley.

I sat there not knowing how to answer him. He needed someone to tell him if it would be the right thing to do, but how was I to know? I took a deep breath. "I guess, if it were me, I guess I'd like that."

Evan nodded and sat back, letting his shoulders relax. Slowly it grew dusky and then quickly dark.

"My mom's going to be worried," I said finally. It was the only thing that would make me break the spell of being alone with Evan, worrying about my mom worrying about me. "I didn't tell her I was with you."

"You're right. We'd better get you home."

I hated the way he had said it, like I was a baby. I wanted to protest, but the thought of my mom panicking when I didn't show up by dinner time stopped me. It didn't matter how long I was willing to stay huddled in the cold of Evan's car, I had to go home.

Evan turned the engine on but he didn't put it into drive. I put my hands up to the vents, waiting for the first warm air to blow through, my fingers burning from the cold. I wondered why Evan wasn't telling his friends from high school this stuff instead of me. I didn't know if he'd even seen any of them yet. Somewhere, deep inside of me, I knew it wasn't because I was more special than them. The idea came to me like Portia creeping into my head, but this time I only had myself to resent.

"Sorry," he said. "I didn't think about how cold you probably are."

"It's okay." My teeth started chattering uncontrollably.

Evan laughed. "You're always a trouper, Bug, you know that?"

"Yeah," I said. An idea was forming in my head about Evan not traveling all the way to Bloomington without someone with him, especially to visit the widow of his dead friend.

"Is Mike home yet?" If Evan would take his best friend with him when he went to see this woman, somehow I'd feel better about the whole thing.

Evan put the car in reverse. "I don't know," he said, as though that answered the question I was really asking. I figured OU had to be on break. The colleges always ended before the high schools.

"You haven't talked to him?"

"I saw him on Halloween night, at the Kove. He was home for the weekend. He was pretty surprised to see me. Why? Do you want me to fix you up with him or something? He's too old for you."

"No," I said, with enough sincerity that Evan didn't follow up with any teasing. *Please tell me he didn't say something stupid about your hand.*

"None of us expected you until February or March," I said as a lame excuse for whatever stupid thing Mike must have said.

I wanted to argue with him that Mike wasn't too old for me since that meant he was, too, but he would have just thought I did have a crush on Mike.

Evan shrugged, turning the radio on as we pulled out to the main road. *Aquarius* filled the air and I couldn't think of anything to say to make the conversation go the way I wanted it to.

"He told me not to talk about it," Evan said, his words striking like firecrackers on a quiet night.

"Your hand?"

"No, Bug. Vietnam. He said that, as my friend, he was telling me that, if I were smart, I wouldn't ever mention Vietnam to anyone. He said no one thinks the war is a good idea, and no one cares about what it's like over there. He told me, as my friend, that the best thing I could do was just forget I was ever over there and pretend like it hadn't happened. And then he looked at my hand and told me, as my friend, that I should keep a low profile. And that was before My Lai broke."

Anger flooded through me, red hot. The idea that Mike could tell Evan not to talk about his life for the last two years because people were tired of the war or didn't agree with it made me want to slap Mike right in the face. Did he think Vietnam was Evan's idea? Evan did what his country told him to do, just like my dad had, and nobody hated his generation for it. I wanted to go find Mike and tell him off. But somewhere in that flood of anger, I lost my footing and started swirling in a whirlpool of crystallized realization.

I looked out the window at the big, old houses lining Mantua Street. "People have been tired of the war for a long time. So they blame the troops."

It didn't matter if someone was against the war or supported it. Both sides were sick of it. Since My Lai, the war protestors had been calling the troops "baby killers," while the establishment people had a long list of hateful names for the protestors, most of them coined by Vice-President Agnew. But none of them wanted to actually see Vietnam coming home on planes, wounded or in flag draped caskets. That part of Vietnam wasn't supposed to exist. The protestors used the dead soldiers to tell everyone how wrong the war was, but they didn't care about the Evans who were right in front of them, while the establishment people just wanted their heroes to be stoic, riding into the sunset like good little cowboys.

"Funny that the people who aren't doing the fighting are the most tired of it," Evan said. "We never knew anything about people being sick of it, or protests, or people thinking we were the bad guys. All our news was censored. We thought everyone would be proud of us, like they are of our dads. We were out there, putting everything on the line every day because that's what our country told us to do, under conditions that would make a saint afraid to look God in the face, and we were doing our best. I knew there were a few anti-war protests before I left, but I never expected it to be like this.

"When I got off the plane in San Francisco, people wouldn't make eye contact with me. They looked away from me like, I don't know, like I wasn't clean enough to even set eyes on. At first, I thought it was because of my hand."

"But they must have told you about the violent protestors, like the Weathermen?"

"I read about how they protested the Democratic National Convention before I left, but nothing else. I didn't know they staged that riot during the Chicago Seven trial until I got back."

The Weathermen had broken off from the Students for a Democratic Society because they didn't think the SDS was radical enough. "They want to force a revolution with riots and bombs. They named themselves after Bob Dylan's *You Don't Need a Weatherman to Know Which Way the Wind Blows*. Just more proof that rock music is the devil's work."

Evan smiled at my sarcasm. "They never told us any of that."

"You know we landed on the moon, right?" He smiled a little more.

"That we heard about. And the Yankees scores, and well, you always wrote me about stuff or sent me articles. Like when the Cuyahoga caught on fire. I remember the things you wrote to me more than what they told us over Armed Forces Radio. That always sounded like propaganda worthy of the Japanese. And when we landed on the moon, it didn't seem real, hunkered down in that filthy jungle, the canopy so thick you couldn't even see the moon sometimes. But then I got your letter, and I believed it could have happened. But they didn't tell us anything that didn't make America sound invincible."

"I guess they didn't want to mess up your morale."

"Yeah, we definitely needed a bunch of spoiled brat kids on deferment telling us how pointless the war was. We would never have figured that out by ourselves, over there getting our butts kicked by a bunch of ghosts in black pajamas, half of them under the age of fifteen, using our own unexploded bombs to booby trap us. Knowing that a bunch of deferment jerks were protesting the war would've really messed up our great morale."

I tried to smile, but it came out a whispered, "I'm sorry."

"I'm getting how things are real quick." His voice had the edge of bitter black coffee.

Evan pulled the car into his driveway. It was wrong. Every part of it. And maybe Mike had meant to protect Evan by telling him to forget the war. Maybe he'd actually been kinder than I thought at first. Maybe he really didn't understand that war isn't something you just forget because it's more convenient for everyone else that way. But as I watched Evan climb out of the Mustang he only had because of his disability pay, I still felt like slapping Mike right in the face.

11

TWO DAYS LATER, we went to get our Christmas tree. It was a strange family ritual, since we all looked forward to it even though my dad was sure to have one of his rages and make us miserable eventually. None of us would have wanted an outsider to see it, but Evan wasn't an outsider.

Sometime in the late morning, much later than any of us wanted, my dad was finally ready to go and we piled into the Buick. After he'd screamed about not being able to find the tree saw and then the cord to tie the tree to the roof. My mom sat in the middle up front, between my dad and Evan, and Willa got the middle seat in the back.

"It's so good to have you home, Evan," my mom said.

Portia batted her eyelashes at me over Willa's head. I mouthed *shut up*. Willa giggled, making Evan turn his head.

"What's so funny, Willa?" he asked.

"Oh, nothing," she said, her face becoming serious, "it's just really nice to have you back."

"Thanks, Willa," Evan said, sweeping his gaze over me before he turned back around.

We drove into the country which didn't take very long, but it took us four tries to find a tree farm that hadn't sheared all of their trees. My mom hated sheared trees, saying that people always had to ruin nature in their quest for modernization.

We tumbled out of the car and Evan's face broke into a huge smile despite the fact that he was standing in a freezing field in the middle of nowhere Ohio, looking for the perfect imperfect Christmas tree with my not-quite-perfect family.

We took off in different directions, my mom and I heading up a small hill to the long needled trees. I hated shorted needled trees because they left marks on my arms. And I was the one who would decorate it. Willa always said she wanted to help, but by the time the lights were strung she'd be too busy watching TV. Portia never cared about decorating the tree.

"I think we should get this one," Portia called from the opposite hill, Evan following behind her with the tree saw.

"It's too blue and too skinny," I called back. She turned and said something to Evan and that made him laugh, then they both looked back toward me. Portia had never really forgiven me for being born. I walked further down the line of trees to distance myself from the image of them laughing at me together.

"Oh, Rachel, look at this one," my mom said, standing before a thirteen foot White Pine.

"It's beautiful. We should tell dad we like the one next to it, and then he'll probably pick this one."

My mom giggled.

"Dad, look at this one," I called to him, pointing to the tree next to the one we liked.

"Well," he said when he had huffed his way over to us. "I guess if that's the kind of tree you like."

"Well, do you see a better one?" I asked, pretty sure I had him this time. But my father wasn't that easy. He looked past our beautiful pine to one on the other side.

"That's a better tree there," he said. "Every tree here is."

Portia, Willa, and Evan came up the hill to us.

"Let's get this one," Portia said, pointing to the one my mom and I had picked out. "It's the prettiest here."

"That tree's no good," my dad said. "Look at that huge bare spot near the bottom."

Everyone began arguing about which was the best tree, except for Evan and me. When I was thirteen, he'd told me how pointless it was to argue with my dad when it made him so happy to pick an ugly tree. And somehow, the way Evan had explained it, I had seen the logic in giving in to my dad. That year I realized that scrawny, ugly trees allow the ornaments to hang, filling in the empty spaces with a unique kind of beauty. Part of me still wanted the beautiful pine my mom and I liked, but I was learning to see the beauty in the lopsided, bare trees my dad chose. Standing there in the cold, I thought maybe Evan's hand could be like that. Maybe there was some beauty that could fill the empty space of his missing fingers. But I couldn't think of any.

When the argument was finally over, Evan had cut one of the ugliest, short-needled trees on the lot, while my dad complained that he was cutting it crookedly and we would lose another foot just to fix it. But Evan just smiled, because my dad was the only guy in the world who would treat him like nothing had changed. It had been hard for him to hold the saw as he moved it back and forth, the empty fingers of his glove flopping back and forth as though they were searching for what was missing, too.

When we got home, Evan and my dad brought the tree in and set it up in the tree stand in the living room, in front of the big picture window.

"Is it straight?" my dad asked, still breathing hard from the exertion of carrying the tree. He and Evan were on either side of it and my mom had the unenviable job of tightening the tree stand bolts.

"No, it needs to come to the right," I said. "No, too far, go back about an inch."

"Oh for cryin' out loud, Rachel," my dad yelled, "that can't be right." He wiped the sweat from his forehead with the back of his leather work glove. My dad was an imposing figure when he was happy. Angry he was like a hurricane bearing down on you. There was so much uncontained anger pulsing from his frame.

The tree slipped from Evan's hold and went lopsided again.

"Aw, for Christ's sake," my dad yelled. "Can't anyone give me any help here?"

"Sorry, Art," Evan said.

I no longer cared if the tree were straight. Just like always, my dad had taken the joy out of the whole thing. The hurt in Evan's voice was sharp like a note that's off. I started thinking how great it would be not to have to live through my dad's tantrums if I got to go to New York.

"Art, really," my mom said.

"Now what do we have to do?" my dad asked, the tone in his voice letting us know he was ignoring any protests.

"It needs to come to the left, about two inches," I said. "There, that's perfect."

"That can't be right," he said, shaking his head at me, anger dripping from his words.

"Then come see," I replied, walking over and taking his post so that he could see the tree from across the room. He walked over and stood there looking, not wanting to give in.

"Well, you've put the worst side on the front, but the hell with it, if that's how you want it" he said. "Tighten it, Ree," he told my mom. "Willa, run out to the garage and bring my drill in."

It was time for the part where he drilled holes into the trunk to fill in the really bare spots with extra branches that would have to be glued and wired in place. That was always worse than picking the tree or putting it in the stand.

"I'll go," I told Willa, not wanting her to get caught in my dad's mad trap.

Every time my dad had one of his rages it melted into the last one, which melted into the one before that, as far back into my childhood as I could remember. They flooded together, a giant vat of molten wax threatening to spill over and burn me into oblivion. Maybe it was part of the reason getting away from KSU was so important to me. All I knew was that I couldn't wait to be grown up and in control of my life.

When I came back, my dad yelled at me for bringing the wrong sized bit so Evan followed me out to the garage to help me get the right one, or at least shoulder the blame if my dad still wasn't satisfied. It was cold and I snapped the light on, hurrying over to my dad's work bench.

"Thanks," I said.

"It's no big deal," Evan said softly, following me.

I stopped a minute, some part of me frozen, but shifting and boiling underneath like a geyser.

"Someday, when I have a house of my own, and kids of my own, I'm only going to have happy Christmases. I'm never going to let anything ruin them." I couldn't look at Evan.

There were tears in my eyes I didn't want him to see, even if he knew they were there.

He slipped his arm around my shoulder and pulled me into his chest. "Someday, Bug, you'll only have happy Christmases," he whispered, the words drifting down on me from above like falling snow.

"What's taking so long? Dad wants to know," Willa's voice burst upon me and I jerked away from Evan and hid my face while I wiped my cheeks.

"I think we found it," Evan said. "Come on, Bug."

We went back to the living room and Evan handed my dad the drill bit. My mom had the wood glue and wire, and the operation went on much as it always did, with a lot of yelling and swearing. I watched Evan and I wasn't sure if that moment in the garage had really happened or if I had finally gone off the deep end and fallen straight into one of my daydreams. But he smiled at me, and the real crashed into me. He wanted to protect me from my dad the way I always tried to protect Willa.

When the extra branches were finally secured in the base of the tree, my dad rocked back on his heels and wiped his forehead with his handkerchief.

"I need a coffee," he said. The annual battle was over. My dad would be his normal self until Christmas Eve, when he'd get crazy again.

We had hot chocolate, and I put Christmas music on the stereo and hung the bee lights. Willa and Evan brought the ornament boxes up from the basement and started going through them. My mom gave each of us a keepsake ornament every year, and had given one to Evan for the last few years before he left. We each had a small box that held our ornaments wrapped in tissue paper.

Evan opened his box and unwrapped the electric guitar ornament my mom had given him three years ago. He stared at it for a few moments, and then he put the box aside and went in the kitchen with my parents.

After dinner, I went back to finish the tree while Portia and Evan helped my mom clear the table. Willa sat glued in front of the television, but I listened to the laughter coming from the kitchen. I envied Portia every look Evan must be giving her, every time he spoke to her. They had never been close the way we were, but Portia was always prettier than me, always smarter, always more at ease. She could have had her pick from any boy on the KSU campus, but she was holding out for something better when she got to law school. She didn't understand Evan, the way his China blue eyes were like the hues in the finest Delftware. She didn't understand that Evan was capable of changing lives and the world had misplaced him. She didn't know that Evan needed a hero as much as he needed to be one. But she understood how much I loved him.

A little after nine, Willa finally came to add her ornaments.

"Portia, Evan," she called, "come and put your ornaments on. Rachel's finished."

I was standing ankle deep in bits of tissue paper and boxes and discarded pieces of unusable ornaments beginning to gather them, the sap on my fingers making the tissue stick to me. Portia took her box and unwrapped her ornaments.

"Should I put this here?" she asked, turning and smiling at us, her dark hair perfectly curled at the bottom, her make-up still fresh. The ornament was a porcelain pair of ballet slippers my mom had given to her when she was in ninth grade. She had taken ballet until she was a junior in high school, but my mom had let me quit when I was eight because I couldn't follow what everyone else was doing and always stood out like an ugly duckling among swans.

I wouldn't be able to blame Evan if he did fall in love with her. Maybe he had always loved her and I hadn't realized, but I didn't think so. I was pretty sure I would have noticed something as painful as that.

"I'm going to bed," Willa announced, just as my dad started yelling for my mom from upstairs because he couldn't find a light bulb and the lamp in his study had gone out.

"I'd better get going, too," Evan said before I even had a chance to wish Portia out of the room.

"Don't you want to hang your ornaments?" I asked him.

He shook his head as he walked into the hallway and picked up his canvas coat from a chair. I followed him to the doorway. "No, Bug," he said, "you can do it for me, like you did the last two years."

He remembered the letters I'd sent, telling him that I put his ornaments on the tree for him. He was still supposed to be in Vietnam now. He was supposed to have two months left on his tour. I thought about all the what ifs, and whether I was glad he was with us even if it meant that he'd lost all of his dreams. If he hadn't lost his fingers, maybe he would have come home in February with his left hand okay. Or maybe two more months would have taken his life. Or his sight. Or his legs. I thought about how much worse it could have been, but somehow glad wasn't quite what I felt.

"Night," he said, and the weariness in his voice fell on me, heavy and cold.

"Night," I said, watching him disappear into the dark before closing the front door.

Portia turned the television off. I walked over to the coffee table and picked up the box with Evan's ornaments, carefully hanging the guitar on the back side of the tree, near the window where he wouldn't have to see it. Then I scattered the rest of his ornaments, blending them into the whole.

"He's changed," Portia said. "He's haunted by spirits."

There was something in her voice I didn't like, something resembling recognition or compassion that had never been there before.

I looked over at her, standing perfect in the doorway, watching me claim Evan's share of our Christmas tree. Her face, delicate as an orchid in the glow of the twinkling lights, was filled with pity. I just wasn't sure if that pity was for Evan or for me.

12

THERE WAS SOMETHING about my dad's Christmas Eve rage that set it apart from the others. Maybe it was the intensity, or the predictability. It ended an hour or so before the first guests arrived. My father transformed like a spirit possessed from a troll into a prince, so that no one outside our family but Evan ever knew what he had been capable of only a few hours before.

The Olessons always came on Christmas Eve since they didn't celebrate it otherwise, but went on Christmas day to Dr. Olesson's sister, Kate. Mrs. Olesson didn't like to have company because it messed her house up. My Aunt Mary and her husband Armand came from Pittsburgh, and my dad's brother, John, and his family brought my grandfather from Cleveland. Two of my dad's professor friends came every year with their wives and kids, and then there was always a stray or two that my dad managed to drag home at the last minute. Ray, the grad student from Colorado, was coming this year, along with his roommate, Doug.

Even the farmhouse table wasn't long enough for everyone, so we put up a second table that my dad fashioned out of the base of an old oak table and a top that he put together of antique pine planks. The rest of us knotted up like fishing line when the time came to put it together, knowing this was the most likely thing to set my dad off. I hated his rages the most when he made Willa or my mom cry. In those moments, I hated him. So much that I couldn't remember he'd spent the Christmas of 1944 fighting in the Pacific, knowing his brother had been captured by the Germans, and the Christmas of 1945 occupying China.

Evan was the first person to show up. He strode into the kitchen from the front hall like a young Cary Grant. "I hope it's all right that I came early," he said to my mom, like he didn't normally come over whenever he wanted, handing her a bouquet of winter roses.

My mom hugged him. "Merry Christmas Evan. It's so wonderful to have you home!"

He looked almost like a little boy, the smile spreading over his face like a clear sunrise after a long spell of clouds. It was the first time since he'd been home that there was more of the before Vietnam Evan on his face than the after Vietnam Evan.

The back door shot open and my Uncle Armand and Aunt Mary came bustling in, handing their luggage to Willa and me to take upstairs, packages falling out of their arms. Aunt Mary threw on an apron. She was my mom's oldest sister and the closest thing to a grandmother I ever had, since both of my grandmothers died before I was born. She wasn't even five feet tall, but she ran my mother's kitchen like a five-star hotel. Every pan sparkled, every onion was minced to perfection.

The house began to fill with people. The sizzle of frying smelts crackled like music. Willa and I buzzed around the frying pan, snatching the hot salted fish while my Aunt Mary swatted her slotted spoon at us, trying to save them for the buffet. But they were never as good as when they first came from the pan, crisp and tender. Evan leaned against the counter and helped himself while my Aunt Mary smiled at him, as glad to have him home as the rest of us. Christmas songs on the stereo drifted from the living room where a fire popped and the tree shimmered. Candles and oil lamps glowed alongside the soft lamplight, the house like a fairy palace, smelling of warm food and burning wood.

Evan pulled me aside as I restocked crackers for the cheese plate. "How was it?" he asked.

"Like always."

"There's something about the holiday that really gets him."

"This year she hadn't bought enough Coke. That one really made him crazy. She had ruined Christmas for everyone. If he were a dictator, he would have had her shot."

"I should have come earlier. Sometimes he's not as bad when I'm here."

"It's over now," I said, shrugging. "Some things you just have to live through."

Evan looked at me like he was a little too amused by my youthful wisdom. Across the room, my father was rageless, as charming as a king in an enchanted forest with his court bowed before him, listening to his stories with an attention any priest would have coveted. And Evan was as susceptible as the rest, glancing at my dad with the same boyish admiration he'd always had. But he knew both sides of my dad.

"I'll try to talk your art up during dinner, since he's always in such a good mood then," Evan said, turning back to me.

I looked up, surprised. It was the first time he'd even hinted that he might be thinking about helping me get to Pratt. "Thanks," I practically stammered as his mom called him over to meet Ray.

"Is that the Frog Prince?" Evan asked, smiling.

I nodded and he laughed as he sauntered away. I helped my mom and Aunt Mary get the food to the long sideboard where we laid the buffet. Clams in a roux with white wine, marinated shrimp, boiled shrimp, spaghetti with tuna in tomato sauce, fried smelts, roasted asparagus, sautéed finocchio, salad. Evan filled his plate as though he were making up for the last two years.

"Seconds are allowed," I said as I passed him in the swirl of the buffet line, enjoying the way I could always make him smile.

He sat down next to my dad while Portia jockeyed with my Uncle John to sit on the other side of him. I sat at the designated kids' table with my cousins like always because Portia wouldn't and my mom didn't think it was proper for some of the hosts not to sit at both.

Afterwards, we passed around platters of pizzelles, cutout cookies, fried knots, almond macaroons, and chocolate candies. This year, I had made Snickerdoodles, too, because Evan liked them. He looked up at me as he took a couple when the plate went past.

Ever since he was elelven, Evan had played the guitar after dinner. There had been plenty of nervous glances sent his way, watching, waiting for the moment that he must be remembering. But Evan didn't need anything to remind him. His left hand had been trying to form chords all night, distractedly, clumsily, against his thigh as he'd talked with people. The urge to play glistened in his eyes. The unhappy humming of a song brushed my ears as I bent over him to set his teacup down on the table.

Some of the guests stayed in the dining room, mesmerized by my dad. He was telling war stories. The funny, innocuous ones that made everyone forget that war could leave you without fingers, or legs, or a soul.

Others wandered into the living room with more coffee and sweets. Willa and some of my little cousins were still young enough to beg for it to be time to hand out presents. There was some small gift for everyone. Evan stopped me as I walked past his chair, asking what we had gotten the frog prince and his roommate.

Portia overheard him and leaned closer to separate us.

"Bug's going to kiss him and take the curse away," she said, a smile spread across her face.

Evan laughed, and my heart contracted into a fist. I wished I could think of some snappy retort, but instead I blushed stupidly and forced myself to smile as if I appreciated the joke. Just like when we were little and played checkers, or jump rope, or Monopoly, Portia had beaten me. Sometimes I just wished she would stop.

Mrs. Olesson was telling my Uncle John, "I just want them to finish the job. They have to end this, just like the allies did with Hitler. I don't want Evan's—" she paused, her eye twitching, her face intent on bringing Uncle John into her fold, "experience, to have been wasted."

I grabbed some empty wine glasses off the table and hurried to the sink. Mrs. Olesson loved her son, but she didn't understand him, or his "experience." Evan didn't care what happened in Vietnam anymore. It was a thousand times more irrelevant to him than I was.

My Aunt Mary shooed me from the kitchen just as my Aunt Grace called me into the living room to ask about school and if I was looking forward to starting KSU in the fall. The question landed like a kick in my stomach. I tried to say yes, but I couldn't quite bring myself to it. There was no 'starting KSU.' I'd been there my whole life already.

"I don't really know," I finally said. Across the room, Willa was handing Evan his present from me. I hadn't even seen him come into the room. The drawing was rolled up like a scroll with a ribbon around it, sitting in the Snoopy shaving mug. I had placed it up on a bookshelf, so that I could tell him about it before anyone gave it to him but somehow Willa had noticed it. I tried to slip between people to get across the room and stop him until I could explain, but it was too late.

He unrolled the drawing and his face grew still, losing all expression. He stared at it until I was sure my heart would stop.

"What is it?" Robby asked, leaning over Evan's shoulder. "Hey, that's you!"

Evan nodded, and several people started crowding him.

"Who's the guy handing out the presents?" Willa asked.

"Did Rachel draw this?" Professor Donaldson asked. My Aunt Grace walked over to see.

"That's exceptional, she's very talented," Doug said.

Their voices sounded like something far away, the blood pounding through my head demanding a response from Evan. He was looking at it so intently it gave me the same feeling I got whenever he stared into my eyes.

"Rachel, it's lovely," my Aunt Grace said, squeezing my arm as she walked back into the kitchen.

"Thank you," I murmured, not able to take my eyes off of Evan. He looked up then, searching the room for me. I mouthed "I'm sorry," and his face was transfused with an expression I had never seen before and couldn't name.

He nodded to me and mouthed "thanks," but his face had this terrible weight of sadness on it, and then he handed the drawing to my grandfather who had asked to see it. He pulled back from everyone else and slipped behind them, moving to the doorway that led to the hall.

I tried to follow him, to try to explain why I had done it, to try and make him understand that I hadn't meant to hurt him, but my grandfather called me over to his chair by the fire, asking me what the picture meant.

"It's a drawing of Evan and some of the guys in his unit, and one of them is a friend of his who died in Vietnam, Nonno," I told him. "It's a scene Evan told me about in one of his letters. They had been pinned down for a couple of days without enough supplies, and when they finally had some rations and ammunition dropped to them from a helicopter, Evan's friend, Tom Foley, said 'must be Christmas, boys,' and all of the guys started laughing and calling him Santa Claus because he was handing them stuff from the package."

"Hmmph," my grandfather said. I leaned over and hugged him. He smelled of tobacco and tweed and some cologne that could have been made by the Old English furniture polish company.

"Bring me an espresso, huh, bella?" he asked, patting my arm.

"Coming," I said, choking back the rising desperation to find Evan and explain. I kissed my mom for having anticipated my Nonno's wish, standing there taking the espresso pot off of the stove.

"For your grandfather?" she asked as I handed her a little yellow cup and saucer. My hand shook.

"Yes," I said, grabbing a plate and putting a couple of pizzelles on it so he would be distracted enough to let me go. As soon as I had made my delivery, I started looking for Evan. He wasn't in the kitchen or living room, and he had walked into the front hall so I dashed up the steps and checked my dad's empty study. I ran back downstairs and grabbed a coat from the closet. I had to find him. I had to try to make him understand. The only problem was that, with every passing second, I was growing more certain that I was the one who didn't understand anything at all.

13

THE AIR WAS SO COLD it hurt my lungs as I drew my first few breaths of the winter night. I thought maybe Evan would be sitting in his car, but the Mustang sat abandoned and dark. He wouldn't have gone back to his house and I stood there a moment not sure where to look as the magnitude of what I had done sunk into me. I headed to the only place I could think of.

Evan was sitting on the ground, his back against one of the hammock trees, staring up at the stars.

"I'm so sorry," I said, running over to him, my heels wobbly on the frozen grass, unable to check the tears stinging at my face. "I didn't mean to make it worse. I thought maybe it would help you to have a good memory of him, something that was tangible, to remember there's light beneath the sadness. I didn't mean to—" I gasped for air and fell to my knees beside him, a twig on the ground ripping through my nylons. Judas could not have wanted forgiveness as much as I did.

"Stop, Bug," he said, shaking his head. "What you did was—"

He paused, as though he were searching for the word to describe it, and my chest tightened like something inside it was shrinking and snapping into pieces and I cried even harder.

But Evan just looked at me, his eyes wet. "It's beautiful."

My breath shuddered. I pushed the air out trying to clear my head to be sure I had heard him right.

"I'm so sorry I hurt you."

Evan laughed and searched the stars as if he expected them to agree with him. "You didn't hurt me, Bug. Vietnam did. Life did. I did. You've never hurt me once in your whole life. Well, except that time you hit me in the head with the baseball bat." He gave me a sideways smile as a tear hit his cheek.

"That was an accident," I said, smiling and sniffling. "And I only grazed you."

"Oh, and that time you ran me over with your bike."

"Most people swerve to the right to avoid a collision," I reminded him. And then my smile faded. Another reminder that he was left handed. Another time when it had cost him more than it should have, including four stitches in his leg.

"Times like these, I wish I smoked," he said, looking back at the stars, his voice husky. "Everybody in Nam smoked. 'Give me a 'borough,' 'hey, you got a 'borough?' 'I need a 'borough!' All the time. And every time somebody would die, or lose a body part, or find out his girl had dumped him, or his dog died back home, I'd wish I smoked with the rest of them. But then I'd think of your dad, sitting at the kitchen table, coughing and spitting up that nasty yellow mucous into his handkerchief, or my dad, his fingers stained all yellow and smelling foul as he works on your teeth, and I wouldn't light it. I'd sit there with it in my fingers and stare at it and wonder if it even mattered. If I started smoking and died before I came home, what difference would it have made? But if I started smoking and I made it home, I didn't want to be like them. And all the guys wanted the ones in my rations. 'You gonna smoke that or just make love to it with your eyes?' they'd say to me, and I'd toss it to the closest guy."

Evan sniffed.

"I'm glad you didn't start smoking," I said stupidly.

"Yeah, I'd think of you and Willa, too, when I was over there, always trying to get Art to quit."

I followed Evan's gaze up to the stars and we sat there for a few minutes, just quiet, the way we were in summer with the hammock beneath us. I wished my side was against him, the way it always was when gravity pulled us together in the hammock. Even the cold seemed to understand how much I loved him. It was the kind that makes you feel like climbing mountains, sharp and clean.

"Could you make a copy?" he asked.

He kept staring into the navy sky.

"Of the drawing, you mean?"

"Yeah."

"I guess so."

"How long would it take?"

"I don't know." I found my pockets to protect my bare hands from the soft breeze. "A few days, I think."

"Could you do it by Saturday morning?"

"Sure, I guess I could if I really worked at it. Why?" His eyes looked so dark in the night, but it was the kind of dark that makes you want to curl up safe and happy, knowing the morning will be clear.

"I'd like to give one to his wife. I think she'd like it. You captured him perfectly. If you don't mind."

"No, of course not. I'll make you one."

"I was thinking of leaving Saturday. Maybe stopping in Cincinnati to see my Aunt Margaret." Evan shrugged, like he wasn't sure any of it mattered. "Could you do it by then?"

I nodded.

"Thanks, Bug. Hey, d'you get your present?"

"No, not yet."

"Come on," he said, sniffing and standing and offering me his left hand. "You're gonna love it."

I slipped my hand into his and he pulled me up. When I was on my feet he let go, and I shoved my fingers back in my pocket before the cold could steal the warmth of his touch.

"Sometimes, I still feel them," he said, holding his hand out, his voice ghostly. "Like just now, it felt like I had all my fingers when I pulled you up."

"It seemed like it to me, too."

"The doctors said it's normal to still feel what's missing for a while. Weird."

"Yeah, weird," I echoed. I followed him back to the house. We slipped in the front door and hung up our coats. No one seemed to have noticed we'd been gone.

Evan grabbed for a box tucked underneath the lowest branch of the tree. It was wrapped perfectly. He couldn't wrap a present even when he had had all of his fingers.

"The store wrapped it, Smarty Pants," he said, reading my face. "Just open it."

It was kind of heavy as I tore the wrapping. It wasn't a book like he usually gave me, or a Peanuts comb, or a wall calendar. As the green foil paper fell away, I realized what it was. A Canon EX EE SLR camera.

My mouth dropped open and I looked up, his grin raining down on me. "Do you like it? I almost bought a Nikon, but this one has this new technology that the salesman says is state of the art for quick loading the film. And the lens is supposed to be easily changeable. They just came out in September."

"It's incredible."

Evan started showing me all of the features the salesman had taught him, standing so close to me, his head bent over mine that I couldn't understand anything he was saying. I just nodded and said "yes," when it seemed like I should.

"But it's so expensive."

"What did Miss Dictionary say? 'Something tangibly good out of the sadness,' or some Hallmark card crap like that?"

Evan had always made fun of my vocabulary. But I had forgotten he used to call me "Miss Dictionary."

Portia's voice exploded into my world like thunder. "That must have cost a lot!" she said, and I felt a flicker of triumph that she knew, even if it was only Evan spending his disability money like a reckless sailor.

"Oh, Evan," my mom said, "Rachel can't possibly keep something that expensive. It's far too generous!"

She had on her cautionary face, and suddenly everyone was staring at me.

"It's fine, Rita," Evan said, "the money's not important, and Bug should have a good camera."

"I know you want to be generous," she said, "but, really, this must have cost a good deal. You should save your money for college. The GI bill won't pay for everything."

Evan looked at me and then back to my mom, and then at Portia. "Can I speak to you?" he said to my mom, nodding his head at the doorway. They walked into the hall and I could see Evan pleading his case. I stood paralyzed, wishing again that I had some control of my life, waiting to see my mother's scale tip one way or the other. But it only took Evan a few sentences before my mom conceded. I could tell by the look on her face and the way she nodded.

He came back over to me, his smile announcing his victory. "So you like it? You wouldn't rather have had the Nikon?"

"This is incredible," I said.

"I think Miss Dictionary used that one already," he replied.

I loaded the role of film he had set inside the box ready to try it out. Portia dragged Evan over by the tree so that she would be in my first picture. Willa was next and I took several more, but I wanted to save some of the film for after I had read the directions.

Evan came over as I put the camera back in the box. "We need some music," he said.

I couldn't help it, bringing my skeptical gaze up to his. "Not me, Bug, you. Willa told me you learned to play 'Revolution' while I was gone. I want to hear you."

"Well, I did, but, I—" I hesitated, not knowing how to ask him if he was sure. There were so many people.

"So you don't know how to play it?"

"Oh, I can play it," I said, "but it won't sound right on—" I stopped. It wasn't really my guitar, but it wasn't his anymore either. "The electric guitar."

"I brought my acoustic," he said, "it's in the hall closet."

Evan retrieved the guitar and pulled it from its case, holding it a moment as if it were The Lady of Shalott and he were Lancelot suddenly stunned by her. Then he handed it to me.

"Just play it," he said.

Soon Willa and my cousins were singing along and then Robby and Doug.

When I finished, everyone clapped.

"Not bad, Bug, not bad," Evan said.

"Play some Christmas music," Willa said.

I played the songs I knew, *What Child is This, Winter Wonderland, Holly Jolly Christmas,* and *Happy New Year Darling.*

Everyone was singing along and laughing. I kept looking at Evan, but he seemed to be okay, just quieter than usual.

"Can you play *Baby It's Cold Outside?*" Portia asked.

I shook my head. "I can't play by ear the way Evan can."

"I can help Bug if someone can sing it," Evan said.

"I'll sing it," Robby said, and a laugh rippled through those of us who knew him since he was perfect for the role of the wolf. Robby and Portia sang the duet while Evan sat close to me, whispering the chords into my ear, every inch of me fighting to concentrate on what he was saying. I made a few mistakes which made him chuckle, and then he put his arm around me and guided me on a chord I was struggling with, his index finger and thumb running over my fingers so quickly it was like his hand was still whole. I stumbled over the tune again and suddenly everyone in the room was silent and we looked up to see them watching us, the ghostliness of Evan helping me play reflected on their faces. Evan shrank back.

"Well," I said as cheerfully as I could manage, "I think I need a break!"

Evan turned away. Others joined me, saying they didn't realize it was past one o'clock, and what a wonderful evening it had been, while my mother offered more coffee. But the mood had changed and everyone began heading home. The Olessons were the last to leave and I watched through the front window as they walked across the frosted ground, the evening ending the way my time with Evan always did, with aching regret.

14

FOUR DAYS LATER, I took a breath of the clear afternoon air and rang the Olesson's doorbell, sending Karma a little telepathic request to let anyone other than Evan's mom answer it.

The door swung open. Slowly. Robby stood in the foyer and I let go of the breath I'd been holding. His bare feet stuck out beneath bell bottom jeans and a plaid button down shirt draped his slender shoulders. His curly hair was getting long enough to cover his ears, and he tossed his head to get it out of his eyes.

"Oh, hey Bug," he said. "I suppose you're here to see Evan?"

He was being sarcastic, knowing that I'd never come for any other reason unless my mom sent me over on an errand.

I stepped inside. Evan was home because his Mustang was parked in the driveway. Robby wasn't in any hurry to announce me.

"Is he home?" I asked after an awkward silence.

"Up in his room," he said, "listening to *Paint It, Black* for the millionth time."

I didn't think Mrs. Olesson would like me barging upstairs, but I didn't like to have to ask Robby to go get Evan for me since he was already playing with me about it.

"She's not here, you're safe," he said, reading my mind.

My face burned, but I was relieved, too.

"She's at her Friday afternoon bridge club. She won't be back for at least a half hour." He raised his eyebrows just a little and smirked at me. "You could do a lot better than Evan," he said. "Especially now. Wanna go to the movies tonight? We could see *On Her Majesty's Secret Service*. You can French me when it gets dark."

"Thanks for the tempting offer, but I'll pass. I can't imagine anyone playing Bond besides Sean Connery."

"Suit yourself," he said with a shrug and walked into the kitchen, giving his hair another flip. I smiled, thinking how crazy that must make his mom.

I took the stairs two at a time. It had been ages since I'd been upstairs at the Olessons. *Paint It, Black* slipped from under his door. I took a breath and knocked.

"Yeah?"

The heavy glass knob was cool in my hand. I peeked in. Evan was lying on his back on his bed, as though he'd just been staring up at the ceiling. His feet were pressed against the wall over the wooden headboard. A tennis ball lay on his stomach.

"Oh, hey Bug," he said, sounding just like Robby as he sat up.

"I brought you the drawing," I said, holding the rolled up paper out to him. The paper struggled against his left hand as he unrolled it.

"Yours is the one on top. Although, I guess it doesn't really matter."

"No," he said, examining them. "They look identical. It's amazing. How did you ever manage to make it look so realistic?"

"It's all in the shading, and the stippling and hatching and crosshatching."

"I don't know what any of that means," he said, "but thanks."

I shrugged, not mentioning that I had been working on it almost non-stop since he'd asked for it.

"You're welcome." I stood there, not wanting to leave but not wanting to stay if he didn't want me to. Nothing seemed to have changed since the last time I had been there. The queen bed his mom had gotten him in tenth grade when he'd reached six feet tall and was still growing, the old oak bookcase, his stereo resting on the top shelf, the posters of guitars and the Beatles and Jimi Hendrix. His acoustic guitar was leaning against the wall in the corner.

"I went to the camera store this morning with Michelle," I said. "I took the first role of film to be developed, so I guess we'll see how good I am at using an SLR camera." I smiled, and he returned it.

"You'll have to show me the pictures when I get back."

I nodded. I wanted more than anything to ask him when that would be, but somehow it didn't seem as though I should. I thought about the day he had come by my room, the day he told me that he'd gotten into Berklee, but this time I was the one standing there awkwardly, with more to say than I knew how.

"I hope she likes the drawing," I said.

"Yeah, me, too."

"So what did you say to my mom to convince her to let me keep the camera?"

Evan tilted his head, just looking at me a moment. "I told her that your whole family has always been there for me and that you always made sure I had mail when I was in Vietnam. I told her it was my way of saying thanks, and besides, the camera was on sale and I had plenty of money saved, since I never spent any over there. Except for the silk robe I sent my mom for Christmas last year."

I nodded.

"How come you didn't ask her yourself?"

"I did."

He laughed just a little. "Well, what'd she say?"

"She said it was because you were homesick when you were in Vietnam and I always sent you cookies and mail." I didn't tell him that she had, with eyes full of worry, warned me not to read too much into it, not to think it meant more than it did. She had been her usual sweet self, but she had let me know I shouldn't romanticize it, that it was just the gratitude of a lost boy who remembered being scared and homesick. And I didn't tell him that I had been frantically trying to listen to her every minute since, hushing the desperate, crazy hope that she was wrong. Because if I didn't, it just might kill me.

Evan didn't say anything. "I'd better go," I said, suddenly afraid his mom might come home and find me there.

"Thanks for doing this, Bug," he said as I reached the door.

I stopped but didn't turn around. "You're welcome," I said. "Drive safely."

I sprinted down the steps and out the front door before Robby could give me a hard time.

The next morning from the window, I watched Evan throw an old duffle bag into the trunk of the Mustang. He had the drawing, rolled up and wrapped in plain brown paper in his hand. He drove away through a light veil of snow.

I went up to my room and lay on the floor, staring at the ceiling. Not knowing when Evan would be back reminded me of when he'd left for the Marines. This time it was only for a couple of days, but soon enough it would be for the rest of his life.

I pulled out my New York City guide book that I'd bought at the campus bookstore and studied it, trying to figure out the number of blocks from Pratt to the Empire State Building. I wondered how far it was from Pratt to Berklee, until it occurred to me that they were a lifetime from each other.

The cold outside seeped into me over the next few days. Michelle and I walked to Main, but the street was empty of its usual bustle. It was almost as if Kent didn't exist with all the students home for the holidays. I read *Tess of the D'urbervilles* again. I had read it when I was fourteen, because it was the reason I'd been named Rachel. My dad had wanted to name me Tess, but my mom had argued that her life was too tragic. So they had settled on Rachel, from the scene where Angel Clare carries her over the water. This time I cried so much my mom told me I was only allowed to reread Jane Austen. I studied my physics, but decided that was pointless as I wasn't getting any better at it. I drew Evan, sitting in the Mustang. I drew him lying on the hammock, looking at the stars. I took pictures with my new camera. Slowly, Saturday turned into Sunday, and Sunday into Monday. Tuesday came like a dull ache. Evan had only been back for two months, and I was completely dependent on knowing he was just there. It was dangerous and I had to learn not to indulge it, but I also knew it couldn't last much longer. Kent wouldn't hold Evan for very long, even if it kept me its prisoner forever, and I was like an addict who wasn't willing to waste an ounce of the drug that brought such sweet relief even if the withdrawal was going to kill me some day.

"Rachel!" my dad yelled up the stairs late in the morning. "Rachel, come down here a minute. Hurry up!"

He had gone to his office for a few hours and I couldn't imagine what could be so important. He was in the kitchen with a copy paper box on the table, fumbling with a cigarette.

"What?"

"Come here," he said, motioning me over. There were small cries coming from the box, and holes in the lid.

"Dad, what on earth—" I started to say, but he pulled the top of the box off and there were two tiny kittens crawling around helplessly on the cardboard.

"Oh my God!" I said, picking one up. "Where did you get them? Mom's gonna flip!"

He was smiling now. "The janitor for our building found them out back near the trash dumpster. The mom was too weak to take care of them. Bill Dawson took her home with him. I thought we should take these two."

"Mom's terrified of cats!"

"But these are kittens," he said. "It's just because she got scratched by the neighbor's cat when she was a kid. These little guys can't hurt anyone."

"Are you sure they're guys?" I asked, holding up the tail of the little black one I held. If there were any boy parts there, I couldn't see them.

My dad shook his head. "I'm going to call a vet. I don't know what they need."

"What who need?" my mom asked, walking into the room. "Oh, no, Art," she said when she saw me with the kitten.

"They were abandoned, Mom," I said holding the kitten beside my face. "Look how cute this green one is!" I added, picking that one up, too.

"*Only* until you find a home for them," she said, her features unusually firm. "And I'm not taking care of them."

"He's brown," my dad said, contracting his eyebrows.

"Maybe the strands of his fur are, but all together they make him look green. Trust me, Dad, I know about these things."

"I guess that's why you want to be an artist," he replied, his voice tinged with regret. He couldn't even bring himself to acknowledge that I was going to be one. Only that I wanted to be one.

I spent the next two days learning everything there was to know about kittens. Even my mom had to admit they were ridiculously cute.

"It's all part of my master plan," I heard my dad telling her the next evening as I was about to enter the kitchen. Something made me stop, some feeling that whatever he was saying had to do with me.

"I don't see how kittens are part of a master plan," my mom said.

"She's never going to want to leave home if we have these kittens," my dad replied.

"Cats. They'll be cats by September."

"Okay," my dad said. "Cats. Rachel will never want to leave home if we have these cats that she's raised from helpless kittens. She'll forget all about this Pratt nonsense and settle down to KSU without any fuss at all."

"I don't know about that," my mom said so quietly I could barely hear her. "Just because she hasn't been talking about it doesn't mean that she doesn't still have her heart set on it. She still has that map of New York sitting on her desk, open."

"Well, New York might have Pratt, but we have kittens. She's not going, and this way she'll accept it and move on. You'll see."

"Cats," my mom said.

I turned and walked away from the kitchen. The kittens were curled up together on a towel I had put in front of a heating vent in the hall, sound asleep. I pet them, but they didn't stir. "You guys understand it's not nonsense, right?" I asked in a whisper. Whatever Evan had said about my art on Christmas Eve hadn't made any impression. My dad was determined I wasn't going to go. The kittens were just a way to appease me so that I didn't make his life miserable in the process.

Money was part of it. Pratt was a lot more than KSU. But with my tuition allowance from his faculty benefits, it wasn't going to be impossible for me to go to Pratt. Maybe I could even find a scholarship. But the money wasn't as important to him as keeping me at home. He wanted me in Kent, where he thought I belonged. He didn't want me to be an artist and he really didn't want me going away.

Even if I defied my dad and tried to go without his blessing, I wouldn't be eighteen for another year so I'd lose a whole year of school. But I wasn't the kind of girl who defied her parents. I didn't even know where to start, and I couldn't realistically imagine living completely on my own if they weren't willing to help me. There was no job I was going to qualify for that would pay for Pratt, and I wasn't going to get a job out of college as an art major that would pay for the kinds of student loans I would need. I had to figure out a way to convince my dad he was wrong, but I had time. I didn't expect to hear from Pratt until at least February. There was a big maybe that I wouldn't even get in.

The phone rang on the drop leaf table beside me.

"Hello?"

"Hey, it's me," Michelle's voice came over the line. "How are the kittens?"

"Just as cute as when you saw them yesterday."

"Did you name them?"

"Mmmhmm. In keeping with family tradition, we had a rousing debate about authors and characters. Shakespeare and Voltaire lost. Charles and Dickens won."

"Which one got Dickens?" Michelle asked. "The bad green one or the black one?

"The bad one."

"Hey, you are coming to the party tomorrow night, right? It's going to be huge. End of the decade, after all!"

"No," I said, "I'm going to stay here with Willa. My parents are going to a party at Professor Stevens' house. I don't want Willa to be alone on New Year's Eve."

"You've never liked New Year's Eve," Michelle said. "You're too sentimental."

"You celebrate for me. I promised my mom I'd stay with Willa."

"Okay, Scrooge," Michelle replied.

I laughed. She had gone with Colin to the winter formal and been bored out of her skull by him, but she still thought she should be wringing out every bit of fun there was to be had in senior year. She had only admitted that you shouldn't go out with someone just because you feel sorry for them. I told her about my dad's plan to use the kittens against me, but I didn't tell her about the drawing I had given Evan or that he asked me to copy it. I didn't even tell her my new camera was from him, and she just assumed my parents had gotten it for me. Just like Evan was learning not to talk about Vietnam, I was learning not to talk about Evan.

15

I CHECKED THE OLESSON'S DRIVEWAY the next morning, but Evan's Mustang still hadn't materialized. I peeked through the window every few hours, telling myself not to expect to see his car, but somehow my disappointment still rose each time. I wanted him to want to be with us, the way he always had before the war, but the fact that he wasn't coming home said New Year's at our house didn't matter to him anymore.

Even Willa noticed. "I wish Evan had come home," she said, as we watched my parents pull out of the drive to go to their party. I closed the door against the cold and gave Willa a quick squeeze. And I wondered where in the world Evan was spending this New Year's Eve, just as I had the past two years.

"Can we play Monopoly?" Willa asked.

"I guess so. You set it up. I'm going to put another log on the fire."

We tried to play, but the kittens insisted on crawling all over the board, climbing up the sofa and jumping onto the coffee table where the board sat. They batted the pieces around with their tiny paws until we finally gave up and just played with them.

Around ten o'clock, the kittens fell asleep in a bundle on the sofa, soft purrs filling the room. Guy Lombardo's New Year's Eve show was on TV. The Christmas tree still twinkled across the room from the fireplace. I always took the ornaments off on New Year's Day, while my dad, Mr. Olesson, Evan, and Robby watched the bowl games. I had thought Evan would just slip into the routine again once he came home, but he was gone again, this time of his own volition.

"You know what I love most about Evan?" Willa asked as though she had caught me thinking about him.

"What?"

"The way, when he smiles, it makes you feel just like you do when the weather is absolutely perfect. You know, like late September, and you think anything is possible just because the day is so heavenly. That's the way Evan smiles."

I pressed my lips together. That was exactly the way Evan smiled.

"So what do you love most about Evan?" she asked. No one had ever asked me what I loved about Evan. Everyone had just always made fun of the fact that I did.

"I don't know."

"Yes, you do. So, what is it?"

I hesitated. I'd been so careful lately not to talk about him, even if I did think about him all the time.

"I guess it's that the way he smiles is the real him. Like at Christmas. Everyone should have been making things easy for him, but he was the one who smoothed the whole evening out, like when he helped me play the guitar so there would be music. He sees what's funny and what matters. He's strong, but in a sweet way."

"I hope someday he decides to love you the way you love him."

"Love isn't something you decide, Willa," I said, shaking my head. "It's either there or it's not. But thanks for wishing it."

"Will you make us popcorn?" she asked, the gears in her head shifting like the engine in a sports car. "Mom bought Jiffy Pop."

"Mom never buys Jiffy Pop."

"I asked her to."

"She spoils you," I said, but I understood because Willa was easy to spoil. We laughed at the way the foil expanded into a giant ball.

"It looks like something from 'Lost in Space,'" Willa said. We settled down on the sofa with pop corn and Kool-Aid and waited for midnight.

There was a sharp knock on the door and Willa jumped. "Who'd be coming over now?"

"It's probably Robby because his date dumped him," I said, which made her laugh.

I looked through one of the small glass panes that framed the sides of the front door. Evan was standing on the porch, shivering in his canvas coat despite the shearling lining. I grabbed the knob and pulled the door open.

"Hey, can I join the party?" he asked, stepping inside. "I saw the lights."

"I didn't think you'd be back." I was almost afraid I was daydreaming.

"I was beginning to think I wasn't going to make it, too. Some of the roads were pretty bad west of here."

"Evan!" Willa exclaimed, running into the hall and hugging him.

"Hey, Squirt," he said, squeezing her.

"We have pop corn," she told him, dragging him into the living room. "Jiffy Pop popcorn!" I went to the kitchen and brought him a Coke.

"Thanks, Bug."

Willa already had one of the kittens in Evan's lap and was almost finished telling him the story of their miraculous appearance.

"And your mom went for this?" Evan asked. "She's terrified of cats."

"Mmmm," I said. "It's all part of my dad's sinister plot to keep me from going to Pratt. He thinks I'm too soft to leave if I raise them."

"I don't want you to go either," Willa said.

"Well, I doubt if I'll get the chance. Even if I get in, Dad's not going to let me go."

"You don't know that," Evan said with a slight shake of his head. "You need to take some knockout pictures with that camera and show him why it's a good idea."

It was the first time he'd really said anything helpful about Pratt, except for his promise on Christmas Eve to talk my art up to my dad. But he'd given me the camera to help me show my dad that I deserved to be at a real art school, and that was better than talking about it. Maybe I could convince my dad through pictures.

The countdown came and we stood and the numbers spilled from us until we finally cried out "Happy New Year!" Evan gave Willa a kiss on the cheek, and then leaned over and kissed my cheek, too, so close to my lips that it singed them.

"Happy New Year, Bug," I heard through the buzz making the room float. His gaze fell on mine, melting my lips together so I couldn't even smile. Then Auld Lang Syne was being sung on the television and Evan and I put our arms around Willa's shoulders as she stood between us, swaying gently from side to side. When the song ended, we broke apart but I could still feel the burn of Evan's lips on my cheek.

Couples as old as our parents and grandparents floated across the television screen, dancing to a Nat King Cole song in perfect waves.

"We need a New Year's Eve show for our generation," Evan said. "You know, something with rock bands playing."

"People our age are supposed to be out at parties, like our parents." I said. His parents were at a dinner dance at the Twin Lakes Country Club with all the elite "Kentites."

Evan laughed. "Not watching TV."

"I bet it will happen though. Things are changing so quickly," I said. "A few years ago, women were still wearing dresses all the time and white gloves if they left their house. Women are still 'Mrs. John Smith' in the newspaper, but they're changing their image. It's just a matter of time until there's a New Year's Eve show for us."

"In mom's day, Portia wouldn't have been able to go to law school," Willa said.

"I think Vietnam has a lot to do with changing things," I said.

"What do you mean?" Evan studied me as he asked.

"I don't know, I guess it's made us ask why. Our parents' never ask why, they just do whatever they're told. Wear white gloves. Wear dresses instead of pants. Drive a Chevy. Work the same job your whole life. Vote for the status quo. Go to war." I shrugged. "I mean, I think that's what scares them so much about the 'long hairs.' It's not that their hair is past their ears, or that they wear colorful clothes and listen to different music. It's that they demand to know why they have to do stuff that doesn't make sense to them."

"I think you understand an awful lot for someone who's never really been out of Kent," Evan said.

But for all my wisdom, Evan still didn't seem to think I was old enough for him.

Willa yawned. "You'd better go upstairs now," I told her. "I promised Mom you'd be in bed by 12:30."

"Do I have to?"

"Yes," Evan said, "or you'll be too tired to watch the games with us tomorrow."

Willa relented then, kissing Evan and me on the cheeks one more time before heading upstairs. I was afraid he would leave, but he settled back down on the sofa.

"Do you have any leftovers?" he asked.

"Just polenta." It was the one thing my mom made that Evan didn't like very much. My dad and I loved it when it was leftover and fried in butter. "I could make you something."

"Such as?" he asked, taunting me with his skepticism.

"I don't know," I said, "such as a grilled cheese sandwich, or eggs and toast. This isn't an all night diner. And the toast has to be Italian bread, that's all we have."

"Eggs and Italian toast would be great."

He followed me into the kitchen and lifted himself up to sit on the counter while I made his meal. The cotton of his long sleeve t-shirt caught the outline of his arm muscles and shoulders, and I tucked the memory away to draw it later. Michelle would be mad at me, but I couldn't help thinking how lucky some girl would be someday, the one who got to marry him, the one who got to be like this with him forever.

"So, I didn't want to say anything in front of Willa," he said, "but Ann Foley really liked your drawing."

"She did?"

"She said you must be a great artist, because it seemed so much like him."

"I was afraid she might not like it. You know, that she might be offended that I tried to capture him when I never even knew him."

"No, she was really happy."

I slipped his scrambled eggs and toast on a plate, and we went back into the living room. He ate quietly for a few minutes, the TV filling the silence. He was getting a little better at eating with his right hand.

He set his empty plate down on the coffee table and pushed it away. "When I got there, I didn't know what to do, you know?" he said. "I just stood there. I had practiced in my head what I should say, I don't know how many times on the way there. But standing at her door, I couldn't remember any of it. She was looking at me like she knew why I was there, but she didn't know what to say either. Finally I just said 'I served with Tom,' and handed her the picture, and she unrolled it and looked at it and when she looked up at me, I knew I had done the right thing, going to see her like that."

"I was afraid maybe I had told you the wrong thing. I was afraid maybe I shouldn't have said you should go."

"No, it was good. She called his parents and they came over. We had dinner and I told them all about Tom, everything I could remember. But no matter how much I told them, it was like they couldn't hear enough. They just wanted to touch him, you know? I guess I did, too."

He stopped, and I wished I knew what to say. The wall clock kept ticking loudly, but my mind was stubbornly frozen, unable to come up with a single necessary word.

"And he's got this little boy, Tommy, and he wouldn't leave my side," Evan said at last. "As soon as his mom told him I had served with his dad, he stood beside me, or sat on my lap, or right next to me. And they asked me about how Tom died, and I didn't want to tell them in front of Tommy, but Ann said he had a right to know, so I told them."

His face twitched, but all I could do was sit beside him quietly, waiting for him to be ready to go on.

"And then his parents left," he said after a few moments, "and she asked me if I'd help her put Tommy to bed. So we went up to his room, and I told him nice things about Vietnam. It was a real struggle to remember anything nice. There wasn't much. I told him how beautiful the ocean is there, and how the white beaches stretch for miles like something you'd see on a post card. I told him how bright the stars are at night, out in the valleys of the green mountains where there aren't any cities. And I told him how the children would run up to us for candy and how his dad always had some in his pockets for them. And then his mom turned out the light, and we stayed there in the dark, with just his nightlight humming until he fell asleep. It was weird, sitting in the dark like that with them, but it was right somehow, too, you know?"

He stopped, and I realized how far away the television and the room had become. He rubbed the side of his hair with his hand and took a big breath.

"She said it was the first night since they found out about Tom that he'd gone to bed without a fuss."

Evan picked up his glass and took a long drink of his Coke. He set the glass back down on the coffee table, but he kept his hand on it, staring at it.

"I felt so—" he stopped, turning his head to look at me like he didn't know if the word existed to describe his feelings.

"Grief-stricken?"

He shook his head.

"No, Bug. Guilty. I felt so *guilty*. If it had been my turn to take point, or anyone else's, that little boy's dad might still be alive, tucking him in at night. I had been point the day before, Bug. The day before! If we had crossed that rice paddy the day before—"

"You can't think in ifs," I interrupted. "The list would be endless." But his "if" was ringing in my head like the liberty bell being struck.

He slumped back into the sofa. The hurt inside of him flooded onto his face, pinching his features until he reminded me of his mother. My heart fractured, splintering into a thousand little pieces of uncontained sorrow.

"I know you're right," he said, and the unspoken words "but I still feel so guilty" thickened the air.

"I don't know if things happen for a reason or not. Evan. If they do, then it's seems pretty pointless to ask why. There's a reason and we have to struggle through it. And if things don't happen for a reason, well, they're still final, so it isn't any less pointless. Sometimes, we just have to accept what life deals us. Sometimes, that's the only option we get. It's not very prophetic, but it is true."

Evan stared at the fire, and I worried that I'd said the wrong thing. Again.

"You know," he said at last, "when I lost my fingers, I knew there were guys who had it a lot worse than me. I watched guys lose their legs, or be paralyzed, or burned until you just can't understand how they don't want to die. There were weeks where we had so many casualties, we couldn't get the helo's in fast enough. The smell of blood and burnt flesh stuck in your nostrils until it seemed normal. You'd see a piece of a foot or an arm stuck in a tree limb and you wouldn't even flinch, guys were losing them so fast. Or you'd be walking along and you'd come across a VC body that some sick mother had posed, you know, like he'd be propped against a tree with a cigarette in his hand, all decomposed and maggoty, and you knew whoever had done it had been in country way too long. And that was even worse than knowing some guy had left his foot behind. And if it had just been my fingers I left there, I would've been glad to get a ticket home."

My stomach scrunched into a tight ball as he was talking. But I knew why he was saying it, where he was going with these raw thoughts burning like dry ice against skin. He turned and looked me in the eye, his voice coming in a whisper.

"Some days I can't even bear to hear music. I go through whole days of silence from it. But there are days I miss it so much, I just—"

He stopped, flexing his hand as he stared at it with a look of betrayal. He meant playing the guitar. I had watched him too many times holding a guitar like it was a part of him, his fingers running over it as though he'd been born with it attached to him, not to understand how much he missed it.

"Ache," I said.

Evan nodded covering his face with his hands, sitting forward so that his elbows were on his knees. He sat still a moment and then took a deep breath and looked at me.

"A couple of weeks ago, I drove up to Detroit. I went to this club a guy told me about before I went down south."

"Down south?" I asked, calculating in my head how many hours it would take to drive to Detroit and back.

"It's what we called Nam when we were in Okinawa. I met this sergeant once at a supply point and he heard one of the guys call me 'strings.' That was my nickname over there, after some of the guys found out I could play. Everybody had a nickname. I guess it's a way to get close to the guy next to you and stay detached all at the same time. Anyway, this sergeant started talking to me because he played, too. He was from Detroit, and he told me about this club and said when I got back I should go check it out because they had some of the best jazz guitarists you'd ever want to hear. I don't know, but it stuck in my head, and so, once I had wheels, I decided to go."

I thought about the miles Evan had put on his car, and the nights he had come home late enough to wake me with the strangeness of the sound of a car on our street, and I wished I could have been there for him.

"I sat there watching this band, and I mean, Bug, this one guy was solid," Evan said. "I just sat at the table, watching him, and it was like I could feel every move he was making. When they took a break, he came over to me, asked me if I played.

"'I used to,' I told him, pulling my hand up and putting it on the table. He just nodded at me. 'I thought so,' he said. 'You were looking at me like a booze hound looks at a bottle of whiskey. Now I understand why.'" Evan laughed at the memory, and I managed a weak smile.

"So he sat down with me, and we talked about music and shared a couple beers and he showed me his guitar, which was signed by B.B. King. And then he had to do the next set, and he got up on stage and said 'this one is for my new friend sitting over here,' and I watched how magical it was to see him play, and I felt like I was walking through the desert without a drop of water."

"You could still play," I said, not able to make my voice loud enough to sound convincing.

An article I had read before he came home tricled back to me, and I was grasping to remember how the words were written on the page, placing them in order to make sense of the information I hadn't thought important at the time.

"Like Jimi Hendrix or Paul McCartney," I said. "I read an article about Paul McCartney. He had trouble learning to play right handed, and then he saw Slim Whitman playing left handed on a guitar that had been altered and he realized that was what he needed to do. That's how he learned. But sometimes he plays a customized left handed guitar. You could alter a guitar, or get a left handed one. I'm sure Hoefler's could help you alter your guitar to make it play left handed. And I know it means you'd have to relearn how to play, because the strings would be backward, but you could do that. I know you could."

"Everything sounds so easy when it falls from your mouth."

He was being sarcastic. "Look, I never said it would be easy. There's no doubt in my mind that if you'd gone to Berklee like you were supposed to, you'd have been the lead guitarist for a rock band that would've become famous. You probably would've even ended up being a legend and gotten a fat head and started living fast and doing drugs and you would have died in a hotel somewhere of an overdose. You were that good. You know you were. Berklee knew you were."

He was smiling in a lopsided way.

"And if that's all the guitar is to you, then you're right, you shouldn't pick one up again. But if it's like drawing is to me, if it's your—I don't know—your voice, then what do you have to lose?"

"I can't fail anymore, Bug. I've stepped backwards so many times in the last two years I don't even know how to move forward anymore."

"Yes, you do," I said, channeling Willa's practical tone. "And if you get stuck, I'm here to pull you forward."

His gaze stayed on me like a branding iron, but I held it. He wasn't going to make me back down when I was so close to pulling him back.

He sighed, rubbing his hands over his jeans in a nervous way. "Okay, I'll try," he said at last. "I'll see about a guitar. And my old man's been on me to go to school. Maybe I'll start looking."

I wanted to tell him he should look at schools in New York and apply to KSU, but that was stupid. Evan was Ivy League material and even if I was going to get stuck at KSU, there was no reason he should.

"You could still go to school for music. You're a great song writer, and there are all kinds of music programs that don't require that you play an instrument to get in. Aren't there?"

"I guess so," Evan said. The lights from my dad's car swept the room as he pulled into the driveway.

"I should go," Evan said, standing up quickly. He walked to the front hall and grabbed his coat off a chair.

"Thanks, Bug," he said, as he slipped his arms into the sleeves and opened the door. "And Happy New Year."

"Happy New Year, Evan," I said, closing the door behind him slowly, wondering if I had helped round up some of the evil spilling out of Pandora's Box, or if I had only propped the box wide open.

16

MY MOM, clad in her camel hair coat, came into the living room where we were all watching the bowl games. "I'm going over to St. Patrick's," she said, slipping her gloves on. "Does anyone want to come?"

"You're going to mass?" I asked. But the sound came out in stereo. Evan, my dad, and Willa had asked the same thing at the same time.

My mom smiled. "Don't be silly. I'm going to a peace vigil."

I scanned the faces around me. My dad was too preoccupied with the game to pay much attention, but Dr. Olesson was looking uncomfortable. I didn't know if he shared Mrs. Olesson's "finish the job" view, but his look was like a match against the growing grain of rebellion to the war living inside of me.

"I'll go," I said, standing up from the floor where I had been sitting. I gave a quick glance to Evan, a little afraid that he might disapprove, but he was looking back at me with an ambivalent face.

"I'll come, too," Willa said, raising her gaze from Evan's hand, which was resting on his leg. She pushed herself up from the spot on the sofa where she had been happily wedged between my dad and Evan and ran to get her coat. I turned and followed her.

"I'll come."

Evan's voice reached me like someone running up to grab me from behind. I wheeled around and we collided.

"Sorry," I said, trying to catch a glimpse of Dr. Olesson's face. But he was hidden from my view by Evan, who was laughing as he turned me around and pushed me out of the living room.

We could have walked, but it was so cold that Evan warmed up the Mustang and we all piled in. Willa and I jumped into the small back seat so my mom could sit up front, and it seemed strange not to have shotgun.

"How did you even know there's going to be a peace vigil?" I asked my mom, since she certainly hadn't read it in the church bulletin.

"I read the papers, dear. I talk to people, too," she replied with an amused tone. "Just because I don't believe in organized religion doesn't mean I don't know what goes on, or when they use their powers for good." She nodded at Evan like that explained the universe.

I looked in the rear view mirror and saw Evan's lips curling into his delicious smile. He was thoroughly enjoying the idea of his harem of heathen neighbors attending a church peace vigil against the war, knowing we were all there in his honor.

We walked into the dim chill of St. Patrick's Catholic Church and stood there a moment, huddled together, foreigners in a foreign land. Evan stepped forward. "Come on," he said, leading us down the aisle about half the way before he stopped and ushered us into a pew. My mom genuflected and started to cross herself, but when she caught my surprised face, she stopped and just shrugged to tell me that old habits die hard. There were peace pamphlets sitting on the bench and I picked a couple up and handed them to the others.

The church was dappled with people. Father Loperfido introduced himself and ministers from different churches around Kent. The Reverend Spearman of the Kent Presbyterian Church, where the Olessons went every Sunday, was there, and I tried to imagine the sermons he sent Evan's way and how Evan must see him. Evan wasn't much of a believer before he went to Vietnam, only going to church because his parents expected it. But I didn't know if the war had changed him there, too. It didn't seem like it. There were even Sundays when he didn't go at all, despite the scowls his mother sent his way for the rest of the day. But maybe today he thought differently of Reverend Spearman.

There were other ministers there, too, and they talked about peace and the need for change to come through nonviolent protest and about Ghandi and God and hope. A woman played classical music on the organ and another played some Christmas music. The church was quiet and cold and somber, but I had this sense of happiness in purpose, as these people had come together to stand up in this quiet way for an end to the war.

A candle burned near the altar, which was to be extinguished at the close of the vigil, when another candle would be lighted in a church in Ann Arbor, Michigan. The same thing would happen there, and then a candle would be lit in another church, and another, and it was supposed to go on until the war ended. I didn't believe there were enough churches in the whole country.

A group of people came in together, maybe twenty or so, most of them middle-aged, and walked to the front few pews. People stared at them as they went by. One of them carried an American flag. I recognized Mr. Purtill, a lawyer from town. They sat down, but most of the people scattered in the pews were looking at them, a palpable tension running through the church. Then Mr Purtill stood up and tore some of the peace pamphlets before taking them to the altar and laying them by a manger scene.

"What are they doing?" Willa asked in a hushed tone.

"They seem to be protesting the peace vigil," my mom whispered.

"They think anyone who is against the war is a subversive," Evan added.

"That's ridiculous," Willa said. My mom and I smiled at each other, but the whole church seemed suddenly to be spinning like a penny on its side, and we waited a little breathlessly for it to land on one side or the other.

Father Loperfido looked about nervously but kept going forward with the program, his voice resonating in a resistance of his own. Even here, the conflict of the war pressed against me. Then Father Loperfido introduced Tom and Tim DeFrange, who went to the altar and started playing folk songs on the guitar.

"I know the younger brother, a little," I said to my mom and Evan. "Tim. He goes to KSU. I've seen him at the Hub when I was there with Portia a few times. He says his mom is against the war but his dad supports it. Their brother died in Vietnam last summer. Don't you remember, Mom, it was in the papers? He'd only been there a month or two."

"Oh, yes, I do remember, now," my mom whispered, as the DeFrange boys sang *Where Have All the Flowers Gone* and *Blowing in the Wind*. A young woman in the pew in front of us swayed, while others around us tapped their hands gently against their knees, and I wished that all the Evans still trapped in Vietnam could see this, if only for a few moments.

We must have sat there for an hour or so listening to the speeches and music, but it seemed to me that time was transfixed, huddled in the cold glow of the candles. The protestors stayed for a little while and then left. The frigid air seemed lighter to me once they were gone.

When we were ready to go, Evan said he'd warm the car up for us and he slipped out of the pew. We waited a few minutes and then followed him. On the way out, I passed John Davis from school and we smiled at each other. I was glad, now, that he'd stood on that milk crate and challenged the war, even if it had been futile. Something was better than nothing.

The next morning, the Record Courier splashed Kent's big war protest across the front page. "Peace Vigil Meets 'Silent Majority' at St. Patrick's." My dad and I were at the kitchen table reading the paper when Evan knocked on the sliding glass door. I slipped out of my chair and unlocked it for him.

"Pancakes?" he asked hopefully.

"We're waiting for Portia to get up," I said.

"Well, we've given her long enough," my mom said. "Sit down, Evan, they'll be ready in a few minutes."

"Did you see the paper?" I asked him.

There was a crackle through the air as my mom put some bacon into a hot frying pan.

"No."

"Mr. Purtill says the peace pamphlets at the vigil are 'communist propaganda.'"

"He's a moron," my dad said from behind the sports section. Evan and I smiled at each other.

I read from the paper: "Roger Slease, an organizer of the peace vigil said 'Too bad those who came into the church to protest the vigil did not stay around to see the whole program.

They would have seen there were no Weathermen (SDS) or radicals here, just people who wanted peace.'"

"People are really afraid of the Weathermen, aren't they?" Evan asked.

"I think they have a right to be afraid of the Weathermen," my dad replied. "It's the SDS I don't get. Those kids couldn't organize a puppet show. They're about as capable of igniting a revolution as a bunch of Catholic schoolgirls. They call meetings and hand out pamphlets, but no one really pays any attention to them. If they get two dozen at a meeting, it's a banner turn out."

"They go about it all wrong," I said. "I know a lot of kids are against the war, but every time I see an SDS guy trying to convince someone to join the cause he's so belligerent about it that it's no wonder no one takes them seriously. They're so caught up in shocking you they forget the point of the whole thing, dressing like hippies on skid row and swearing about everything. If they'd just act normal, maybe people would get involved."

"I don't know, that church wasn't exactly filled yesterday and no one could accuse Father Loperfido of being a hippie," Evan said. "But you do have a point, Bug. During that anti-war march in November, there were kids carrying the Vietnamese flag saying they hated America for oppressing the Vietnamese. You're never going to get anyone to listen if you start out like that, saying you hate your country just because your government is doing the wrong thing. And what a joke. All we did was help the South Vietnamese oppress themselves so that the 'wrong' Vietnamese weren't oppressing them instead. It didn't much matter to the peasants which side was in charge, either way they were getting the shaft. The VC let them keep more of their farm yields, but they still screwed the poor over one way or another. The whole thing is one big fu—." He stopped and looked up at my mom. "Freakin' joke."

She smiled a thank you at him and I got up to help her bring the food over.

Willa and Portia floated into the room.

"Mmmmm, I'm sooooo hungry," Willa said. Portia slid into my seat next to Evan, looking like she had just left a beauty salon instead of her bed. I made Evan a big glass of Néstle's Quick, putting an extra teaspoon of mix in it.

"Thanks, Bug," he said as I set it before him. "What else is in the paper?"

"Leroy Satrum has assumed office as Kent's first full-time mayor," I said as if it were actually important news, handing him the plastic bottle of fake syrup before sitting down across from him.

"Now that's a headline," Evan said, dousing his pancakes. "Anything else?"

"President Nixon has created a Council on Environmental Quality. He says the fight against air and water pollution is a 'now or never' task and if we don't move to protect the environment, our world will become a poisonous place to live."

"Sounds like he's declaring another war," Evan said.

My dad sputtered his coffee.

Portia reached across Evan and picked up the syrup bottle. "At least he's figured out that when a river like the Cuyahoga catches fire, you probably need to do something to clean it up."

Evan shot Portia an approving look, and she caught it easily. I was never going to be like that. Maybe that was why my dad didn't think I belonged anywhere but Kent.

"The inquest in Mary Jo Kopechne's drowning is this week," I said to change the subject. I wanted the Chappaquiddick accident to be an innocent mistake, even though it was naïve. I didn't think Teddy Kennedy had let her die intentionally, but he wouldn't have panicked about her in the first place if it hadn't been wrong for her to be with him. He would've gotten help right away, and maybe she would have been rescued.

"Another Kennedy assassination," Portia said, "only this one was self inflicted."

My dad pushed his coffee cup toward me. "Get me another, would you, honey?"

The cup was still warm as I crossed paths with my mom who was bringing more pancakes over. I pulled the glass carafe from the electric coffee maker, the sweet smell of roasted beans thick in the air, and filled his mug two thirds of the way, then topped it off with half and half.

"He won't lose his Senate seat," my dad said as I set his mug down beside him. "But he'll never be president, now."

He was right. The era of the Kennedys was over. We were never going to have another Camelot. Evan was never going to soar on his guitar, and I was never going to leave Kent. The only thing that was going to stay the same was how much I loved Evan.

"What about the Farm Corner?" he asked, making fun of the entire section the Record Courier devoted to farm news.

"Corn prices are expected to be flat."

He laughed. "So, is that the whole wrap up of the news?"

I nodded. "Except the editors predict the 'frantic sixties' will be replaced by the 'glorious seventies.'"

"Glorious, huh?"

"Apparently," I replied, and we smiled at each other.

I didn't tell him about the story on the draft lottery, saying that everyone subject to the draft was confused about the way it was supposed to work. I didn't tell him that the Nixon Administration was seriously considering whether to abandon the draft all together and just have a volunteer army. It was too late for him, but based on the kids I saw at KSU and Roosevelt High, I didn't think there would be a silent majority rush to sign up. Most of the boys seemed determined to avoid the draft any way they could. Looking across the table at Evan, riddled with missing pieces without even knowing the reason, it wasn't hard to understand why.

17

A FEW WEEKS LATER, a thud landed somewhere in my dream just as Mr. Johnson, my physics teacher, was approaching my desk his hand outstretched for my homework, which happened to be incomplete because I hadn't figured out most of the answers. I opened my eyes as another thud landed in my ears. *Bombs away,* I thought, remembering the way Evan and Robby used to yell it when they pelted us with snowballs when we were kids. I sat up. A fat wad of snow was sliding slowly to the bottom of the window pane before falling off. I got out of bed and reached the window as another snowball hit the glass, making me blink.

I scratched the frosted panes with my fingernails to get a better view. Evan was standing in the driveway, looking up at me. His nose was red from the cold and his breath steamed the air. He pulled a large piece of paper from behind his back, tilting it so I could read it. *Happy Birthday* was written in bright blue, shaky lettering.

I smiled, pressing my teeth into my lower lip. I tried to open the window, but it was frozen shut. He laughed and pointed to his wrist, then he turned and ran back to his house, dodging snow drifts like he was running an obstacle course.

It was freezing by the window and the sweatshirt and flannel pajama pants I had slept in weren't enough to ward off the chill. I grabbed my flannel robe, threw my hair into a ponytail, shoved my icy toes into slippers, and ran downstairs. Willa was in the living room playing with the kittens and watching her favorite new cartoon, *Scooby-doo, Where Are you!*

"Rachel, you're awake!" she said, jumping up from the floor and running over to hug me. "Happy birthday! Mom said we had to let you sleep in. Shaggy's my favorite. Who's your favorite?"

My mom came over and kissed me and my dad pulled the paper aside to wish me happy birthday. A haze of smoke surrounded him, the ashtray beside him on the table filled. Portia had already left for her new job at Ivy's flower shop down on Main.

"Thanks," I said. I didn't tell them that someone else had already wished me happy birthday.

My mom made pancakes and hot chocolate and afterward my dad got up to go shovel the driveway.

"I'm sorry it's so cold on your birthday," my mom said as I helped her clear the table. The "glorious seventies" had come roaring in on an arctic train, and maybe the bitter cold was a sign that the decade ahead wasn't going to be as enlightening as we all hoped it would be. Every window was frosted over, and the floor boards felt like you were stepping on popsicles. Night time temperatures were below freezing, and the week before, on the day the paper had proclaimed the American death toll in Vietnam had reached 40,000, the high had been two degrees below zero.

"It's okay."

"This is the worst winter I can remember since we came here."

"What made Dad pick KSU?" I asked, suddenly wondering at the mysticism that had made kent my destiny. "I mean, he had other job offers, didn't he? I thought he had one from some college in Virginia, too."

My mom pulled herself up a little and thought a minute. "Yes, he had an offer from Virginia Polytechnic Institute, and one from some small school in New Jersey. I don't even remember the name of that one." She turned on the hot water and waited, the greasy pot she had boiled the sausage in hanging in her hands. "He thought that Kent would be a good place to raise children. We talked about it, because I was pregnant with Portia at the time, and he thought you could have a nice, safe life here, and still not be that far from cities, like Pittsburgh and Cleveland. And of course that meant family, too. Blacksburg was so far away from anything, tucked into the mountains in Virginia. I didn't want to go to New Jersey. We had been there once for a wedding for one of my second cousins, and I just remembered it being all factories and smoke."

Kent had always made sense to me, being so close to my dad's family in Cleveland and my mom's in Pittsburgh. But now I wondered why, of all the colleges in the country, my dad had ended up in a small town like Kent. KSU wasn't a small school, but it wasn't exactly the epicenter of academic enlightenment either.

"I know you're curious about that big world out there, Rachel," my mom said. "But sometimes you discover that, while things may seem very different on the surface, underneath every place is pretty much the same."

"It's not that, Mom," I said. "I just want to go to the best art school I can get in to, and if Pratt would take me, I think I could really give myself a good chance to make a living doing what I love. I want my art to matter. I want people to look at it and see something that makes them say 'oh, that's a Rachel Morelli.'"

My mom pressed her lips into an unhappy smile. "And I had to quit art school."

"I know," I said. My mom had always told us that her girls would go to college, because she'd had to drop out of night classes when her dad died in '46. She was working during the day in the display department at Gimbel's department store, but there wasn't enough money to pay for art school, even at night.

"I've always been determined that you girls would have the chances I didn't," she said as she rinsed the pot and set it on the drying rack. "Things were so different in my day. There was war, but everything was different."

"Because people believed in the war effort?"

"Because everyone was affected. Everyone had a stake," she said. "All the boys were gone, not just some of them, and the ones who couldn't be shipped overseas were drafted to stay and run the army here unless they were 4F. Every family had someone serving."

"And everyone understood why we were fighting," I said. "I still don't understand why we're in Vietnam. Who cares if they want to be communist? Why does it even matter?"

"I don't know, Rachel," my mom said. "But I think it's a good thing your generation is asking that question."

"So, if questions are a good thing, why isn't it good that I want to question why I can't go to Pratt instead of KSU?"

My mom jerked, as if I were the family dog suddenly threatening to attack her. "Rachel," she said, "your dad and I only want what's best for you. Surely you realize that? Your dad knows about these things, and I think we should trust him." She gave me a quick, dismissive hug, and I went upstairs to shower and dress, tucking my frustration back down inside of me as if it were a handkerchief pushed into a pocket.

I stared into my closet, unimpressed with my choices. Evan was right about bell bottoms, especially on short people. They just made everyone notice how close to the ground you actually were. They were made for tall, slender Twiggy types, the kind of girls who would look natural on the arm of Evan Olesson.

Willa walked into my room. "What are you going to wear?" she asked. "It has to be something that will make Evan drool."

"Maybe you should pick it out, then," I told her, "since I don't seem to know what makes Evan drool."

She scrolled through the blouses on my hangers. "This one," she said, handing me a white linen top with macramé fringe.

"Okay," I said, "but what am I going to wear with it?"

She opened her eyes wide. "That silky blue skirt that Portia just bought!"

"She'd never let me wear that."

"We could tell her it makes her look fat."

I laughed. "She'll never believe that, Willa."

"I guess not. But I'll ask her for the skirt anyway when she gets home."

I didn't believe Portia would let me wear her skirt, but decided to wait until the last minute to pick something out, since that way I wouldn't torture myself over it all day. I threw on some jeans to stay warm, or at least warmer, and went down to help my mom.

We polished the silverware and I rubbed the crystal wine glasses. We laid a linen cloth on the old table and I set the good china out. My mom always made a fuss over our birthdays because she said no one ever bothered about them in her family when she was growing up. Too many kids she said.

Portia came home and brought me flowers.

"Aren't they nice, Bug?" she asked, apparently just noticing the fact.

"They're beautiful," I said. "Thanks."

"Oh, they really are!" my mom exclaimed, giving her more credit than she deserved for them. "Rachel, you should finish getting dressed."

I went upstairs and faced my closet, laying an old plaid skirt on my bed, but the more I looked at it, the uglier it became.

"How about this?" Portia's voice came to me from the doorway. I looked over and she was holding up the blue mini skirt.

"Really?" I asked, not able to keep the skepticism out of my voice.

"Willa told me you wanted to borrow it. Consider it another birthday present."

"Okay, thanks."

"And don't spill anything on it!"

"I won't, I promise," I said, slipping it on before she could change her mind.

Evan was just coming in the back door when I came downstairs. He stomped the snow off of his shoes onto the braided cotton rug by the door. "Hey, Bug, Happy Birthday!"

"Thanks," I said. He had a store wrapped present in his hands and he pulled me aside.

"Listen," he said quietly, his hand resting on my forearm, "don't make a fuss when you open this, even though you're gonna love it." He smiled as he tilted his head toward the box. "Seriously, it was expensive, but just act like it's not that big of a deal and I bet no one else will realize it cost a lot, okay?"

"What is it?"

"You'll see. Just act normal, 'cause you are gonna love it," he said, going out of his way to torment me.

All through dinner, I thought about what was in the box and why it was expensive and why Evan had bought me something expensive. Again. The dinner conversation wasn't our usual party fare. No one talked about the war, or politics, or current world events. You wouldn't have known that B-52's were pounding the Me Kong Delta, wherever that was, or that doctors were saying The Pill could cause cancer or strokes and safety studies on it were inadequate, or even that PanAm had just launched their first Boeing 747 flight between New York and London. We talked about the weather, and the cupcakes at Hahn's bakery, and the new library being built at KSU.

"We're kind of boring tonight," I said with a vague smile.

"That's okay," Evan replied. "It's better than being at my house, listening to my dad drone on about college, and all the great colleges there are in Ohio, and my mom saying that at least now I won't be wasting my time on music."

His hand twitched like it always did when he formed chords in his head. Except that his fingers weren't there to do his bidding. His mother's words hung in the air like a swarm of bees getting ready to attack.

"The arts are never a waste of time," my mother said. "Whatever you decide to do, you'll do beautifully."

The bees suddenly disbanded and flew away.

"Thanks, Rita," Evan said.

We had Duncan Hines chocolate cake with boiled white icing. Evan's voice, mostly clean with just a hint of gravel to it, perfectly suited for the lead singer of a rock band, floated through the others as they sang the obtuse lyrics of the Happy Birthday song.

After cake, we went into the living room by the fire and I opened my presents. My parents gave me a garnet pendant, and Willa, with my parent's help, gave me a beautiful old copy of Arthur Guptill's *Rendering in Pen and Ink*. Portia was content with the flowers she'd given me. Or maybe her conscience had pricked her into lending me her skirt because she knew she was being cheap.

"I guess that just leaves me," Evan said. He handed me his present. "It's a snoopy pencil cup," he said and I laughed.

I opened the box and had to catch my breath not to exclaim. He was right. I loved it.

"Thanks," I said, trying to act nonchalant about it.

"What is it?" Portia asked, looking at the box as though it held a science experiment.

"It's a camera lens," I replied, holding the box up. I looked around, worried someone would ask how much it cost. But none of them seemed to suspect it could be more expensive than the camera was. They didn't have a clue how special a 500 mm lens was.

"Well, I like it. Thanks, Evan," I said.

He nodded casually and everyone let it drop.

"We should all go ice skating up at Twin Lakes tomorrow," Willa said. "To celebrate Rachel's birthday weekend."

"I haven't been ice skating in ages," Portia said.

"Could we?" Willa asked.

"Sure, Squirt, if you want to," Evan said. Then he turned his head toward me. "Bug, you haven't said anything."

"I can't." I gave a quick look at my dad to make sure he was paying attention to my mom and not me. "I have a test in physics on Wednesday and I'm not ready for it."

"Wednesday, Bug?" Portia asked, "that's plenty of time to study!"

"If you understand what you're studying in the first place," I muttered.

"You having trouble with physics?" Evan asked.

I nodded.

"Why didn't you say something?" he asked. "I'll help you."

I didn't want him to know how stupid I was when it came to science, but I was in way too deep in physics. And the chance to spend time with him, for any reason, was too good to pass up.

"It's too cold to skate anyway," Evan said. "We'll go soon. The way this winter is going, the lakes will be frozen 'til June."

As he got ready to leave, he sauntered over to me and whispered, "You love it, don't you?"

My stomach pooled into melted chocolate as I nodded, loving the way his voice fell on me when he stood so close. "It's incredible," I said, not able to meet his eyes even though I could feel them penetrating me. His smile tickled the edges of my vision, another something that was just between us. So many things between us, all of them pulling us together and pushing us apart. "I can't thank you enough."

"You just take the best pictures of your life," he said, "and show your dad exactly why you belong at Pratt. That's all the thanks I need."

My eyes stung. He believed in me. But he could let me go, too. And that kept it from being too good to believe. It sobered me, making my mother's words ring through my mind. *It was just the gratitude of a lost boy who remembered being scared and homesick.*

"Okay," I forced out, smiling because Evan deserved it, because Evan was generous and loyal and always knew the right thing to do.

"That's my girl," he said quietly, and I wanted that statement to be true as much as I wanted to breathe.

18

I STOPPED AT HOEFLER'S on my way home from school the following week. I still had some birthday money left and I wanted to get *Fire and Rain* with it and maybe The Guess Who's *No Time*. I held the 45 of *Fire and Rain* as I leafed through stacks of records, checking out the album cover artwork on them like I always did.

Evan's voice fell on me so suddenly I dropped the 45 as I looked up. "You should get the whole album," he said.

"I didn't see you come in."

He laughed as he stooped and picked the record up for me. "I know. You were completely engrossed in studying covers. Seriously, you should get the whole album. The guy has an amazing voice. And after you listen to it, you can let me borrow it." He grinned.

"I was thinking of getting *No Time*, too. I don't have enough for that and a whole album."

"I'll buy it for you, if you want."

"No, thanks." I needed to become less dependent on him making things easy for me. "I'll just get The Guess Who another time." Evan pulled out a copy of *Sweet Baby James* and handed it to me.

"Are you going home?" he asked as we walked over to the counter so I could pay for it.

"No, I have to go to Dubois' and pick up a copy of *A Midsummer Night's Dream*."

"Your dad has to have at least four copies of that."

"I know, but I want to be able to write my own notes in the margins," I replied. "It's going to be a big part of our final grade in English."

Evan laughed at me. I paid for the album and we walked out of the store. Grey clouds rolled over a frowning sky. The dry sidewalk was crunchy with salt and islands of ice that refused to melt.

Evan took my backpack from me, slinging it over his left shoulder as he fell into step beside me up the hill toward campus.

"Are you sure you're not in law school?" he asked, shifting the weight of my books.

"I'm always afraid I'm going to need them if I leave them at school."

He shook his head, an amused look on his face. "When guys first get to Nam, they want to bring all kinds of gear on patrol. And you'd tell them, 'you don't need half that stuff. You're gonna be sorry a few hours from now when it's slowin' you down.' Usually they wouldn't listen, but every once in a while you'd get a guy who'd take your advice. That guy was good to go. Otherwise he was just a Foxtrot November Golf."

"Foxtrot November Golf?"

"Fucking New Guy. They were dangerous. Half the guys in Nam were too green to keep themselves alive, and the other half, I guess we were the lucky ones. We lived long enough not to be cherries, and the last thing we wanted was to be stuck with a Foxtrot November Golf and end up dead with him."

"It's a good thing I'm not in Nam then, I guess." It was a dumb thing to say, and I regretted it as soon as it had left my lips.

Evan didn't seem to notice though, changing the subject without a beat. "I wish you could go to JB's with me tonight."

I looked up at him. There was no way my parents would let me go to JB's, even if I managed not to get carded and even if I was with Evan. But my heart did a cartwheel that he even wanted me to go.

"I wish you could hear this Joe Walsh guy. He's really something," he said. "He's going places, and it's not Akron, you know?"

"I've heard kids talk about him." It would be another eleven months before I could go to a bar and listen to music. For just a moment I wondered if Evan would wait that long, but then reality paid me an unwelcome visit. In another year, Evan would be in college somewhere far away from Ohio, while I'd still be in Kent, born and raised and stuck forever just like the Townie I technically was, old enough to go to a bar and hear Joe Walsh play if I wanted to. But Evan Olesson and Joe Walsh would both be long gone.

It was windy and Evan turned with me onto South Lincoln instead of handing me my backpack and heading home. We hurried up the sidewalk to the low, ugly yellow brick building that housed Dubois' Books. The trimester was far enough along that the little store was pretty empty. Evan waited indulgently while I checked to make sure there weren't any new novels I had missed. I didn't care what Michelle would say, I savored the sense of him nearby, waiting for me, storing up my memory for the desolate, endless winter that was somewhere ahead of me when he would be gone again.

"I'm just waiting for her," I heard Evan say. I turned around.

"Oh, hi Rachel, I didn't see you come in," the boy behind the counter said.

"Hi Steve," I said. "Nothing new, huh?"

"No," he said. "Our spring shipment is supposed to be here in a couple of weeks. What did you think of *Crime and Punishment*?"

"Oh, I loved it. It was hard to follow sometimes, all those Russian names that are almost the same. But you were right, it's really intense."

"I'm glad you liked it. Where've you been? I've missed seeing you around here."

"It's been too cold," I said. "I haven't been coming to campus at all." Evan was looking at Steve, and I realized they hadn't been introduced. They nodded at each other as I repeated their names, and Evan let out a stiff "Hi."

"Yeah, this winter's been brutal." Steve said, turning his gaze back to me. "Hey, I've got your dad this trimester."

"Don't remind him you know me. He'd probably call on you just for that." I handed him *A Midsummer Night's Dream* and two dollars.

"Thanks for the warning," he said. "He's a pretty cool cat, though. I like him."

"Yeah, he's a pretty cool cat," I replied, *especially when you don't have to live with him.* I looked at Evan who just smiled.

Steve handed me my change. "Maybe I'll see you at the Hub sometime," he said, as he gave Evan a glance. I had suspected once or twice that maybe Steve liked me, but he had never said anything like that before.

"Yeah, maybe," I replied, not sure if he'd said it to see if Evan reacted like a boyfriend or because it was so obvious that Evan wasn't my boyfriend. If I had never known Evan, I might have had a crush on Steve. He had big brown eyes and even though he kept his hair a little bit long, it was neat. He was an English major and knew all about the classics, and his eyes lit up when he talked about them. He wanted to be a writer and he always asked me about my art. But I did know Evan. I took the book from Steve as he reached for a paper bag to put it in.

"Don't bother," I said. "I'll just put it in my backpack." Evan turned and bent his knees so that I could reach the zipper and I dropped the book in. When he turned around, it was Steve he was smiling at. "Nice to meet you."

"Yeah, same here," Steve replied, but I had the feeling that neither of them really thought so. I waved to Steve and walked out of the bookstore with Evan, wondering if I could be wrong that Evan didn't feel anything more than friendship for me. My pulse started ticking a little bit faster.

"Let's go to the Hub," Evan said when we were on the sidewalk, "I don't feel like going home." Even though he was technically a townie, Evan knew the KSU campus as well as I did. Most people from Kent treated the campus like it was some secret government lab, mysterious and frightening even if their kids ended up here. But Evan had grown up going to football games with us. He knew my dad's office and the library, the student union, and the bookstore as well as Portia and Willa and I did.

We crossed Lincoln and cut across campus.

It was too early for the dinner crowd and the only other people in the Hub were a few stray commuter students and a couple of professors grabbing a late lunch.

We got a couple of cheeseburgers and some French fries to share and two cokes. We picked a table near the windows and started toward it.

"Hey, would you grab a paper? I want to get the basketball news," Evan said as he balanced the tray of food.

"Sure," I said, "but you know there's no Farm Corner in the Stater, right?" I watched him smile before walking across the room to a little metal stand that held the school newspaper, *The Kent Stater*. I grabbed one and started back to the table when a kid with shoulder length blonde hair stepped in front of me.

"Hey, you're in my music class, aren't you?" he asked. He had on a Grateful Dead t-shirt under a winter coat, and his jeans were too long for him and frayed on the bottom.

"No, sorry."

"Yeah, sure you are," he said. "What's your name, again?"

"I don't go to school here. I'm not the right girl."

I tried to walk past him, but he caught my arm.

"A foxy girl like you is always the right girl," he said. "How about you and I spend some time together?" He had a glazed look in his eyes like he was high, and I was glad we were in a public place.

"No thanks," I said, wrenching my arm from his grip.

"Come on, angel. I'll sneak you into my room and show you a real good time. I've got some premium stuff, you know?" He reached for me again. I pulled away, but Evan suddenly sprang past me like a raging bull, grasping the kid and slamming him into the wall in front of me.

"She's not your angel," Evan said, his teeth clenched as he pinned the kid to the wall with his good arm.

"Evan, what are you doing? Let go of him!"

"Hey man, I didn't know she was your chick. I thought she was alone," the blonde kid said, his eyes trying to focus on the person who had him jammed against the wall.

"She's not my chick. Apologize to her. Now!"

"Stop, please, he's not worth it." I moved closer, trying to distract him from his target. The veins on Evan's neck stood out like a three dimensional map to his heart.

"I'm sorry, man, I'm sorry," the kid sputtered. "You're hurting me!" Evan pushed his arm further against the kid's throat, making him gurgle helplessly. I grasped Evan's arm, the muscle in his bicep taut. I squeezed as hard as I could and he relaxed slowly and then released his hold. The kid staggered sideways away from us, coughing, looking like he thought we were completely crazy.

"Just go, please," I said.

"What's wrong over there?" someone called out from behind us.

I spun around to see the cashier craning his neck in our direction. "Nothing, nothing, it's just a misunderstanding. It's all right now," I called back. Evan's face was red, but the blonde kid didn't wait to see what he'd do next. He took off practically running, muttering about us being "freaking crazy." I clasped Evan's arm in case he tried to go after him, but he turned to me.

"Are you okay?"

I looked at him without even trying to cover my surprise. He had to care about me after all. But he had scared me so much I couldn't feel happy. "Yeah, I'm fine. You?" He ignored my sarcasm.

"Come on," he said, nodding his head toward our table. We walked back, the stares of the cashier and the few people in the cafeteria following us. At one of the tables we passed, I caught the eye of Dr. Glenn Frank, who taught in the Geology department with Michelle's dad. I nodded casually as my face flushed, thinking he would probably tell Michelle's dad and mine when he saw them. I mumbled hello and he replied, his gaze following us to our table. I laid the crumpled *Kent Stater* down and unwrapped my cheeseburger. Evan watched the blonde kid disappearing over the hill through the window.

He tossed me a packet of ketchup. "Could you open this please?" he asked, but it sounded more like a command than a question.

I tore it open and squeezed it onto the fries for him. We ate in silence. I only took a couple bites of my burger, pushing the rest over to him. He didn't eat it, though, and we threw our trash away and headed home. I wanted to talk to him, but I didn't know how to form the words so I kept waiting for him to do it.

When we turned onto our street, he made a comment about the days finally getting longer and I nodded. He handed my backpack to me at my house.

"Here you go," he said.

"Thanks."

"I'll see ya."

"Yeah, see ya." I turned and went inside, all the words we both needed to say suspended in the air, crushing us.

I went up to my room and sat in the window seat, pulling my pencils into my fingers, letting the soft anchoring wood sink into me. I started to draw, feverishly filling a crisp page of my sketch book with the image in my head. I drew a bull, after the picadors have tormented him, in that moment before he is ready to surrender. His large, dark eyes held the same expression as Evan's had this afternoon. I put him in a field of cork trees, like Munro Leaf, but there were no flowers, just a jagged bolt of lightning and clouds as dark as coal. I stared at it for a long time after I was finished, feeling like I had pressed Evan's soul onto the paper against his will. The bull stared back at me, haunting reproach in his eyes. Evan didn't want to be left alone like Ferdinand. He wanted the picadors to suffer. But the picadors had been kinder to Ferdinand. I turned my head toward the window, my gaze falling to the place I loved best. Evan was leaning against the farthest tree where the hammock hung in summer, watching me. Watching me like I was the picador.

I stared back, hoping he would wave me down, but he stood motionless. There was defiance in the way he leaned against the tree, one leg pulled up, his foot pressing against it, his eyes locked on mine. I couldn't move. Then he shifted, ever so slightly, nodding his head to ask me to come down. My clenched fingers softened and dropped the sketch pad, and I ran downstairs.

I slipped my coat and gloves on as I slid out the door. I hesitated on the porch, but Evan was still there.

"Hey," he said as I reached him.

"Hey."

I looked away then, across the yard at the bare rose bushes and empty flower beds.

"Look, about today," he said, stopping as though he wanted me to supply the rest of his sentence. Except I didn't know what the rest of the sentence was.

I tried to bring "it's okay," to my lips, but the words were trapped beneath the confusion.

"I'm sorry," he said at last. "I know I overreacted and made you mad."

"You didn't make me mad." I looked him in the eye and had to force the words so they came out husky. "You scared me."

Evan stepped back as though I had shoved him, the fog of our breath creating a mist to separate us.

"I get so mad, sometimes, Bug. I don't even know why. I should be happy. I mean, I'm home, alive. But it's just in me, all the time, this anger I can't even explain, rubbing me raw. And sometimes it just gets to be too much and I snap. That jerk never should've treated you like that."

It was my turn to feel like I'd been shoved, as it sunk into me that it wasn't jealously driving him to react the way he had. "No, he shouldn't have," I said. "But, Evan, you could've killed him."

"I know exactly how much it takes to kill a man, Bug, and that wasn't it." He shook his head at my ignorance, or maybe at his knowledge.

I let out a sharp breath, suspended between relief that he hadn't almost killed that kid and my own share of disgust at what my country had done to the boy I grew up with.

"You can't beat a guy up just because he's a jerk," I said, refusing to give up my advantage.

He shrugged defensively. *Fuck you, Picador* ran through my head as if he were saying it out loud. I looked down at my shoes, counting the rows of laces to push back the tears.

"Maybe I'll end up like your dad, full of irrational rages, banging through the house looking for bacon when I know it isn't there," Evan said, his voice changing somewhere in that sentence until I heard the anger melting away, replaced by a nameless fear we both shared.

"Maybe," I replied. Evan looked at me, and we smiled at each other, gingerly, like we were meeting for the first time. The back door of his house opened and his mother stuck her head out.

"Evan," she said, her voice rushing over the yard faster than the winter wind. "Supper is on the table."

Evan shrugged his "I'd better go," the way he used to when we were growing up. I nodded and turned back to my house.

I hung my coat up on the hook by the door and walked past my mom, her back to me as she stood at the stovetop. She didn't hear me over the sizzle of the breaded veal she was frying and I was glad, heading to my room for a while before dinner.

As I climbed the stairs, I wiped a tear off of my face. Portia was right about one thing. Evan was haunted by spirits. So many, there wasn't any room left for me.

19

A FEW DAYS LATER, Evan and I were sitting at a table in the KSU library. He was explaining the principle of kinetic energy being directly proportional to the square of an object's speed to me. I was trying to concentrate, but I couldn't help thinking that I liked the way the muscles in his long neck moved when he spoke, and the way he'd scratch at his ear when he paused to think about how to explain something.

"No wonder you're not doing well in physics," he said, looking at the drawings all over my notebook. "You must spend all of your class time day-doodling."

"Day dreaming is boring," I said, making him crack his seriousness, and he asked me about the little caricatures of people from school strewn through my notes. He laughed as I described people. I was glad I had torn out the last few pages, filled with pictures of him, and tucked them into my desk at home. I would never have been able to explain those. But it was after nine, and even though our time together was running out, I took a breath and tried to focus on the open book in front of me. I had to keep up my grades just in case Pratt accepted me and just in case I could convince my dad I should go. It was already the second week of February. A letter was due any day.

Someone moving toward us caught my peripheral vision, and I looked up to see John Davis. I hadn't thought about him much since I'd seen him at the peace vigil, but all of the activists had been driven inside by the cold. Even the guys who stood on the street corners downtown to preach against the war had scurried like grasshoppers to their hidden winter dens weeks ago.

"Hi Rachel," John said, pushing his hair off of his face. "I called your house and I think it was your little sister, she told me you were here." He looked at Evan as he spoke, fidgeting with the gloves he held in his hands. "I hope you don't mind me coming to find you, but I need to ask you something."

"Sure," I said. I couldn't imagine what John would want to ask me that would make him look for me this late at night.

John glanced at Evan again.

"I have to hit the head," Evan said. He stood up and walked past John toward the hallway.

"The 'head'?" John asked.

"He was in the Marines. That's what they call the bathroom."

John nodded and sat down opposite me in Evan's chair. "Is he your boyfriend or just a friend?"

"He's a friend," I replied, purposely leaving out the word "just." There was nothing "just" about what Evan was to me. "Why?"

"Nothing, only he looks like he's been in the military, and I didn't want to offend him."

"Why would you offend him?"

"Well, you know, since I'm part of the anti-war movement, I didn't want to cause any problems for you."

"Evan won't care that you're against Vietnam. He's not exactly a big fan of it himself these days."

John's face relaxed. "Oh, that's good. I didn't want to talk to you in front of him if he wouldn't be cool about me being against the war."

"You can protest Vietnam as much as you want. President Nixon doesn't seem to be in any hurry with his 'peace with honor' agenda."

"Did you hear Jerry Gordon when he was here the other day?" he asked, talking about the Cleveland attorney who had defended some KSU students after they'd been arrested for protesting last spring.

"No," I said, "but I heard he said imprisoning the KSU demonstrators was part of a national attempt to crush movements if they question things too much."

"He said there's another anti-war demonstration planned for April that will be even bigger than the Moratorium was. They're hoping to rally five million to march in Washington. Man, I'd love to go to that, you know?"

"I can definitely see you there."

He nodded, but it was obvious he hadn't tracked me down to tell me about Jerry Gordon or some demonstration planned for April. We looked at each other awkwardly.

"Does your friend go to school here?"

"No, he just got back a few months ago. He hasn't decided where he's going to go, but it sure won't be here." I looked around, dissatisfied with everything KSU had to offer.

"There are worse schools," John said.

"I know, but Evan's the 4.0 type, and he needs to put some distance between him and his family."

"I know the feeling," John said, raising his eyebrows.

Evan came into view behind John and looked at me, his face asking if I wanted him to come save me. I waved him over and introduced him to John.

"So what did you want to ask me?" I said.

"Oh, right," John said and cleared his throat. "Well, you know that I've been speaking out against Vietnam a lot."

I nodded.

"Well, I went to the Moratorium back in November in Washington, and my old man was pretty pissed off at me for it. You see, my cousin, Danny, he was over there at the time, and my dad thought if I wasn't supporting the war, then I wasn't supporting Danny, either. But I didn't see it that way." He noticed Evan's hand.

"Anyway," he said, "Danny was killed last week in a helicopter crash."

"Oh, John, I'm so sorry," I said.

"That's rough, man, I'm sorry," Evan said.

John sniffed a little. "Well, last night my old man and I got into it about Danny and the war and the whole thing. We really had it out. He said our generation is a bunch of spoiled brats and we have no business questioning the President because all we do is run around to bars and chase girls and think up ways to spend our parents' hard earned money." He stopped and looked at me, as though I should understand what all this had to do with me.

"I'm really sorry," I said. "I wish there was something I could do to help."

"Well, you see, Rachel, that's why I came looking for you," John said. "You see, my old man, he threw me out of the house."

"He threw you out?" There wasn't anything that would make my parents throw me out, they just weren't like that. But the war was tearing more and more families apart, one way or another. Evan touched my thigh under the table to remind me to be more tactful.

"Well, I turned eighteen a couple of months ago," he said, staring at his gloves lying on the table and pushing them around slowly. "So he told me I could take care of myself since I thought I knew more than the people in charge. I've got that job down at the gas station over on Summit Street after school and on Saturdays, and I've got a little saved, but it's not much."

"I wish I could help you, I really do," I said.

"Well, see, I was thinking, your older sister goes here, and your dad teaches here, so I thought maybe they might know of some guys with an apartment who'd let me stay with them until I can figure this out. I mean, I'd pay my way. I just need a couch to crash on for a few weeks, anyplace really, as long as it's cheap. Do you think maybe they'd know anybody who would help me out?"

He had a look of desperation on his face, and it was so cold outside. It was going to be hard for him to finish high school and support himself. Maybe he wouldn't even be able to go to Ohio State in the fall like he'd planned. "I'm sure they will, if they can," I said. "Why don't you come home with us and we'll ask them. We were almost done, anyway."

"Thanks, Rachel, this is really great of you. You've always been one of the nicest girls in school," John said. "I knew you'd help me."

I figured John was just buttering me up, but I wished he hadn't said it in front of Evan. Nice didn't seem to be the in thing anymore. From what I could tell, the popular girls were the ones burning their bras or dressing like Raquel Welch.

I put my books into my backpack and Evan grabbed it off the table. "I'll warm up the car," he said. "Give me a couple minutes head start."

He started to walk away and then turned. "Bug, maybe you should give your folks a heads up that you're bringing someone home."

I looked at John and nodded. "It's getting late. I probably should let them know."

"Sure, sure," John said.

I walked with Evan toward the front doors, slipping into a phone booth as I watched him saunter out of the library into the darkness. John was standing nearby, looking uncomfortable, like he didn't know what to do with himself. He took out a cigarette and lit it.

I dropped my dime in the slot on the phone and dialed. My mom answered and I told her that a friend of mine from school needed some help and that Evan and I were bringing him home to talk to dad. She didn't question me, she only said, "Okay dear."

I hung up and opened the door. "It's fine," I said and John smiled as we headed outside.

We reached Evan's car and he got out and held his door open for me. Then he looked over at John and said "Sorry, man, there's no smoking in the Mustang."

I slipped into the back seat, while John said "Oh, yeah, hey, I can dig that," flicking the cigarette away. It fizzled as it hit an ice patch.

My dad was sitting in the kitchen reading the newspaper and I introduced John and explained why I'd brought him home with me.

My dad lit a cigarette and blew the smoke out slowly, up above his head the way he always did when he was thinking. Then he leaned forward and tapped the ash off into the ashtray in front him. The smoke rising made my nose itch.

"Why don't you go get Portia," he said to me. I ran upstairs to tell her what was going on. When we got back to the kitchen, the table was filled with plates of salami and cheese and crackers, and my mom was serving coffee. John watched Evan with a look of envy as Evan stuffed a cracker with a thick slice of brick cheese into his mouth. I pushed the plate closer to John and he smiled at me as he helped himself.

"There's a boy in one of my classes who lives in an apartment off of Lincoln somewhere," my dad was saying, "and he's a nice kid. You'd be okay with him. Rachel, you know him. What's his name?"

My dad was always sure the rest of us were telepathic, but I had no idea whom he meant, so I shook my head.

"Oh, come on," my dad said to me, "you know! That lanky kid who works in the book store. The one who gets the puppy dog eyes every time you walk in, trying to pick you up."

I flushed. "Oh, Steve, you mean. He doesn't try to pick me up."

"Yes, he does," Evan said quietly and I wanted to look at him but I didn't have the courage. His words started pounding in my ears.

"Anyway," my dad said, "I know he lives in an apartment on the south side of campus with a couple of other boys. I could ask him. Or maybe Rachel should ask him," my dad added. "She's more likely to get him to say yes. Portia, do you know anyone?"

"Sure," she said, "a lot of the seniors are in apartments. I could ask around."

"That would be groovy," John said, smiling at her, his face getting the same stupid expression all boys got when Portia looked at them. I was nice. Portia was beautiful.

"You can stay here on our couch, until we find you someplace," my dad said, "We can't let you wander the streets."

"Oh, I'm staying with a friend from school," John said. "His dad said I could crash for a few days, but he doesn't want to get in between my dad and me, so he said I have to hurry up and find someplace." He took another cracker and some salami.

My dad nodded. "Well, no one's going to be looking for roommates in early February, but I'm sure there's a group of boys who could find room for one more somewhere on campus. They're always looking for a way to share costs. But you should apologize to your dad, regardless. It's not right for a father and son not to get along. You need to show him the respect he deserves just because he's your father. You don't have to agree with him to show him respect."

"Yes, sir," John said. "I really appreciate this, Professor Morelli." He was watching my dad's cigarette, looking anxious for another smoke. I was pretty sure he hadn't heard much of my dad's lecture on familial duty.

John stood up. "I should go now, it's getting late."

Evan stood, too. "I'll drive you," he said. "It's too cold to walk. Where's your friend live?"

"Over on Cuyahoga Street," John answered. Evan nodded and they put their coats on.

"Call me tomorrow after school," my dad said to John. "Rachel, you can give him my office number at school tomorrow."

"Yes, sir," John replied. "I can't thank you all enough."

My dad nodded and I followed Evan and John to the door. Evan stopped on his way out. "Seriously," he said to me, "you should ask that kid, Steve, after school tomorrow. He looked like he'd do anything for you."

I dropped his gaze as the heat prickled up my neck and across my face, but it didn't sound like there was any jealousy in voice as he encouraged me to go ask Steve for help.

"And John's right about you," he added. "You are really nice."

"Thanks," I said, not able to meet his eye. I was a nice person, and I knew he meant it as a compliment. But I didn't want to be nice. I wanted to be the kind of girl Evan Olesson couldn't resist.

20

THE NEXT DAY, I stopped at Hoefler's before going to the bookstore to ask Steve if he could help John. Evan's birthday was coming up, and I hadn't seen a single sign that he'd done anything about getting himself a guitar. I had even asked Robby just to make sure, and he told me Evan's acoustic guitar was sitting in the corner of his room untouched as far as he could tell since I had played it at Christmas.

I thumbed through the catalog for left-handed guitars, but I was short for even the least expensive one. I thought about asking Michelle to loan me some money, but she was forever broke. There was only one person I knew who always managed to squirrel away money, and that was Willa. I just hoped she would have enough. I knew she'd lend it to me once she knew what it was for.

I left Hoefler's and headed for Dubois'. It was sunny, but still chilly. Winter was hanging on, pushing back any sign of spring that tried to give us some hope that it might someday be warm again.

The smell of paper and ink surrounded me as soon as I stepped into the bookstore. I inhaled deeply, stopping to take my gloves off. Steve was shelving poetry books.

"Hey Rachel," he said. "Where's your *Crime and Punishment* friend?"

"My *Crime and Punishment* friend?"

"That guy you came into the store with that one day. He came back a day or two later and bought a copy."

"He did?"

"Yeah, I figured he'd mention it, since you two seemed pretty tight." His tone was nonchalant, but his gaze was intent on me, examining me.

"I wish you hadn't sold it to him."

"Why? Too deep for him?" Steve asked with a smile.

"Something like that."

"Sorry," Steve said, "but that's what he asked for." He pulled the tape off the empty cardboard shipping box and folded it up.

"It's just that he's only been home a few months, and he's just starting to get his bearings. He doesn't need to think about crime and guilt and the inevitability of punishment. Not now."

Steve looked at me a long moment without saying anything, the smile leaving his face. "He's lucky to have a girl like you."

"I'm not his girl," I said, the words prickling in my mouth.

"Maybe not, but you wish you were. Like I said, he's lucky."

I wasn't sure what to say, so I shrugged. It was nice to think someone would consider it lucky to have the devotion I lavished on Evan so uselessly. Maybe Michelle was right, and I should be trying not to love him so much. But it still seemed like a formidable task, and for now all I could manage was planting a little seed of doubt.

"Actually, I wish he were with you now," Steve said. "I wanted to ask him something about the army."

"He was in the Marines."

"Oh, well, he'd probably still know why the army would withhold the cause of death from a family. Could you ask him for me?"

The little knot that was always in my stomach since Evan had come home began to grow.

"My brother's best friend was killed, and the army isn't telling the family what happened. They're going nuts, and the dad's been asking but no one will talk. They just keep getting the run around."

"They must have told them something?"

"Only that he died in an explosion. They won't tell them the circumstances."

I looked away, thinking of all the things Evan had told me about how people died in Vietnam. Some of them commit suicide, he said, and some were killed by mistakes.

"Maybe it was friendly fire. The military doesn't like to talk about that."

"What's friendly fire?"

"Evan says it's when we kill our own. When the bombers come in with the wrong coordinates, or when someone slips on a muddy hillside and his weapon discharges and kills the guy in front of him. Stuff like that."

"But why wouldn't they just say it was an accident? Especially with the family asking questions. He'd only been there a few months. A brand new lieutenant and such a great guy. Everyone loved him."

"I'll ask Evan, if you want me to."

"Yeah, that would be great. Thanks."

"Now I have a favor to ask you," I said. I told Steve about John, making his situation sound as desperate and heroic as I could, just a kid standing up for his ideals against his dad who stood with the establishment. It didn't take me long to convince Steve to help him, which was going to make my dad gloat that he was right to send me to be the one to ask. But I wanted to help John not just because he was a nice guy, but because I was as tired of the war as anyone.

Afterwards, I headed home, going straight up to Willa's room.

"Hey Squirt," I said, using Evan's nickname for her and plopping down on her bed in between all the stuffed animals.

"What do you need?"

"Why do you just assume I need something?" She lowered her head and stared at me.

I laughed. "Do you have any money I could borrow?"

"Maybe," she said, her big grey eyes studying me like an owl's. "How much do you need and why?"

"Sixty-two dollars. To help me buy Evan a left-handed guitar for his birthday."

Willa got up from the floor where she'd been reading and went to her dresser. She opened her underwear drawer and pulled out an old candy box. She lifted the lid and counted out sixty-two dollars from what must have been almost a hundred and handed it to me.

"Why doesn't he just buy it himself?"

"He told me he would on New Year's Eve, but he hasn't. I guess it's been harder for him to do than he thought it would be. I figure if I get him the guitar, he won't have any excuses holding him back and he can start trying again. He'll never play like he used to, but he still needs to play."

"Can it be from me, too?"

"Absolutely. Come on, let's go to Hoefler's before dinner and order it."

We walked back to the music store as fast as we could. It smelled almost like the book store, but with an edge of vinyl. I showed Willa the catalog and we bought Evan a Gibson SG standard left-handed guitar. In cherry.

"It'll be here next Tuesday, probably," the boy working that day told us.

"Thanks," I said.

"What will we give him if it doesn't come in time?" Willa asked as we walked home.

"It will come," I told her, "it has to." I was feeling the urgency of needing to drag Evan back into the present, even if bits and pieces of Vietnam clung to him like shrapnel forever.

That night, Evan took me to the library. He was trying to explain notes and how longitudinal waves of sound are the creation of compressions and rarefactions within the air. "Like a string, vibrating forward and backward," he said "pushing the sound out horizontally."

"I have a question," I said, interrupting him to tell him about Steve's question.

"It's an interesting combination of circumstance," Evan said, staring off into the nothingness above my head. "He might've been fragged."

"What's 'fragged'?"

"He could have been killed by a fragmentation grenade. It was happening a lot before I left. Especially in the army."

"I don't understand." There was way too much that I didn't understand. I was never going to catch up to Evan. I was never going to be old enough for him.

"It's a kind of grenade we use."

"You mean another American could have killed him with a grenade? You're saying he could have been murdered by a fellow soldier?" I fought not to sound too incredulous.

"It's possible, that's all I'm saying."

"Why? Why would an American soldier murder another American?"

Evan looked at me, his face the mixture of patience and protectiveness that melted me to eight again and the day he tried to explain why the thrush in my hand had died after it hit our window. I looked away, hating myself for being so naïve, and hating the world even more for being so cruel.

"Not everybody in the service wants to be there, Bug. Some of these guys come from the rough side of the tracks. Some of them pick the army over jail and then get to Nam and wish they had picked prison. It's that bad. Some of them get there without a firm grip to start with and a few weeks in country will unhinge them before they even get snapped in."

"So they just murder their fellow Americans?"

"I'm not saying it's right, I'm just telling you it happens. Guys like that can get pissed off at the brass and decide to get even. Like last year, there was a whole company from the First Air Calvary Division that refused to go down a road because they thought it was dangerous. I mean, no one got fragged then, but that kind of stuff sets a crazy guy off, thinking the brass is going to get them killed. Some of them would do it just for being told not to do drugs. A fragmentation grenade is an easy way to 'get back.' It's quick, plentiful, and almost impossible to trace to the man who threw it."

I stared at Evan, trying to process the idea that murderers walked among heroes. But then I remembered My Lai.

"His rank and time in country would have made him unpopular with some of the guys who'd already been there too long. If one of them thought this guy was dangerous to him making it out alive, it's possible. It never happened in my unit, but a buddy of mine in artillery told me it happened in his. Someone had a beef with a gunny and lobbed one into his bunker while he slept, but it didn't go off and the gunny woke up and found it. The guy who did it was long gone by the time the gunny ran out of the bunker, and when the brass asked if anyone knew anything, everyone said 'no, sir,' even though they all knew who it was. I guess the brass had a pretty good idea, too, 'cause a week later the joker got transferred to an infantry unit."

"So the military is just pretending it's not happening?"

"The U.S. military is never going to admit it doesn't have a handle on what's going on in Nam. They weren't even admitting it to us when I was there. You just heard things through the underground. In the army, especially, it was a real problem. Look, I can't tell you that's how this guy died. But it would make sense, based on what you told me. Not everyone dies heroically over there. Sometimes it's better not to know."

Evan pulled my physics book toward him and stared at the open page.

"Notes," I said to bring his memory back from wherever it had wandered.

"A string, vibrating forward and backward," he said, his eyes darting up to look at me, "pushing the sound out horizontally."

I dropped my gaze to the diagram on the page. Evan and I were like notes being pushed around in a world that didn't make any sense.

"What are you thinking?" he asked.

"I'm thinking it's wrong to take something as beautiful as a note and dissect it."

Evans lips curled into a half smile. "I think you're right. Some things are better left alone." He closed my book. "Come on, I'll take you home."

We packed my things up and left. A cold rain obscured Evan's soft reflection in the car window, the droplets running down the glass to their destiny. I was slowly getting used to the continual wave of the war pounding against us, but I couldn't help worrying just how many more heartaches Vietnam carried that I didn't want to even know about.

21

I WENT TO HOEFLER'S after school on Monday, just in case, and on Tuesday, but the guitar still hadn't come. On Wednesday it was there, and I took it to my dad's office and made him put it in the trunk of his car. He looked at my choice skeptically, but he saved his lecture on why it was the wrong present for home when my mom was there to back him up.

On Thursday, Willa and I came home from school eager for Evan's mandatory dinner with his parents at the country club to be over. He was coming to our house afterwards to be fawned over by his fan club, and Willa and I were ready.

Evan came in looking like a young Atticus Finch after a long day in a hot courtroom. He loosened his thin tie as he walked through the front hallway to the kitchen, the weariness of the day he'd had draped over him. He took his suit jacket off, his crisp, white dress shirt outlining his shoulders and contrasting his eyes. Looking at him was like looking at a Rembrandt, every delicate detail blending into a wispy reality. I brought him a coke while my mother fussed over the cake she'd made for him, putting candles on it and setting out her best dessert plates.

We sang happy birthday, and Portia handed Evan the cake knife to cut the first slice.

"Wait," I said as he went to blow out the candles. "Don't forget to make a wish."

"Guess I'm a little rusty at this birthday stuff," he said.

"Well, I hope you remember how to open presents," I said, "because you're going to love what Willa and I got you."

"Getting even for your birthday, huh? I think I remember." He took a breath and said "I wish for Bug to become a famous artist," and he blew out the candles.

He was giving my parents a big hint. "You can't say what you wish for out loud," I said. "It won't come true." I forced a smile because he had meant well, but the ominous echo of impossibility kept ringing in my head.

"Sorry," Evan said, "I told you I was rusty at this birthday stuff."

"That's just silly superstition, anyway," my mom said, handing him a box. Evan unwrapped his present, struggling with the tape on the corners to find the watch she and my dad had gotten him.

"It's inscribed," my mom told him, and he turned it over. He read the inscription, *Always with us, wherever you go*, and sat there completely still for a moment. "Thanks Rita. Thanks Art," he said his voice cracking just a little.

My dad coughed his thick, rattling smoker's cough and lit another cigarette. "To replace the one we gave you for your graduation that got ruined over there," he said. He'd been wearing it when the explosion hit him.

"Here," Portia said, breaking the tension by handing Evan her gift. She looked so lovely sitting there across from him maybe he thought it was a present just to have her smiling at him like that. But if he did, it didn't show on his face as he took the small package and unwrapped a *Chicago* 8-track.

"It's for your car," she said.

"It's great, thanks," Evan told her. He looked at me. "So?"

Willa handed him a small box. "You're gonna *love* it," she said with a huge grin.

"You keep saying that," he said.

"It's a Snoopy pencil holder," I told him, and something inside me lit like fire as I watched his lips try not to curl. He tore the paper, revealing a box with a Peanuts pencil holder in it. He smiled and raised his eyebrows, like he couldn't believe we'd actually gotten him that.

"Thanks," he said, trying to act like it was funnier than it was.

"Oh, and there's one more thing," I said. Willa ran into the living room and reappeared with the guitar in its case, a bright blue ribbon tied around the neck. Evan's face transformed into surprise as Willa placed the guitar on the table in front of him.

He looked at it, his face suddenly emotionless, and the haunting fear my parents had expressed that this was the wrong thing to give him, that what he really needed was to forget all about the guitar, began to churn through me like ice water.

"Well, open it!" Willa said.

He pulled the ribbon off and lifted the lid and stared at the guitar lying inside like snow white in her golden coffin. He dropped his chin to his chest and my heart constricted. Willa grabbed my hand.

"I'm sorry," I said. "We didn't mean to make you unhappy. It's my fault, not Willa's. You don't have to take it if you don't want to. I'm sure Hoefler's will help me resell it." It was hard to keep my voice steady as the muscles in my throat tightened. I could feel my dad's disapproving stare without having to look up to see it.

"This guitar is amazing," Evan said with a shake of his head. "You're not taking it back!"

Willa and I burst into smiles, the strain hovering in the room only a moment before dissipating in an instant. I turned my head to blink back tears. Evan took the guitar out of its case and carefully started tuning it, the awkwardness of working in reverse and strumming with only his index finger and thumb making him stumble over what used to be so natural to him. He slowly picked out random chords, the pacing hesitation of his mind showing in his eyes as he worked to reconfigure everything he knew about playing. Like the soft beating of a hawk's wing, the chords slowly began to rise in a recognizable pattern.

He started singing *Blackbird*, his voice and the chords folding into each other like broken wings.

"*...and learn to fly-*"

Watching him, I wasn't sure if this was the moment that was going to free him, or even if that moment could ever exist, but he was tired of waiting to be free, and if nothing else, John Lennon and Paul McCartney had understood what it felt like to be caged.

"I used to sing that, in my head, at night when we were out in the bush, and try to remember what it was like back in the world."

"Back in the world?" Willa asked.

"It's what we called home. There was Vietnam, and there was the world. And never the twain shall meet. Sometimes it was like thinking about heaven, something you weren't quite sure was real but wanted to believe in so badly. Sometimes the only thing that could make me believe it was real was one of Bug's chatterbox letters." He cleared his throat and gently placed the guitar back in its case. "So, I guess when Bug wants you to do something, you're gonna do it."

"You seemed to need a little nudge," I said.

"I guess I did."

I was afraid he might say, "Thanks, Bug, this was nice of you."

"I should go," he said suddenly. "You kids all have school tomorrow." He grinned at us like we were the unlucky ones, even though he didn't relish his long days at home with his mom. But at least now he could work on his music again.

He slipped his suit jacket back on and gathered his presents awkwardly in his hands. It wasn't easy anymore for him to hold a bunch of things.

"Do you want some help carrying your stuff over?" I asked.

"No, I got it," he said, with the same tone he had used when his dad offered to carry his sea bag that first day home. I opened the door for him and he turned around and thanked us all one more time before he left.

I closed the door behind him, Willa at my side.

"He loved it, didn't he?" she asked me.

"I think he did, Willa. I think he did."

22

THE WEEK AFTER, Evan and I were back at the library. I pulled my books from my backpack and a copy of Anthony Trollope's *He knew He Was Right* slid out on top of my physics book. Evan picked it up and read the back cover. "New?"

"I got it today."

"Did he ask you out?"

My face crinkled with heat. "Who?" I asked as though I didn't know.

"That Steve guy from the bookstore."

"No."

"He will."

"I don't think so."

"You sound disappointed."

I shook my head and wished he'd stop tormenting me. If the whole world knew how much I loved him, then he must know. I stifled the desire to throw something at him and pushed my book over to him instead.

"Okay," he said, "I can take a hint. Discussion of Bug's love life is off limits."

I have no love life, thanks to you. For once, I wasn't having much trouble concentrating on the stupid principles of physics.

We had spent almost an hour dryly going over the importance of the law of reflection, and refraction at a boundary, and plane mirrors when Portia walked over with a friend.

"Hi Bug, Evan," she said. "This is Linda. Linda, this is my little sister and our neighbor."

We said the polite things to say. Linda's perfect blond hair and perky little nose, making her look like the ideal of all cheerleaders, fit perfectly with Portia. They looked like the yin and yang of beauty, light meeting dark, but equally and obnoxiously exquisite.

"I know you," Linda said to Evan. "You were in the class behind us at Roosevelt, and had a band. 'The Curfew,' or something you called yourselves."

Evan's face broke into a broad smile. "Two classes, actually," he said. "You have a good memory."

"You played at some of the parties the year Portia and I graduated."

Evan nodded.

"You were great," she said.

I must have been scowling because Portia kicked her foot against mine, which made me wince and realign my features. I tapped a pencil against my leg under the table and wished they'd go away.

"So, are you in school here?" Linda asked Evan. I didn't like the green makeup she used to highlight her eyes, or the way she fixed those eyes on Evan. And she didn't even know he owned a chick mobile.

"No, I just got back from Nam," he said, gesturing his hands apart like he hadn't had time to get to school yet, and her face made that slight recognition of impact everyone had when they realized Evan was missing some of his hand. I was pretty sure he had seen it, too, but he didn't seem to mind. Why would he, though, with her standing there smiling at him like he was a piece of her favorite candy.

"Hey," she said to him, "some of us are going to J.B.'s in a little while to hear Joe Walsh. You wanna come?" Of course he would want to go to J.B.'s and hear Joe Walsh. Her smiling lips were the color of Eve's apple. Then she looked at me like I was an afterthought. "You too, Bug."

"My name's Rachel," I said. Portia made a face at me to tell me to stop being rude. I almost added "and I'm not old enough to go to J.B.'s," but I caught myself, refusing to give either of them the satisfaction of hearing me say it.

"Oh, I'm sorry," Linda said, "I thought Portia said you were called 'Bug.' Anyway," she added to Evan, "you should join us, it's going to be a gas."

Evan shook his head, but he smiled at her. "Bug and I have a lot to cover yet," he said. Maybe he just didn't want to hurt my feelings, since the other two didn't seem to mind in the least that I was being excluded.

I tried to tell him it was okay if he wanted to go, rooting the words up from some swamp of lie-dom, when Linda said "Oh, well, we won't be going til at least 10:00 or 10:30. You could join us when you're done." She smiled sweetly at me like I was a little kid who would be put to bed soon.

"Yeah, maybe," Evan replied. "After I take Bug home."

My eyes started to sting and I looked down at my book forcing myself to think about refracting angles and points of light.

"Come on," Portia said, suddenly tugging at Linda's sleeve, "we'll catch you later." She turned and walked away, Linda following her with a little wave to Evan.

She had to know it was killing me to watch that girl flirt with Evan right in front of me. She had to know how much it would hurt me if Evan went to J.B.'s and took up with that girl. Or any girl.

"Don't let Portia get to you," Evan said, breaking into my thoughts.

I smiled like I didn't care. Or at least, I tried to smile that way. "Portia is Portia."

He laughed. "Yeah, Portia is Portia."

We finished going over the chapter and Evan closed the book.

"I'll go warm up the car," he said. He took my backpack and slung it onto his shoulder.

"I'll wait by the door." I didn't want to see Portia or Linda again.

"I wish it were summer," Evan said as we walked toward the entrance. "I feel like going for an ice cream."

"You're the one who told the weather Gods you didn't ever want to be hot and wet again."

"I didn't say I wanted to spend my life as a freaking popsicle," he said, but he was smiling. "And it was the groundhog who didn't see his shadow, if you remember, Miss Dictionary. Maybe Brady's is still open. I'll buy you a hot chocolate if it is."

"You really know how to treat a girl."

"First class with me, baby," he said and a blast of cold air hit me as he opened the door. I watched him walk across the snowy parking lot, a warm feeling creeping over me. *He might not go.* Or maybe he was just in a good mood because a pretty girl had flirted with him.

I only gave him a couple of minutes head start and then made a dash for the Mustang. The heater wasn't blowing warm air yet and the seats were hard and frigid.

"You have no patience, you know that." Evan laughed at me as I shivered. I thought about my dad, telling me to give Evan time, even though patience wasn't my strong suit. But how much time was too much? I didn't want him getting sucked in by some girl like Linda just because he was bored. If he was going to fall in love with someone else, it had to be some brainy Princeton girl who taught him to love opera or something equally ridiculous. Some girl who could at least appreciate him the way I did.

We pulled into Brady's coffeehouse, which was usually packed. But at this time of night the only kids in it were the super studious and the socially disadvantaged, who were usually one and the same. We sat at a table away from the few kids scattered through the place and ordered hot chocolate. And we talked about art. Evan started asking me questions, which was weird because he never asked me about my art. Who were my favorite artists? Why? I watched his reflection in the window beside us, lean and clear and strong, making it hard for me to concentrate on what he was even asking me.

"Well?" he pressed me.

I told him Rembrandt and Wyeth, because they made color convey the emotion as much as the lines forming the subject matter.

"So, it's like refraction?" he asked, making me laugh.

"Yeah, I guess so."

"So, it's like physics," he said.

"I get it," I said.

He smiled and took a sip of his cocoa. "So why do you love this Raskolnikov guy?" He wasn't smiling anymore.

"I didn't say I loved Raskolnikov. I said I loved the book."

"But he's pretty much a selfish jerk through the whole thing."

"Until he finds love, and then he finds atonement."

He shook his head. "I don't believe people change like that. The guys I saw in Nam, they stayed the same. They just got more of whatever they started out as. If a guy was a good guy, then the war broke him down and made him soft and crazy. If a guy was a street kicker, then he just got harder and colder and meaner. Where's the atonement in that?"

"I don't know exactly." He stared at me waiting for me to tell him some worldly truth, as if he believed I had any to tell. "It's different for Raskolniknov," I said, "because he's a nihilist. He believes he's superior to the rest of society and disconnected from it. And so he commits his crimes wantonly to prove it, and thinks he doesn't have to pay for them. But the emptiness of rejecting society makes him turn to love, and he has to embrace his punishment to do that."

He was still staring at me. "But maybe it's the same after all," I said. "Maybe atonement can only be found in love."

The eager expression on his face turned flat. I was a stupid Pollyanna, thinking that love made the world go round.

"Atonement. It's the real thing," he said, mimicking the Coca-Cola commercial.

"Yeah," I echoed, my throat tight. "It's the real thing."

He stared at his mug.

"Anyway, it's different," I added. "Raskolnikov didn't play by the rules, so he had to accept his punishment to fit in his society. You played by the rules your society gave you."

His eyes searched mine. "Such as they were, huh?"

I shrugged, just a little.

"So why am I still being punished?" he asked, that one little word encapsulating his lost dreams, and the way people treated him like he no longer fit into our neat little society, and the way the pain of having been both predator and prey ate at him. I reached across the table and laid my fingers over his broken hand. He flinched, just a little before he rolled it and took mine.

"One thing's for sure," he said, picking my hand up and then setting it back down on the table. "Raskolnikov got off easy. I'd trade a few years in Siberia to be free of Vietnam in a heartbeat."

I wished all over again that Steve had sold Evan any other book in the store.

Evan swigged the last of his hot chocolate.

"You ready?" he asked. I nodded and we stood and put our coats on while he threw enough money on the table to cover the drinks and tip. We walked out into the cold and he fired up the Mustang and drove the short distance home, both of us quiet.

He pulled into his drive and shut the engine off.

"Are you going to J.B.'s?" I asked, knowing I'd only have myself to blame if I didn't like the answer. I held my breath, worried I might not be strong enough to hide my heartbreak if he said yes.

"No," he said. "I'm worn out from all this physics." He smiled, turning his head and his delicious smile settled on me with its full effect. I let the edges of my lips curl up slowly, satisfied. We got out and turned to face each other as we shut the car doors.

"Night," Evan said.

"Night."

I started to walk to the back porch.

"Hey Bug," Evan called. I turned around. He was still standing by his car, his right hand resting against the top of it. "Sweet dreams."

I couldn't see his expression in the dark, but his voice was gentle and indulgent like he was talking to a child.

"Yeah, sweet dreams."

I walked into my house and, closing the door, wondered what sweet things there could even be for Evan and Raskolnikov to dream about.

23

EVAN'S REFLECTION in the plate glass window of Brady's moved like a living painting, gold and blue pulsing within dark hues of night. It had been a couple of weeks and we hadn't seen Linda or Portia at the library even once. I was glad.

"What's so interesting out there?" he asked, tilting his head to look where I was looking.

"Nothing," I said, too quickly. "I was 'day-doodling' in my head."

He smiled and took a sip of his steaming cocoa. Tonight, he hadn't even asked me. He'd just pulled into the parking lot of Brady's and I'd had to bite my lip to keep from smiling. We sat at the same table every time and I had the sense that this time belonged to the two of us alone, moving as slowly as February was. I didn't mind the cold of the glass beside us, tucked away as we were near the corner with the waitress only coming by when she was ready to close the place.

"I think I'm going to go to OU this weekend," Evan said suddenly. I glanced up, warning sirens prickling in my ears.

"Why?" The word sounded unnatural, struggling up from my throat.

"Mike asked me."

I nodded, staring down into my hot chocolate. He hadn't mentioned Mike since that day in the Mustang out by the lake. But they had been best friends before Vietnam. Mike on the drums and Evan on guitar. They had been magic when they played.

Evan's voice, barely more than a whisper, came wafting over me. "I need to get away, Bug. A break from my parents. I promise I'll be back in time for your test next week."

"Is it that bad?"

He leaned back into his seat, running his hand through his hair as if the counter pressure made it more bearable. "My dad's been on me to make a decision. He thinks I should go to OU, and Mike asked me to come sometime, so I just figured it'd be a good time to take a break. She's at me all the time, Bug."

"But you won't go there," I said, a statement rather than a question, and even I could hear the urgency in my voice.

"What do you mean?"

"I don't know. I just think—" I hesitated. "You don't belong there."

Evan smiled, plainly amused. "Where do I belong, Bug?"

"I just always thought, I mean, if you weren't going to go to Berklee, that you'd go somewhere, you know, like Princeton, or Penn, or Georgetown, or Yale."

Evan's smile widened. "You think I'd fit in well with all those WASPs, huh?"

I laughed a little. "No, you're not your mom. It's just that you're smart enough. And Georgetown is a bunch of Catholics anyway, genius."

"Even Ellen wouldn't mind those schools."

I turned my spoon over slowly staring at it.

"OU had that tear gas bomb a few weeks ago," I reminded him. "Outside the campus police station. There are a lot of demonstrations there."

Evan raised his hand in front of me. "If a claymore can't kill me, I don't think a little ol' tear gas bomb is going to do the trick." He was laughing at me, but I couldn't smile back, uneasy digging into me.

The waitress came by and laid the bill on the table between us before walking away. Evan leaned up and pulled his wallet from his jeans' pocket, flipping it open to grab a few dollars. He laid them on the table as I slipped my coat on.

"When are you leaving?"

"I think I'll go on Thursday," he replied, apparently not noticing how pathetically tragic I sounded, but he put his hand on the small of my back as we stepped away from the table, the way men often do when they let a woman go before them. I wished I could own his gesture as mine.

When I walked up the driveway on Thursday afternoon after school, the Mustang was gone. I stood a moment in the cold breeze saying a little prayer to the God of Fortune, begging for Pratt as much to bring a change for me when Evan was gone for good as for all the other reasons I wanted to go. I couldn't bear the thought of Kent becoming more like a prison as the years went on. It would be worse than when he left for Vietnam. Then, I had been too young not to believe he would be back. Then, I had been young enough to believe he would come back able to love me.

I plastered a smile on my face and went in the back door, relieved when my mom wasn't in the kitchen. I slipped the can of Nestle's Quick out of the cupboard, dipping a spoon into it. The little granules of sugar and cocoa melted sticky on my tongue.

I sat down at the table eating Nestle's from the can while I thumbed through the newspaper headlines. *Thirty-four arrested as 1500 toss rocks and bottles near Cal U following a speech by William Kunstler.* The reporter seemed skeptical of the student leaders who said the demonstration didn't have any connection to Kunstler's talk, or the fact that he was the chief defense attorney for the Chicago Seven, but stemmed from long standing problems with the university. He didn't even mention what those problems were, but if California University was anything like KSU, it had to do with racial tension and tuition hikes and the war and students feeling like they should have more say in how curriculum was managed. As far as I could tell, LBJ's great society was still a long way off from being great.

My eyes scanned a second headline saying experts saw a long U.S. stay in Vietnam despite progress. Another story talked about the nineteen GI's killed the week before in a helicopter crash. I dropped my spoon and closed the paper, going up to my room to draw. I drew a picture of Pratt from the brochure I had sent away for the year before and put myself on the lawn by one of the older buildings, an art portfolio dangling from my hand, a backpack hanging from my shoulder. I didn't draw myself very well, or perhaps too well, but the figure looked awkward like it didn't belong somehow. The page tore from the notebook and crumpled easily enough, but my frustration grew. I drew a picture of the beach at Buxton, where we went on vacation every August. I put Evan there, because it was as close as I could come to being with him, walking in bare feet and blue jeans, the wind blowing his t-shirt against the outline of his lean frame, and he was smiling and relaxed, his face slightly unshaven, long and unusual and striking, his incomplete hand balancing out the quirky perfection that was him.

Willa walked into my room. "Mom wants to know why you aren't coming down for dinner. She called you three times."

I looked up, surprised at how dark my room was. "I didn't hear her."

Willa peeked over my shoulder. "Wow."

"Thanks."

"You should give that to him."

I shook my head. It had too much of how I really felt embedded on the paper. I set it down on the window seat and went downstairs.

We were quiet at dinner. Portia had gone out with some friends and my dad had stayed on campus to attend a lecture. I didn't even try to call Michelle. I figured she was hanging out with John. He'd joined us at our lunch table a few days after he'd moved in with Steve to say thanks and the next thing I knew, Michelle was listening to his antiwar rhetoric like a disciple. They'd been spending a lot of time together ever since, at least when John wasn't working to pay his own way with Steve and his roommates. I was happy for her, but it highlighted how isolated I had become. It wasn't safe, to have so much of my happiness depend on Evan just being near, but the thought that he couldn't walk through the door at any moment wouldn't leave me. I resolved to be like Elinor from *Sense and Sensibility*, but my thoughts kept reverting back to Evan and how he wasn't where he should be, worrying about where he was and what he was doing and wishing I could fast forward to Sunday night when he said he would be home. The harder I tried to be like Elinor, the more I realized I was like Marianne. I didn't seem to know how to love Evan without my whole heart being dragged into the process.

Friday and Saturday lumbered along. I walked to Main and took some photos of the river but I couldn't quite forget that

Elinor's nobleness was rewarded in the end. Jane Austen wasn't very useful for the real world.

I was curled up on the sofa watching the Saturday late movie by myself, when a slight tap sounded on the window pane. It was dark outside, the same bitter clouds that had been hanging over Kent all winter still blocking out the moonlight. I laughed at myself. Judith Anderson's Mrs. Danvers was totally creeping me out.

I settled back down but jumped when the tap became clearer, longer, more insistent. I threw off the little acrylic blanket keeping me warm and went toward the window. My dad was snoring away heavily upstairs. My heart was ticking ridiculously fast. And then a hand struck the window. A hand without fingers.

I ran to the front door and unlocked it. Evan met me on the front steps.

"You scared the daylights out of me!"

I pulled him into the front hall and closed the door against the winter. The hallway was dimly lit, just a sliver from the empty kitchen falling along the floorboards in a long ribbon and the flicker of the TV from the living room.

"Sorry," he whispered as I looked up at his face, swollen and bloody, a dark bruise crowding his left eye. "I came home early."

I gasped and touched my hand to his cheek. I turned his head to get a better look.

"I was afraid you might be Portia."

I stopped a moment, the words sweet in my ears, but then I knew better. Portia would have told him to put some ice on it and then she would have gone to bed. He knew I'd at least try to help him.

"Can you fix me up?" he asked. "So she won't be able to tell?"

I shook my head, my mouth hanging open. There was no way I could fix him up enough that his mom wasn't going to know.

"Come in the kitchen," I whispered, leading the way. He sat down and I ran upstairs to get some first aid supplies. When I came back, Evan had his elbows on the table, his face in his hands.

"What the heck happened?" I asked in a hushed tone. He picked his head up and for once I was looking down at him.

"I got in a fight."

"A fight?"

"Just a quick one." He tried to smile, but winced instead.

"I'd hate to see the other guy."

"Other guys," he corrected me. "And they look worse. I think."

I shook my head at him, cleaning off the blood from the cut over his eye with peroxide. He flinched.

"It's not alcohol, you sissy," I whispered. "It won't sting."

I wiped the dried blood away. It wasn't bleeding anymore, but the cut was long, like maybe the buckle of a watch had scraped him. I pressed a clean tissue soaked in peroxide against it, then pushed his face back to look at him. Even beaten up he was beautiful.

"I'm pretty sure you don't need stitches. It's the swelling that's the worst. There's no way your mom isn't gonna flip. Why would you fight a bunch of guys?" I pulled two bandages from the box and covered the cut. Evan had never gotten into a fight before Vietnam. I went to get some ice from the freezer.

"It wasn't a bunch," Evan said, his voice defensive. "It was only two and a little guy who came in toward the end."

I shook my head at him without turning around, knowing he would be watching me.

"And they called me a baby killer."

I stopped where I was, my hand on the ice tray, as frozen as the water at my fingertips. The pendulum clock hanging over the sideboard ticked its loud, regular judgment.

"They called me a baby killer," Evan said again, as if he thought I hadn't heard.

I pulled my hand from the freezer and dropped frozen cubes into the ice pack, screwing the heavy plastic lid on. The sharp smell of vinyl stung my nose. "So? You can't go around fighting with people just because they're morons. You'd have to fight most of the people you meet." Pretty much the same thing I'd said the day he'd gone after that kid at the Hub.

"I knew you'd scold me."

"Your mom's gonna flip," I said again, pressing the bag gently against his face.

"She can't see my like this. I'll never have any peace. Can't you cover it with make-up or something?"

"Maybe in a couple of days," I said, pulling the bag off and looking at him again. His gaze scorched me and I moved the bag back a little too quickly, making him pull away with an "ouch."

"Sorry," I mumbled, pressing it against his face softly. "Where did you park? I didn't hear your car."

"On the street."

"Then she doesn't know you're home. You could go to my grandfather's for a couple of days. Let the swelling go down." I didn't like the idea of sending him away, but the prospect of his mother harping at him was even more terrible. And he'd be safe with my nonno. "You can sleep on the sofa and I'll wake you at 6:00, and by the time you get to Cleveland Nonno will be up. He won't mind."

"You think?"

"You know he adores you." *Just like the rest of us.* "He'll cover for you. Besides, he loves to be in on a secret."

"Sounds like a plan," Evan said, smiling as much as he could. He got up and started rummaging through the refrigerator, making himself a glass of chocolate milk.

"I'll go get you a pillow and blanket." I went upstairs and took the extra pillow from my bed, grabbing a quilt and sheet from a small trunk at the top of the landing. I slipped down to the living room and fixed the sofa up for him. Evan came in and sat down, kicking his sneakers off.

"You won't forget to wake me?"

"I'll set my alarm."

"Aren't you going to say 'I told you so'?"

"Do you need me to?"

He laughed, shaking his head. I went in the kitchen and got the ice pack. When I came back, he was lying down and I sat beside him on the edge of the cushion, letting the ice pack rest against his swollen face. My hip was against his side and I wanted him to be as aware of it as I was. Dickens walked over and jumped on his legs, kneading them and purring before settling down on top of his thighs. Evan closed his eyes.

"It's hard to punch a guy without your fingers," he said, making me sputter.

"You're incorrigible."

"Is that good, Miss Dictionary?" he asked, even though he knew what it meant. He didn't open his eyes when he spoke, though, sinking into our sofa like it was the hammock.

"Go to sleep."

I sat beside him for a long time, holding the ice pack to his face for several minutes and then taking it off again, applying it and taking it off. Evan drifted into a sound sleep, undisturbed by the cold vinyl bag as I pressed it against him. I watched him sleep, a squirrel gathering acorns, hoarding the outline of his features and the smell of his aftershave.

When I went up to my room, I set my alarm clock and placed it under a sweatshirt so it wouldn't wake anyone else when it started buzzing in a few hours. Crawling under the covers, my heart filled with the impression of Evan's nearness and his trust in me, letting me know I had failed the Elinor test, utterly and completely.

24

I WALKED OUT of Roosevelt High a few days later still thinking about the project my art teacher assigned us for our final. Mrs. Anderson said it could be anything we wanted so long as it showed some aspect of the political, racial, or social tension happening in the country. I was thinking of doing some sort of pictorial essay about the town-gown mentality of Kent, using my camera to show how the town fed off of the university without actually liking it. Showing students hanging out and spending money in Kent would be easy, but showing how little the business people liked the students would be a lot harder.

I was standing at the corner of Mantua and Crain waiting for the light to change when Evan's car came up the street. He caught my eye and made the right turn, then pulled up to the curb for me.

"I was afraid I'd missed you," he said as I climbed in. "Where's Tonto?"

I dropped my backpack on the floor. Cinderella couldn't have been as happy to ride in her pumpkin coach as I was to have shotgun in the Mustang. "Michelle's in detention. She got into an argument with our history teacher because they were talking about the difference between the law and morality and she said there's nothing wrong with interracial marriage. Did you just get back?"

He laughed and nodded before looking over his shoulder to pull back into traffic.

"How's your face?" He turned to let me get a good look.

"Much better," I said. "Although your mom is going to know something happened. How was my nonno?"

"He took me to his Italian club. He told all his old cronies I was like his grandson."

"I told you he'd be happy."

"Yeah, they made me drink homemade wine that you could light a bonfire with and then they pulled out the grappa, and I said 'whoa, that's too strong,' and they all laughed their heads off, while your grandfather sat there beaming because he was the one who'd brought the sissy young guy."

I laughed. "You must've made him a celebrity at the Italian club. Those old guys will think that's funny for months. So what are you going to tell your mom?"

"If she asks, I'll tell her I fell out of bed," he said, making me laugh again. "They think I stayed over at OU. They're happy enough at the prospect of me liking OU that they won't ask too many questions. I could've stayed another day or two and let it heal, but you have your test coming up and Ellen's in a tizzy over some package the Marines sent me. Must be some of my stuff they lost when they evac'd me to the hospital."

He pulled the car into his parking space and turned off the engine. "So, you've had a nice break," he said, "but tonight it's back to studying. You have that test in two days."

"Yes, sir," I said, grabbing my backpack and getting out. I was almost to my door when he called to me.

"Yes?" I asked, half turning around.

"Thanks."

He was standing by the car with a serious expression on his face and it made me feel the weight he carried around with him every day as surely as if he had handed me his shackles.

I nodded before going inside.

"Evan must be home," my mom said as I kicked my Keds off. "You're smiling."

I smiled even more ridiculously. She was standing at the sink, peeling apples. The wood floor was cold against my socks and I bent a little to kiss her cheek. "There's plenty of time to be broken hearted yet."

"I hope you'll always be able to make fun of yourself like that," she answered, a worried line wavering in her light tone.

"Me, too," I said doubtfully.

We were still eating dinner when Evan walked in that evening. "You ready to go, Bug?"

I swallowed my mouthful of mashed potatoes and ketchup. "Not quite."

"Willa, get Evan a plate," my dad said.

"That's okay, Art," Evan said, motioning for Willa to stay seated. "I'm not hungry."

My dad shot him a look of surprise and then pushed his empty coffee cup toward my mom.

"I made apple pie, Evan," she said as she got up.

"Thanks, Rita," Evan replied, "but I'll save mine for after the library. Come on, Bug, aren't you ready yet?"

"What's the big rush?" I asked, a half-eaten plate before me.

"No rush," Evan said, shaking his head. But he was jangling the change in his pocket ferociously. The door bell rang. Evan groaned under his breath as he paced behind me.

"I'll get it," Willa volunteered.

I shoved a bite of salad in my mouth and chewed fast, swigging some Kool-Aid to wash it down.

"You ready?" Evan asked again.

"Okay, okay," I said, getting up as Mrs. Olesson walked into the room.

"Oh, I'm sorry to interrupt your dinner," she said.

"Nonsense," said my mom. "Sit down and have some coffee, Ellen."

"Did Evan tell you his news?" Mrs. Olesson asked as she seated herself at the table, holding a big yellow envelope.

There was a chorus of no's.

"What news?" Portia asked.

"It's no big deal, come on, Bug," Evan said as he grabbed my arm.

"Evan was awarded the Bronze Star for valor," Mrs. Olesson said.

I stopped and he dropped his hold on me, cracking us apart.

"Evan, that's wonderful," my mother said.

"Congratulations, Evan," my dad said.

"Wow," Willa added.

Mrs. Olesson pulled out a small, black plastic case from the envelope and opened it to show us Evan's shining medal.

"And this is the citation," she said, sliding a sheet of paper from the envelope and handing it to my dad.

"Rachel, read this, I don't have my glasses," my dad said, handing me the letter. Evan let out a heavy breath beside me.

I started to read, nervously because Evan didn't want me to. The disapproving look on his face was clear in my mind without me needing to look up and see it.

"'For meritorious service in connection with combat operations against the enemy in the Republic of Vietnam when, while serving as a rifleman on 21 September 1969, a heavily fortified North Vietnamese Army platoon ambushed Lance

Corporal Evan J. Olesson's squad and a two hour firefight ensued. After sustaining heavy casualties, including the fire team leader and squad leader, Lance Corporal Olesson rallied his squad, secured a helicopter landing zone, and assisted in the evacuation of three wounded Marines. While under continuous rocket, mortar, and machine gun fire, Lance Corporal Olesson twice returned to his squad's initial defensive position, and with disregard for his personal safety, retrieved the bodies of two fallen members of his squad. His courageous actions saved the lives of three Marines and allowed the safe extraction of the remaining members of the squad. Lance Corporal Olesson's professionalism, bold initiative, and unwavering devotion to duty were in keeping with the highest traditions of the Marine Corps and the United States Naval Service.'"

My voice had become tight. I handed the citation back to Mrs. Olesson.

"You did well, son," my dad said. Portia murmured something and my mom came over and gave Evan a quick hug. "We're very proud of you, darling."

"They made more of it than it was," Evan said. "Are you ready now?" he asked me, his tone angry. I grabbed my backpack and coat.

The night was crisp and clean with hundreds of stars flickering through the empty branches of the trees. The blue of the Mustang floated above the ground as Evan opened the door for me. I slipped into the seat and he closed the door with a sharp clang. He walked around to his side and got in, but he wasn't looking at me or talking.

"She was just doing what moms do," I practically whispered as he backed into the street.

"It's my fault. I should never have opened it in front of her. I had no idea."

"Why?"

"Guys did stuff all the time. There was no telling who they'd put in for a medal."

"No," I said. "I mean, why did you risk your life if—" I stopped. There was no way to ask why he had risked his life if he knew those guys were already dead.

"What, for dead guys?"

"Sorry," I whispered.

He drove a couple of blocks. Then he slowed the car and pulled over to the curb. He slipped it into park and let it idle.

"I'm sorry," he said.

I nodded slowly in agreement.

"Marines take care of their own, Bug, and they never leave another Marine behind. It's hard to explain, but it's the code we live by. You wouldn't have wanted my body left over there if I'd been killed, would you?"

I shook my head no, fighting the tears. I couldn't stand the thought that he could have died trying to bring those other Marines back when it was too late to help them anyway. It was too much for someone to die for people who weren't alive anymore to be helped. I couldn't stand the thought of him dying over there, now that the danger was past and I had finally come to understand how insistent it had been.

"I guess it helped us, knowing we wouldn't be left there to rot if something happened to us. It builds trust, to know the guy next to you will take care of you no matter what. And you know he will, because the group expects it. It's nothing heroic. It doesn't deserve a medal."

We stared at the silent street. A sleek gray cat slid across the pavement, its eyes shining in the Mustang's headlights as it turned toward us. Dirty piles of snow lined the sidewalk thick and low, reflecting the moonlight in dappled pinpoints where ice crystals glowed.

"You're a lot more heroic than you think you are," I said.

"Yeah, you think that, Bug," Evan replied, making me feel like I was seven and he was teasing me for still having training wheels on my bike.

"I mean it," I said, a rumble of defiance giving my voice an edge. "There were other Marines there who could have gone after those guys, but you did. You didn't have to go see Tom Foley's widow, but you did. And you didn't have to ever pick up a guitar again, but you did. You're a lot more heroic than you give yourself credit for." I turned my face toward him, not caring anymore if he saw the tears pooled there.

He looked back at me, his gaze lingering on my face until I felt naked and had to look away. "I think that's maybe something we have in common," he said at last, putting the car in gear and pulling away from the curb.

We went to the library and studied, and then we went to Brady's, because we always did now. But Evan was quiet and when he did talk, his words didn't mean very much. I tried to let him just be, and he seemed relieved. I doodled on a napkin so he didn't have to feel like we had to talk. When we got up to leave, he pulled the napkin over and looked at my drawing. It was Dickens pawing at Charles' tail while he ate, and it made Evan smile.

When we got home and he said good night, I asked him if he was coming in for pie.

"No, ask Rita to save me a piece for breakfast and I'll sneak over tomorrow when Ellen gives herself a cucumber facial." He scrunched up his face and shook his head until I laughed.

Later, when I slipped into bed, the feeling of sitting in the Mustang on the quiet, dark street was all around me and I lay there wondering if I would have made a good Marine if I had been a boy. *Marines take care of their own.* Evan's words rolled through my thoughts like tiny, white-capped waves on the shore of a lake. I didn't know if I'd risk my own life to retrieve someone else's body, but there was one thing I was certain about. As long as I had the chance, I would do whatever I could to take care of Evan James Olesson.

25

A WEEK LATER, the hall was crowded with kids making their way to fourth period. Robby grabbed my arm and pulled me over to the lockers, out of the stream of traffic. "What's wrong with Evan?"

"What do you mean 'what's wrong with him?'"

Robby shook his head at me. "Come on, Bug. He came back from OU looking like Sylvester after Granny beats him with her umbrella and he's having nightmares again, like when he first got home."

"What kind of nightmares?"

"I dunno," he said. "The kind that make a guy mumble crazy stuff in his sleep and wake up wanting to watch the snow on television 'til morning."

It wasn't like Robby to be worried. "Did your mom notice that he was banged up?"

"She didn't say anything to him at the time, but yeah. I think she was afraid he'd been drinking and didn't really want to know. She has no idea what to do with him. Since he's come back, he's been so—I don't know, detached. And he was acting like he was going to start trying to come back, but since he went to OU—"

"He's having a hard time adjusting to how things are here," I said. "You could make it easier for him. Maybe hang out with him. Most of his friends are in school or still serving. He came back to nothing, with people angry at him for giving up everything to do what they asked him to do in the first place. Can't you maybe try to be his friend?"

Robby opened his mouth like he was going to make some sarcastic comment, but then he hesitated. "Yeah, okay, I guess I could do that," he said. "We could play some hoops, like we used to do, or something."

The breath that had been building up inside of me shuddered its way out. "It's hard for him, being stuck in the house with your mom all day."

Robby ticked his head in agreement that that demanded sympathy for anyone.

"Do you need all your fingers to play hoops?" he asked, unable to suppress the worst of him completely. He smiled, his face bursting with the knowledge that he was getting to me.

And just like when we kids, I couldn't rise above it. "If you're going to be a jerk about it, then just—"

"Peace, Bug," Robby said. "You're way too serious. I'll be nice to the walking wounded mental case."

"Okay, you can start by not calling him that," I said. But Robby just sauntered down the hallway leaving me unsure of whether I had made an ally.

It was late on Friday afternoon when I heard voices weaving between the thunking of a basketball in the driveway below. I left my homework and padded over to the window seat. Evan and Robby were in their driveway passing a worn basketball between them, shooting at the rusted out hoop hanging above their garage door. It was only about eight feet high and both of them could reach it just by putting their arms up. But they were smiling and joking like they used to do before Vietnam. I slipped back to my English essay and tried to pretend I couldn't hear Evan's voice, distracting me even when it was too low for me to understand what he was saying, content with knowing Robby was trying.

When I finished my homework, I sat at my desk listening to the thump of the basketball and the rise and fall of their voices as I sketched the two of them until my mom called me down to dinner.

My dad had gone to a cocktail party for a visiting lecturer, and we turned on the television by rote. Not that the news changed from night to night. The war and student protests were always the news, and it never got any better, especially since the North Vietnamese had invaded Cambodia. Cambodia had told them to get out, but the North Vietnamese were refusing to leave and I got the impression they were just laughing at everyone, knowing that if we couldn't beat them in their own country, no one was going to make them leave Cambodia.

Portia had gotten her acceptance letter from Case Western the week before and she talked over the news with her plans for an apartment, a boyfriend on law review with her, and the statistics of women lawyers being hired by big corporations. She had so much confidence.

"Only four percent of lawyers are women," she said. "Did you know that? Only four percent. Someone told me that Columbia's law school has an Employment Rights Project and they're investigating discrimination against women attorneys."

"It's not going to be easy for you," my mom said, bringing the salad over. "It's still a man's world, no matter how many women go around burning their bras."

Willa giggled.

Through the chatter, the words East Liberty reached my mind. "Shhh!" I said, turning toward the TV, but the others had heard it, too. The anchorman was talking about the neighborhood where my Aunt Mary and Uncle Armand lived in Pittsburgh.

"No one was hurt at the shopping mall as the bomb exploded early this morning," the anchorman said.

My mom was already up, heading to the telephone in the front hall. The news moved onto the weather and we followed my mom in a pack.

"All the circuits are busy," my mom said without looking up, pressing the buttons in the cradle down hard before dialing again.

"Mary! We just heard! What's happened?" my mom exclaimed.

We listened to my mom's side of the conversation standing there clustered around her until we were convinced my Aunt Mary and Uncle Armand were all right.

"Why would someone bomb a shopping mall?" Willa asked. I steered her into the living room so my mom could hear my Aunt Mary.

"The world's a little crazy right now," Portia said, like that explained it.

"And getting crazier," I said.

"True," Portia said. "When they set those bombs off the other day in New York it was wrong, but at least you knew they were targeting corporate America. I mean, they hit IBM, and Mobile, and GT&E. What's the point of bombing people trying to shop in East Liberty, for heaven's sake? It's not even a good part of town."

East Liberty was totally depressed, a typical white flight neighborhood with Armand and Mary among the last of the old inhabitants, staying put until the end came to meet them.

"What if Aunt Mary or Uncle Armand had been hurt?" Willa asked.

"They weren't," I said, pushing her hair behind her ears. "Things can't go on like this, it will settle down. You'll see."

"Well," my mom said, walking into the room. "The police think it wasn't meant to actually hurt anyone since it was set off before people were out and shopping. Honestly, I don't know what this world is coming to anymore. The force of it broke windows out all over the street. Armand says it looks like a war zone."

My mom walked over to hug Willa. "Don't cry, love. It's all right, no one was hurt." I put the television on to distract her with a sitcom rerun.

"I never thought all this craziness would reach Pittsburgh," my mom said. "Makes me glad we live in Kent."

"Center of radical thought," I said.

Portia laughed.

"Maybe we should be grateful for that, at least at the moment," my mom said.

"So much for the 'glorious seventies,'" I said.

"Would you please sit with Willa for a while?" my mom asked me, "and I'll clean up the dishes."

"Sure," I said. Portia was going out with some friends and went to get ready. A few minutes later, Evan came over. He'd heard the report, too, and wanted to make sure my Aunt Mary and Uncle Armand were all right.

Willa and I were on the sofa watching *The Partridge Family*, and he sat down on the other side of her.

"I sure could go for some of that Jiffy Pop, Squirt. Do you have any?"

She jumped up and went to make it for him and he shot me a grin. He loved having a harem.

"You should be hearing from Pratt pretty soon, shouldn't you?" he asked.

"I probably would have heard from them already, but my dad's art professor friend at KSU who said he'd write me a recommendation 'forgot' to send the letter until I reminded him last week."

"Come on, Bug," Evan said with a slight smile, "I don't think Art would set you up like that."

"I don't know," I said. "But it seems awfully convenient. They probably figured the later Pratt decided on my application, the more likely I wouldn't get in because they would already have chosen other people."

"But he gave you someone to ask for a recommendation, so why would he tell the guy to send it late?"

"I needed one for KSU, too. He just said he'd do both when I asked him. Then he 'forgot' about the Pratt one."

"Your dad wouldn't be dishonest like that."

"Maybe not," I said. "Not like it matters, he isn't going to let me go even if I do get in. But it would make it easier for him if he didn't have to be the bad guy." I didn't want to give up on Pratt, but I hadn't come up with a single reason that I thought would persuade my dad. The week before, I had tried to talk about Pratt and he'd walked out of the room without even letting me finish my sentence. He didn't think my art mattered, and he didn't approve of me going away. My KSU acceptance had come in February and he'd acted like I'd gotten an acceptance letter from Yale.

"We'll talk him into it," Evan said, the confidence in his voice reminding me that, no matter how much he trusted me, and no matter how much time he spent with me, he wasn't having any trouble with the idea of letting me go.

Postal workers in New York City went on strike the next week crippling mail delivery to and from the city. Maybe it was a bad omen. Maybe the Gods were giving me fair warning that I wasn't going to like my mail when it finally did come through. I was almost grateful when hundreds of mailmen in Akron and Cleveland joined the New York strike, figuring it was better to put off the bad news as long as possible. The only thing worse than not getting into Pratt was the idea of being stuck at KSU when September rolled around and Evan spread those broken wings and flew away to Princeton, or Harvard, or Stanford.

March dragged on, refusing to shed its lion cold even through the very last days. President Nixon went on television to assure us that the mail strike wasn't anything to worry about and then sent the army into New York post offices to sort the mail.

"Do you think he'll be any better at his war on mailmen than he has been at his wars against communism or pollution?" Evan asked me the next night when we were sitting at Brady's.

I laughed. The waitress set down our hot chocolates and the slab of chocolate cake Evan had ordered.

"Did you see the paper this morning?" I asked, wondering as the words came out if I should even mention it.

"You mean the article about that sergeant testifying that the troops were smoking pot the night before My Lai?"

"Do you think that could have been part of it?"

"I don't know. I doubt it."

"Are drugs that bad there?"

"Like here, I guess," he said, pushing the plate of cake in between us and offering me the extra fork. "The army has it worse than the Marines. I guess 'cause it's more draftees."

"But you were drafted."

"Yeah, but it's rare. They just needed to fill a few slots the day I was inducted, and they went through us and pointed at two other guys and me and said 'you volunteer to be a Marine, and you, and you,'" he said, pointing at me as if he were the guy saying it, making me smile.

"I'm not saying there aren't drugs in the Marines, too, it just depends on the unit. We didn't have much of it. Our Lieutenant wouldn't have stood for it. We were pretty deep in the jungle. It was too dangerous to let your guard down. And we were close. None of us would've wanted to be the guy who got Joe killed because we were screwed up."

The edgy feeling I always got when I thought about the danger Evan had lived through for all those months crept over me, and I slipped the fork through the back of the piece of cake to get mostly frosting, letting it melt soft and velvety on my tongue.

"Always going for the icing, Bug, that hasn't changed about you."

I looked up, not sure whether to smile. "Does that mean I'm a little kid or an optimist?"

"I'd say a little of both."

"I don't feel very optimistic," I said, wishing I could convince him I wasn't the little girl he saw me as.

"As soon as you get that acceptance letter, I'll start working on your dad."

Now that Evan was in my corner, I was almost sorry I had wished for it. His eagerness to help me get away was almost as bad as him not caring at all. "He's so against me leaving. He's letting Portia go this year, and he doesn't want to lose both of us. And he thinks because I'm only seventeen that I won't be able to handle it."

"Ah, Bug, it's always darkest before the dawn they say."

"They can afford to be wrong. No one knows who 'they' are."

He laughed, pulling out his wallet to pay the check. But I couldn't shake the feeling that the stars were aligning against me and time wasn't going to help. As we left Brady's and headed home, there was still a lion's roar in the frigid wind making me skeptical that a warm sun was just over the horizon, waiting to illuminate the good hidden beneath the world's ever increasing discord.

26

APRIL CAME WITH NO SIGN of the promised lamb in sight. I couldn't remember a year when the frost of winter clung so tightly to spring. Evan put the hammock up, but it was too cold and rainy to sit in it, even for him. The news was just as chilling, as sour to me as the warm water, whiskey, and sugar mixture my mother used to give us when we were little to cure our stomach aches.

"I can't believe Governor Rhodes is really going to sue *Life* magazine," Portia said one morning, pushing the Courier away from her.

"Do you think he actually has ties to a mobster?" I asked my dad.

"It wouldn't surprise me," he said. "Taft will be a hard man to beat for that Senate seat, and Rhodes can't sit back and do nothing after that article. I'm sure *Life's* lawyers were pretty certain they could beat a defamation suit. Rhodes is going to have to prove he's a friend of the law if he's going to win this election.

"And he's got a real problem now that the Teamsters strike has penetrated Ohio. If the strike isn't settled soon, businesses all over the state are going to be affected. Not a position you want to be in going into an election." My dad smiled and lit a Camel. He hated Governor Rhodes. "If Congress follows through on lowering the voting age to eighteen, you'll be able to vote next year." He blew smoke over my head.

I hoped they would. The first vote I would ever make, no matter how old I had to be to make it, was going to be for an antiwar candidate.

My dad's prediction that Governor Rhodes would show himself as a friend of law and order came true within the week when the mayor of Cleveland requested National Guard support because of race riots at Collinwood High. Governor Rhodes sent seven hundred Guardsmen into the school. My dad did everything except say "I told you so" as he sat reading the newspaper.

"Son of a gun," he said to himself, completely satisfied.

I couldn't imagine army troops standing guard in the halls of Roosevelt. Maybe my mom was right and we should be grateful to live in a boring town like Kent. I started reading the comics and skimming the headlines, but it didn't help. The race riots and bombings and strikes kept rolling through the periphery of my life.

"Did you read the article about McCartney this morning?" Evan asked me a week later, picking at the strings of his new guitar as we sat on my back porch. The temperature was hovering in the 50s, but it seemed almost warm after the relentless cold, leaving only my fingers chilled as I set my guitar down and pulled the sleeves of my sweater over them.

"No, but I heard about it at school. The rumors of his death have been greatly exaggerated."

"And the Beatles are officially over."

"I guess no group could survive all that attention and money and craziness."

"McCartney's pretty bitter," Evan said, his fingers weaving quiet notes across the strings. "I guess that explains why he's been hiding out from the press for all these months."

"I don't know how any of them stood it, people all over them wherever they went."

"You'd never be able to be famous," he said. "You're going to have to be one of those artists whose stuff only becomes valuable after they die."

I shrugged. "I wouldn't want to be a Beatle, that's for sure. I don't blame McCartney."

"No," Evan said, "I can see why he'd want to get away. Like you want to hide when you're in a war, I guess. Except his enemy doesn't want to kill him. They just want a little piece of his fame. Not his legs or his eyes or his life. But I've never been a celebrity. Maybe in its way it's just as bad."

"I doubt if it's as bad."

He began manipulating the strings into a sweet melody. "Do you like this?"

I nodded. "Did you write the lyrics yet?"

He looked at me without answering right away. "It's a work in progress," he said finally. "This guitar is sweet."

"I know it's not what you lost, but it's something."

"Sometimes, something is everything."

I smiled, trying to convince myself to be content. I saw Evan more days than I didn't, and twice a week we went to the library and Brady's when he helped me with my physics. Now that the weather was beginning to thaw, I sometimes found him waiting for me when I walked out of school. I'd slip into the Mustang and we'd drive until we ended up at one of the lakes, sitting on the hood, trying to stay warm between the resting engine beneath us and the late sun above, while Evan scattered bits and pieces of Vietnam before me like die from a Yatzie cup or asked me if I thought the ducks thought we were crazy for sitting there in the cold.

I tried to tell myself it didn't matter when the mail came and there was still no letter from Pratt. I tried not to notice the way Evan had begun to get the mail for his mom and that it meant he was expecting acceptance letters from universities somewhere beyond the second star to the right and straight on to morning. Letters he didn't want his mom to know about until he was ready to tell her. Letters he didn't tell me about either. Letters from destinations I didn't know how to reach, making me wish that, instead of being sensible and responsible, just once in all the years of my childhood, I had learned how to fly the way he and Portia could.

One afternoon in mid April as I came in from school, my mom looked up from the kitchen sink, her face tight. "There's a letter for you on the hall table."

"There is?" I asked, but it wasn't really a question and she had already turned back to the counter where she was pounding cutlets for veal parmesan, one of my dad's favorite meals. I hurried to the hall table where an envelope with a return address of Pratt sat propped against the small lamp. The paper was a thick linen, heavy in my hand, and I stared at the address. I didn't have Evan's confidence that my dad could be talked into letting me go, but I couldn't bear the idea that maybe Pratt didn't even think I was good enough to be accepted. I dropped my backpack on the floor and ran outside, across the lawn to Evan's house.

I stood on his front walk, unable to go to the door and ring the bell. *What if his mom answered?* I couldn't face Mrs. Olesson's questions, especially if it all turned out to be a great big failure and suddenly I felt like running somewhere else, but I couldn't think of anywhere to go. So I just stood there stupidly.

"Hey," Evan said, coming around the side of the house. "Did you open it yet?"

I shook my head. "How did you know?"

"Your mom called me," he said, flashing the Mustang's keys at me.

I followed him to the car and he opened the door for me. I dropped into the seat as if sliding into some old hiding place. Evan got in and I set the letter down between us.

We didn't say anything and he drove up to the Twins and parked where the gravel ended on the north side of West Lake. Late afternoon sparkled across the surface, golden sun against budding greens. Evan didn't make me talk, didn't hand me the letter. We just sat there while I got my courage up.

"Do you suppose the ducks think we're crazy?" I asked after a while, as a mom and seven little ducklings made their way to the cattails.

"You, maybe," he said, and I laughed a little. I picked up the envelope and looked at the address one more time. I turned it over and slid my finger under the flap, breaking the seal slowly so I wouldn't get a paper cut, but really because I was scared. I pulled the letter out, looking over at Evan.

"It's okay, Bug. Either way," he said, and he meant that life goes on no matter how disappointed we are, and that I shouldn't let "no" break my heart. But he wasn't the one who had something to prove. He wasn't the one who would be told he wasn't good enough. He had gotten into his dream school, even if he did blow it afterwards. He wasn't the one who would be stuck in Kent without the person he loved most in the world. He would get into whatever schools he was applying to now. He would leave Kent and forget these months that for me would be the only thing I could remember.

I unfolded the paper. My voice shook a little as I started to read.

"'Dear Miss Morelli, We are pleased to inform you—'" I stopped and laughed and put my hand over my mouth and he took the paper from my trembling hand and read it out loud twice, as if he wanted to make sure I heard him read that I'd been accepted.

"I told you you'd get in," he said, his face reflecting the joy I was just beginning to feel.

"Well, even if my dad doesn't let me go, at least I have this," I said, trying to convince myself it wasn't a bad consolation prize. At least Evan knew I could get in, and now my dad would know, too. My dad would know that Pratt believed in me, even if he didn't. I had actually gotten in.

"About that," Evan said. "I have an idea. But it's kind of a gamble. You'd have to be okay with letting everything ride on one chance." He looked at me steadily.

One chance wasn't much, but I already knew I would trust him. "I'm listening."

"Okay," he said, sinking back in his seat, the leather squeaking with his movement, "so you've been working on your senior art project, right?"

I nodded.

"I think you should go home and tell your folks that you got into Pratt, but then say 'before you say no, I have a proposition.' Your dad will ask what it is, and you tell him that you want to make a deal with him that if you can get an A on your project, then they let you go to Pratt. If not, you never complain about their decision."

"He'll never go for that. I've had straight A's in art since third grade."

"Oh," he said. "Time for you to come up with a brilliant plan, I guess."

"But maybe if I made it rest on his opinion, then he might agree. What do you think?"

"You mean if he thinks your project is first rate, then he lets you go?"

I nodded, but then changed my mind. "Never mind," I said. "I'd be handing him the chance to say no all wrapped up with a neat bow."

"I don't think so, Bug," he said. "Your dad's the most honest guy I know. If he really thinks your project is dynamite, he won't be able to tell you not to go."

"Have you ever heard my dad when he's working a dinner party?" I asked. "Half of every one of his stories is, at best, an exaggeration."

"That's just poetic license, Bug. When it comes to what really matters, your dad's more honest than George Washington. He won't keep you from going to Pratt if he makes a deal with you and really thinks you're good enough to go."

"Even if you're right, there's still another problem. Right now, I haven't come up with anything 'dynamite.' And how will I know what my dad would think is dynamite? I have pictures of students spending money in town, but I still haven't figured out how to show the town's animosity toward them. So much for showing the town-gown mentality through a photo essay."

"Okay, well, then it's time to start brainstorming. Your project isn't due until late next week, right?"

"The Friday after this one, the 8th."

"Well, that gives us thirteen days to come up with something incredible."

"Something incredible," I echoed, not sure I believed it was possible.

Evan leaned forward and turned the key, lighting up the Mustang's engine. "Good. Let's go to Hahn's and celebrate you getting into the best art school in the country. I'll buy you something with so much icing, it'll make you sick."

"Sounds good." I sank back into my seat with a smile, determined to savor this moment with Evan while it lasted, determined not to think about how hard he was trying to help me fly away. I put the letter back in its envelope and set it on the dash, hope burning through me slowly like a warm sip of whiskey.

When we got back to my house, my dad was home. Early. "She must have called him," I said. Evan just pushed me through the door into the kitchen.

"Hey," I said, struggling to smile when I knew they wouldn't share my happiness.

"So, your mom says you got the letter you've been waiting for," my dad said, jumping right in. He leaned his hip against the counter and lit a Camel, taking a deep breath and blowing the smoke out slowly, his gaze locked on mine.

"Yes," I said. I took a deep breath. "And I got in. But before you say "no," I want to ask you, I mean, I want to propose something, I mean…." I stopped. Fumbling over my words wasn't going to convince my dad of anything, but I didn't know how to put it the way Evan had when we were sitting in the Mustang and it sounded so plausible.

"What Bug's trying to say," Evan broke in, "is that she's willing to accept your decision about whether she can go or not, but she's asking you to wait until you see her senior art project. If you see that and still don't think she should go to the best art school she can get into, the best art school in the country really, then she won't complain if you say she can't go. I mean, that's pretty fair, isn't it?"

My dad dragged on his cigarette.

"That sounds reasonable," my mom said. She came over and gave me a quick hug. "We're very proud of you, you know that, don't you?" she asked, slipping my hair behind my ear.

My dad studied me through the haze of smoke he blew out. "So it's your mom's and my decision, based on this one project?"

I nodded.

"And you'll be satisfied if we still say 'no,' that's what you're telling me?"

"Yes," I said, binding myself even though I knew I would never be satisfied.

"It's a deal," my dad said, and I pulled a sharp breath, shooting Evan a look. So far his plan was working. But making a project with what I had so far that my parents couldn't say no to was something else entirely. I couldn't fail.

I spent every waking hour over the next two days trying to come up with a brilliant idea, going over the pictures I had taken already. I wanted to set the photos up in a way that they'd look like dominos starting to fall as we went from the appearance of harmony to the underlying discord. But I still didn't have the right kind of pictures to show the way the Kentites resented the students who drove the town's economy, or a way of displaying them that achieved that domino effect.

I walked through downtown Kent on Tuesday and Wednesday after I got out of school, but I didn't find anything to take a picture of that would be powerful enough to win my parents over.

"Maybe you're approaching this idea from the wrong angle," Evan said to me on Wednesday afternoon as we sat on my back porch.

"What do you mean?"

"The project just has to show some aspect of the social, racial, or political discord happening now, right?"

"Yes."

"So there's no shortage of discord. What about showing people fighting over the environment?" he asked. "Did you take any pictures of that "Earth Day" thing? I mean, they billed it as the first ever, and it got huge crowds all over the country."

"That would've been a good idea, but I didn't even think to go and take pictures of it. Next time, could you have your brainstorm before it's too late?"

He smiled his delicious smile, plummeting me like a roller coaster.

"I'll do my best," he said. "What about the war? I mean, everyone knows Nixon's lying to us. Two weeks ago he said he was pulling one hundred and fifty thousand out by next year, and then last week he says again that he wants to get rid of the student deferments. Why does he need to draft students if he's going to end the war?"

"Are you sure he's lying?"

"He's just trying to quiet the anti-war rhetoric. He has no intention of getting out unless he can make it seem like we won. No president is going to admit he lost the Vietnam War."

"So how would I show the silent majority?" I asked. "Or for that matter, the anti-war movement? I don't think a couple windows with "U.S. out of Vietnam" signs in them or a soap box nut on the corner of Main and Water is going to say much."

"I guess you're right. If this were OU or even OSU there'd be plenty," he said. He shook his head and looked over at his house. "I never thought I'd have to worry about Robby going."

"A lot could happen in a year and a half," I said. "And Congress may not go along with making students draft eligible.

The anti-war movement isn't going away. Nixon's going to have to get us out eventually."

Evan looked at me hard. "I don't think so, Bug. If anything, I think he's going to escalate it."

"What do you mean?"

"He can't let Cambodia fall. Not if we aren't leaving."

A small chill crept over me. "Even if you're right, there's nothing in Kent to show how polarized everyone is through pictures."

"Too bad you can't do something with that trucker getting shot in Western Ohio and Rhodes calling the Guard out on the teamsters' strike."

"'Governor Law-and-order.' That's what my dad calls him," I said.

"We're just going to have to keep thinking."

"I'm running out of time."

"Don't give up yet, Bug."

"It's always darkest before the dawn?" I asked, watching his lips curl into a slender smile.

"Yeah, exactly."

Robby opened the back door of their house and stuck his head out.

"Dinner's ready," he called.

Evan waived at him. "I'll see you later," he said as he gathered his guitar and sauntered across the yard. I watched him disappear into his house, feeling my chances slipping from me as if I were at the carnival ring toss game with only one ring left to throw.

27

I WOKE THE NEXT MORNING to the news that President Nixon had invaded Cambodia. Except he wasn't actually the one doing the invading. Kids he'd never met like Evan were. But he promised to address the nation in the evening. Evan had been right. Nixon had no intention of getting us out of Vietnam.

The President fumbled through his speech that night, determined to prove the war protestors wrong without even understanding what it was they were protesting. He told us that we weren't actually invading Cambodia. We were 'entering' Cambodia to protect American forces in Vietnam once the promised withdrawal of 150,000 troops happened. He told us we were living in an age of anarchy, abroad and at home, as our 'great universities' were 'being systematically destroyed.' He told us that all he wanted was 'a just peace.'

And then his dark, wavering voice told us he would take whatever action he thought was necessary as our commander-in-chief if the North Vietnamese didn't withdraw from Cambodia and South Vietnam.

My family sat quietly around the television. Like I remembered us being when we'd watched President Kennedy's funeral. Like we had been the night Bobby Kennedy was assassinated. Like we had been the night Richard Millhouse Nixon was elected president.

The invasion that wasn't an invasion became the hot topic at school, and Mr. Miller had to talk Colin McEllhenny out of the boys' bathroom again, but this time he called Colin's dad, who Joey Turner said begged Mr. Miller to raise Colin's grade point average to a 3.0 so he could try to get into school somewhere, which wasn't a sure thing anyway since no one knew if the whole college deferment thing was going to go on or not. Joey Turner reminded Mr. Miller that if anyone could get himself killed in Vietnam, though, it was Colin. But Mr. Miller said he couldn't falsify school documents for anyone, even a boy who carried the nickname of Charlie Brown. The last I heard before I left for the day was that some of the varsity band members were helping Colin figure out how to sneak into Canada through Montana. But if it wasn't Colin, it would be some other boy. We just might be lucky enough not to know him.

I walked home slowly, feeling completely frustrated with everything. I didn't know how to make my senior project dynamite. I didn't know how to make Evan love me. And the war had become a constant rattle that drummed in my ears relentlessly. Portia was already home when I got there, filling my mom in on a student protest that had happened on campus earlier.

"They said the President had killed the constitution, so they should give it a proper burial," she said.

"Was anyone there?" I asked, mixing myself some Kool-Aid. "No one takes the SDS seriously."

"It wasn't the SDS, Bug. One of the guys who organized it, Jim Geary, won the Silver Star in Vietnam. He burned his draft card and they gave some speeches and then they buried a copy of the constitution at the victory bell. I don't know how many people were there, but it was a lot. Maybe even five hundred."

"Wow, that is a lot for KSU," I said. It would be the protests at OU and UC Berkeley that made tomorrow's newspaper headlines. But I was still glad someone had done something.

When my dad came home, Portia asked him if he'd seen the protest.

"No, but I heard about it," he said. "It must have been pretty peaceful, because there was a BUS rally a couple of hours later to show support for the black kids who protested at OSU last week, and President White decided things were quiet enough that he could go to his conference in Iowa."

My dad paused and lit a cigarette. The Black United Students didn't like the war, but they never joined up with the SDS because they said that Vietnam was just the racism of the establishment at work. From what Evan had told me, there was a lot of truth to that.

"The rally was pretty calm," Portia said.

"The kids who organized it are grad students in the history department. Not a bunch of rowdies, exactly," my dad said. "Just as well. I really don't feel like running around playing faculty marshal this weekend. Evan's going to help me get that new sink installed in the powder room."

Portia gave me a sly smile. She knew Evan was trying to help me finish my project, but she hadn't been making fun of me about it, so I took that as a sign she was maybe rooting for me to pull it off. But if she wasn't, I didn't really want to hear about it anyway.

Evan came over after dinner to help my dad. They carried the new sink in from the garage, my dad swearing so much I thought the expression should be "cussing like a Marine" instead of a sailor. He was wedged under the sink, yelling at Evan for handing him the wrong wrench, when Portia came into the kitchen.

"God, am I glad Evan's back," she said.

"Better him than us," I echoed, making my mom smile.

"I'm going out with Susan and Lisa and Carl," Portia said to my mom, kissing her on the cheek. "Don't wait up."

"Not too late," my mom cautioned, but Portia was already out the door. I couldn't imagine getting away with that even when I was a senior in college. I pictured myself at thirty, a spinster who still lived at home with an 11:30 curfew, asking my mom if we could buy Jiffy Pop for my big Friday nights sitting at home rereading Jane Austen.

"Ouch, Bug!" Evan said as he walked into the room. "What's with the sour face?"

I shook my head. "Nothing."

Robby walked onto the back porch and I waved him in.

"Hey, can I watch the game over here?" he asked. "Ellen's watching some stupid romance movie."

"What game?" I asked.

"The Lakers and the Knicks are playing their fourth game in the finals tonight," Evan replied, mixing himself some Nestlés.

"Willa will watch anything if it's what Evan wants to watch," I said, making Robby give me a look that might as well have said "And you wouldn't?" I turned my head.

"Evan! Where the hell's that washer?" my dad yelled from the bathroom.

"Hold on, Art," Evan called and walked out, taking his glass with him.

"Oh, man, you didn't tell me your dad had a project going," Robby said.

"Didn't you hear him yelling from your house?"

"Stop, you two," my mom said, but she had a smile on her face.

When the game came on, my dad released Evan from his servitude and they came into the living room to watch. It didn't take him long to have Robby and Evan laughing, as he told them stories about the KSU basketball team when he had to be an assistant coach for them when he was a new professor. My mom and Willa went upstairs around ten-thirty and my dad followed them a half hour later. Evan and Robby and I had just watched the end of the game when Portia came in.

"You're home early," I said.

"You won't believe it when I tell you!" she said, sitting on the edge of one of the armchairs.

"What?" Evan asked, rolling his head to look at her from where he lay sprawled on the sofa. "You couldn't find a single guy out tonight who isn't an astronaut with a doctorate in how to make money?"

Portia made a face at him. "No, funny man, there was a riot downtown and they closed all the bars!"

"What?" the rest of us asked in skeptical stereo.

Portia was nodding furiously. "I don't know how it started, but Ron Sterlaker thought it was the bikers who came in for the parade—"

"Wait," I interrupted. "What parade? With bikers?"

"I told you about him, didn't I?" Portia said. "He belongs to that fake fraternity, the Pit, and every year they run a made up candidate for student council president, and this year they wanted to have this crazy parade, so they asked some biker gangs to come for it, and he thinks they got into a fight and started the whole thing.

"But someone else told me that there were kids in the street stopping cars outside of J.B.'s asking people what they thought about the invasion. Firecrackers were going off and I heard that somebody threw a beer bottle at a police cruiser. We were at the Kove and it was pretty quiet. But then the cops came through and told everyone to go home, that the bars were closing. So everyone goes outside complaining and the next thing I know some kids lit a fire in a trash can and people are throwing rocks and beer bottles through windows!"

"Empty bottles, I hope," Robby said.

"That's brilliant." Evan said with a small laugh. "Push a bunch of drunk college kids out onto the street two hours before closing and expect them to go home quietly."

"A lot of them were probably high, too," I said, since some of the bars were notorious for letting the kids smoke pot like it was tobacco.

"Seriously," Portia said, "it was wild. I mean, they even hit Thompson's."

"Why would anyone break Thompson's windows?" I asked.

Portia shrugged. "I don't know, but they also broke windows in Morton's Shoetique and the bank. That's all I saw, we got out of there. And there was some kind of sit in at the Prentice gate when I was coming home, but all I know about that is that kids were demanding to speak to President White, I think about the curfew being imposed."

"They'll be waiting a while, since he's not even in town," I said. "But dad didn't get called to do his faculty marshal thing so it can't be too bad."

"What's a faculty marshal?" Robby asked.

"They're supposed to go around instilling good behavior in the students if there's some kind of a crisis," I said. "You know, talk the kids into following the rules and stuff. It's mostly professors from the English and Sociology departments. President White set it up last year when he thought the BUS kids might riot."

Robby laughed.

"I think downtown's going to be a real mess tomorrow," Portia said.

"Well, I guess we'll find out half the facts tomorrow when the paper comes," Evan said. "We should go, it's late," he added, standing up and stretching.

I followed them to the door to lock up. As they slipped outside I put my hand on Evan's arm to stop him. "Do you want to go downtown with me tomorrow?" I asked. "I think I might find what I've been looking for."

He nodded. "I'll come by after breakfast."

I watched my coconspirator walk across the lawn to his house. If Evan was going to leave Kent, I might as well get to chase my own dream and, for the first time, Pratt began to feel like it just might be within reach.

28

EVAN AND I BOTH STOPPED when we reached the top of Main Street.

"Wow," I said.

Evan whistled. "Portia wasn't kidding." We started down the hill toward the river and North Water Street.

"Did you see that article about Police Chief Thompson in the paper yesterday?" I asked.

"You mean the one where he was telling the Kiwanis Club that Kent was lucky to have a university with so many well behaved students?"

"I wonder what he's saying today."

"He's saying 'there are, however, those who will dissent in the most criminal and reprehensible fashion,'" Evan replied, deepening his voice as he imitated Vice President Agnew's speech against the war protestors a couple of days earlier, "'and this element will feed on the distaste for war to further its own desire for power through revolution.'" He made a stern face and raised his finger in the air like he was scolding imaginary protestors.

I laughed, but as I looked at Main Street I could see why people were afraid of the 'radical element.'

"I'm glad they didn't hit Hoefler's," I said, as we passed by the unbroken windows of the music store.

"Yeah, me, too."

All along the sloping block to the river and onto North Water Street, shattered store windows opened like wounds. Most of the damage seemed to be on Water, as if the police had gotten a handle on things as they pushed the crowd back up Main toward campus. The Record Courier, Portage

National Bank, Campus Supply, even Ramon's Beauty Shop sat helplessly exposed. Shards of plate glass were strewn across the sidewalk, which was peppered with beer bottles, cans, and cigarette butts. It was hard to believe this was Kent and that students had done all this. It looked like a tornado had blown through.

People were sweeping up glass and nailing in plywood to cover the gaping holes. Some of the people helping out must have been students by the way they were dressed, and a couple even had KSU t-shirts on. I started snapping photos, wondering if the townspeople thought these students were radicals, too, or if it even mattered to them.

We walked around, me taking pictures and Evan talking to some of the store owners. He knew most of the townies, since he was technically one of them. They all liked him because he was clean cut and respectable and had done his duty by his country.

A middle aged man came out of Thompson's drugstore and stopped him.

"Evan, good to see you! Your dad told me you were home. Welcome back, son," he said as they shook hands. His eye flit curiously to Evan's left side, but Evan had already tucked his hand into the pocket of his jeans.

"Thanks, Mr. Donaldson."

"It's these subversive types that come into a place and cause havoc," Mr. Donaldson replied, lowering his voice and waving his hand around like we were in the middle of a conversation about what was going on around us. I aimed my lens at Thompson's storefront.

"Look what they've done to our town," Mr. Donaldson continued. "Mayor Satrom's asked the Governor to put the National Guard on standby, in case there's any more trouble.

There's no telling how many of them are waiting to come here and stir things up."

"I'm sure it will be quiet tonight, Mr. Donaldson," Evan said. "Especially with the bars closed. I don't think you have to worry about any subversives invading Kent."

"These kids need to get jobs, like we had to do," Mr. Donaldson said. "That's what's wrong with your generation. They have it too soft, they don't know how to knuckle down."

I bit my lip to stop myself from reminding him that Evan didn't have some of his knuckles anymore because he hadn't been soft.

Evan smiled like he was talking to a Camaro salesman. "I'm sure you're right."

"I told Chief Thompson we need to be ready for anything," Mr. Donaldson said. "They've probably already looted down here like animals. Just look at what these radicals have done!"

I turned and walked back along Water, less confident in my own patience than Evan's. But Mr. Donaldson's thoughts, in varying words, were covering the sidewalk, cascading from the lips of people cleaning up the debris. A subtle, mass hysteria drifted through the air as people exchanged rumors, each one escalating the supposed danger we were in.

In front of Morton's, an older woman looked me over nervously. "I heard they threatened to poison the water supply," she was telling another woman, her fingers picking at the edges of her house dress. She kept watching me as if she thought I must know something about the plot, standing there with my camera and my youth.

"The police station has been inundated with bomb threats, Bob told me," the other woman replied, her hands clutching a broom. I raised my camera to take their picture, but the suspicious glares they gave me made me lower it and walk on.

Two doors down, a few men were nailing plywood over another broken out store front window.

"These kids have no respect for law and order, that's what's wrong with this country," one of them was saying.

"It's these agitators that come into a place and stir up trouble that I'm worried about," one of his companions said.

"Just look what they've done to our town," the last one said. "They'll take over, if you let them, with their riots and violence. We need to keep those commies out of Kent."

They seemed convinced that a huge mob of radical revolutionaries was just waiting to invade Kent, Ohio. It was funny, but their seriousness kept me from laughing, making a long ribbon of uneasy wrap around me instead.

A police car rolled slowly across the bridge, its windows taped in a crisscrossed pattern to keep them from getting broken if anyone threw a bottle or something. Mr. Donaldson waved at the cruiser and Evan turned from him and headed in my direction.

"Did you get a shot of the cop car all taped up?" he asked when he reached me.

"No, I didn't want them stopping to ask me why I was taking pictures of them."

He nodded. We walked back to the bridge and just looked around. The Williams Brothers' Mill loomed over North Water like an old sentry, while the river slipped away underneath us on its way to the distant Gulf. Evan put his hands on the wall and leaned into it.

"Sometimes when I was over there, it seemed like I had imagined all this," he said, turning his face toward me and squinting in the early afternoon sun. "And when I stand here," he said, looking back out over the river, "it seems like maybe I just imagined Vietnam."

His long, imperfect profile against the backdrop of the town he didn't fit in anymore stood out like a cubist portrait.

"I suppose they couldn't be more different."

"In most ways. But in others, they are exactly alike. I try so hard to forget," he said, his voice quiet, his gaze fixed on the water. "And some of the time it feels like it wasn't really my life at all. Like maybe it was a movie I watched, or some other person whose memories have been given to me to hold for them. But then all of a sudden, for no particular reason, it will feel like I'm still there. Sometimes I have to look around to know where I am." He stopped and looked at me. "I guess that sounds crazy, huh?"

"No," I said. "Sometimes it doesn't seem to me like you could have spent all that time fighting in some place I've never seen, on the other side of the world."

He stared down at the water.

"It's kind of a strange little town," he said after a moment, tilting his head toward the center of Main, "all mixed up forwards and backwards. But it's not really a bad place, all things considered."

I looked around. "No, I suppose it's not such a bad place." But I wasn't sure if I was agreeing with Evan to make him feel better or to convince myself that Kent would be bearable without him.

"I'm hungry," he said. "Let's go get some chow at Ray's. Unless you want pizza. Do you have enough photos?"

"I think I can make it work," I said as we crossed the bridge toward Franklin Street. The police cruiser was turning down by the train station, and this time I stopped and took the shot figuring they were too far away to notice me. "I've gotten all the good shots there are here. At least that I dare to take with everyone so sure there's a conspiracy happening. I wish I had been at that demonstration on campus yesterday when they buried the constitution."

"That would've been good," he said. "I doubt if there'll be any more demonstrations. It's pretty quiet today."

"My dad said Vice President Matson ordered a movie and some doughnuts and coffee for the kids to keep them occupied tonight since the bars will be closed."

"I'm sure that will work," he said with a perfect note of sarcasm.

We went to Ray's Place and had cheeseburgers, and then to Hoefler's where Evan bought Jimi Hendrix's *Band of Gypsys*. Then we walked through campus. Evan was right, things were pretty quiet. It was almost six o'clock when we got back home.

"I'll come by after dinner and let you hear this," he said, lifting the crinkling paper bag with the album.

"Okay," I said. We turned away from each other toward our houses, but I stopped and turned back.

"Evan?"

"Yeah?"

"You don't think Satrom would really call the Guard in, do you?"

"Probably not," he said, but I wasn't sure he believed it.

My mom was getting dinner ready and the tightness that always seemed to be hovering in my stomach anymore pulled just a little tighter. I set my camera down and washed my hands to set the table.

"How bad was it?" my mom asked.

"Bad," I said. "I counted at least forty windows broken. But the thing that was really creepy was how spooked everyone is. It's like they can't spread rumors fast enough."

"I can believe that. This is the most excitement Kent has seen since I've lived here. Were there a lot of people downtown?"

I nodded as I set the forks in their places. "A lot of students were walking around," I said, but before I could say anything else, Willa came running in from outside.

"Mom! Rachel!" she exclaimed. "There're army trucks driving up Crain!" She was breathing hard as she grabbed the sides of my dad's ladderback chair and stared at us.

My mom and I looked at each other, the smile instantly gone from her face.

"Are you sure?" my mom asked.

Willa bobbed her head. "A big long line of them!"

My mom wiped her hands on a dish towel and walked out the door, Willa and I running after her.

We hurried down our block and rounded the corner of the street that flowed into Crain Avenue. We stopped halfway, the parade of army jeeps, trucks, and armored vehicles moving slowly up Crain and into the residential neighborhood right behind ours. Evan and Robby were already on the corner when we got there. Evan flashed a wry smile at me. "I guess Satrom called in the Guard after all."

"Where are they going?" I asked, wishing I had thought to bring my camera.

"I think they must be going to Walls School," my mom said.

"Why would they go to an elementary school?" Willa asked.

"I bet they're going to bivouac there," Evan said. "There's plenty of open space in the parking lot and field."

"Tanks?" Robby said. "In Kent?"

Other people had spilled from their houses, lining up along the avenue to watch the National Guard roll into our neighborhood. Some people waved at them, especially the little kids and older ladies, but the Guardsmen seemed like they didn't want to make eye contact with anyone, most of them looking straight ahead at the street in front of them.

Truck after truck marched by, but somehow it didn't seem possible, as if it were some mistake that would be corrected at any moment.

"Oh," my mom said at last, "my chicken! It'll be burnt to a crisp." She hurried back to our house, the rest of us following slowly. The smell of fuel from their trucks hung heavy in the air.

"Why are they here?" Willa asked. "I mean, the students have to stay on campus tonight anyway."

"It's just to make the townies feel safe, after last night's trouble," Evan said. "It's nothing for you to worry about, Squirt."

"People aren't really going to poison our water, are they?" she asked.

My mouth dropped open for a moment wondering how she could have heard that rumor. "No, of course not! That's just crazy talk," I said, laughing just a little to let her know I meant it. I put my arm around her shoulder as the rumble of military vehicles worked to drown out my words, though, making our quiet world slip just a little bit further off of its axis, like a top teetering just before it falls.

29

WE SAT DOWN to dinner, an unsettled quiet simmering steadily.

My dad set the paper down as I passed him the chicken and polenta. "So, downtown is a real mess?"

I nodded. "Do you think they'll go on campus?"

He slid his butter knife through the soft cornmeal. "I'd be surprised if they didn't."

"But the students didn't destroy anything on campus," Portia said, her supple features realigning themselves into a firm defiance. "It's our campus, what right do they have to just come on it like that?"

I looked over at her, surprised to see how angry she was But I felt the same way, even though it wasn't my school. At least, I hoped it wouldn't be my school. But I'd grown up on that campus and part of KSU would always belong to me in a way, no matter where I went to college. I didn't like the idea of the Guardsmen crawling around the campus and bossing the students anymore than Portia did.

"Portia's right," I said.

My dad laughed, flashing his perfectly shaped teeth, dulled to yellow by tobacco. "I've been waiting seventeen years for this moment," he said. "And it took the National Guard coming to town to get the two of you to agree on something."

I pressed my lips together as Portia said "Funny, Dad."

"Willa, would you get the salad, please?" my mom asked.

"Sure." She got up and headed to the island. The telephone rang, and she set the salad bowl on the table. "I'll get it," she said, swerving toward the hallway.

She was back in a moment. "It's for you, Dad. It's Professor Lewis."

He nodded and pushed his ladder back chair away from the table. My mom's features had the same soft prettiness Portia echoed, even when they were compressed with worry. Professor Lewis would only be calling if he were gathering faculty marshals.

My dad came back a few minutes later and served himself some salad. We waited, knowing he wouldn't tell us anything until he felt like it. He always enjoyed a long dramatic pause. The big old wall clock took over the conversation, while Portia and I exchanged our "I hate it when he does this" look we'd had since we were little.

"I have to be on campus tonight," he said after a swig of coffee. "We have to hand out flyers telling the kids there's a curfew in town and they're to stay put."

"Maybe you should take a squirt gun for protection," Portia said, a sarcastic reference to the big water fight the students had had the weekend before, with kids running all over the quad soaking each other because the weather was finally getting decent.

"Right," my dad said, shaking his head. "Forty-seven years old and I'm a glorified babysitter for a bunch of kids. When I was their age, I was on Okinawa."

"But it's better than having them be like Evan," my mom said and we all stopped and looked at her. She was right, but I swallowed my food down hard. My dad pulled a pack of cigarettes from his shirt pocket, leaning back to get a lighter out of his pants pocket but he came up empty. He nodded at me and I got up and brought him one from the little pile he kept on the island.

"Thanks, baby."

I put a yellow glass ashtray down in front of him so he wouldn't flick his ashes onto his plate.

We finished dinner as quietly as we'd started it. I couldn't do anything with my project because I wouldn't be able to take my pictures to get developed before Monday, so I went to my room and started drawing. I still didn't think I had anything dynamite. I roughed out a sketch of the army trucks rolling down Crain, trying to capture the eerie feeling it had given me and release it onto paper.

A pebble hit my window. Evan and Robby were standing in the yard and Evan had his guitar with him. I opened my window and leaned out.

"You rang?"

"Bring your guitar. There's nothing else to do tonight and it's finally warm enough to sit outside," Evan said.

"Okay."

When I got downstairs, they were already on the back porch with my mom and Portia. Evan was playing *Sentimental Journey* for my mom, who was singing in her quiet, sweet voice. I followed along and sometimes he slowed down a bit to let me catch up.

"Oh, I love that one," my mom said. "You know, I saw Ella Fitzgerald once at a jazz club in Pittsburgh. It was a black club in the Hill District, and you had to go with someone who was black to be let in. I went with a friend of mine from work."

Portia and I nodded, because we'd heard this story before. Evan had probably heard it, too. My mom loved her Ella Fitzgerald story.

The sharp sound of sirens began to wail in the distance.

"I'd like to hear Ella Fitzgerald, someday," Evan said, breaking the stillness as he started playing *It Had to Be You*. My mom and Portia sang along, and Evan looked over at me, his face relaxed and happy.

Willa came and opened the door. "Mom, Mrs. Daniels is on the phone. She's scared about all the Guard and sirens and wants to know if you'd come over for a little while?"

"Tell her I'll be right there." My mom put her hand on Evan's shoulder as she went by him. "Thanks, love," she said, and he looked up at her and smiled like he used to do when he was little. "I'll just be across the street if you kids need me. I guess this is all pretty frightening for some of these older people, especially when they're on their own."

As soon as my mom was gone, Robby said, "Okay, play something good now."

"Shut up," Portia said.

"You're such a dope," I added. Evan laughed and started playing *Yester-me, Yester-you, Yesterday*.

"You don't like that song," I said.

"You were humming it yesterday," he replied, as if it meant nothing and I remembered hearing it coming from a radio in one of the stores as we walked up Water Street.

"You can sing it, it's okay," he said.

He still struggled, playing backwards, but he was definitely getting better. Not Berklee better, but better. He kept playing, songs he knew before he went away and newer ones, melting into the guitar, buttery and smooth. He dedicated *Can't Buy Me Love* to Portia and even she laughed.

Evan was showing me some new chords when Willa came out again. "What am I the receptionist?" she asked, looking at Portia as she added "phone's for you."

Portia went in the house, but was back in a couple of minutes, almost breathless as she broke the news.

"So that was my friend Gwen in the dorms. She said there are a bunch of kids trying to set fire to the old ROTC building and the firemen are there but kids keep trying to cut the hoses."

"That explains the sirens we've been hearing," I said.

"Let's go," Robby said and jumped up from his chair.

Evan and I set our guitars down.

"What about the Guard?" I asked.

"They'll be at the Prentice Gate, but if we crossed east of Music and Speech, they probably wouldn't see us," Evan answered.

"Dad said the curfew was only in town," Portia said. They all started moving, but I hesitated.

"What's wrong, Bug?" Evan asked.

"My dad wouldn't like us going." I shifted on my feet. "And what about leaving Willa alone?"

"I'll tell her we're going for a short walk." Portia headed back to the kitchen door. "We'll be back in a half hour. Willa can call mom at Mrs. Daniels' if she needs her, and I'll handle dad if we run into him. Don't you want to see what's going on?"

"Yes, but what if Willa gets scared?"

"Mom's across the street, Bug," Portia replied. "We'll just see what's going on and come right back. She's watching T.V. She won't even think about us being gone."

"And my parents are next door," Robby added.

I looked at Evan and he ticked his head to the side in agreement.

"Let me get my camera." I ran upstairs to my room. I grabbed my blue sweater and my camera and hurried back down almost afraid they might leave without me.

The four of us walked to Crain and headed east a couple of blocks. Then we turned south again toward East Main. There were few cars and we didn't see any army trucks as we headed across the street. Once we were on campus, we threaded our way to the back side of the commons. Dusk was clinging to the buildings and trees, growing over them like ivy.

We stopped near the north side of Prentice Hall and looked down the hill to the ROTC building. The long, low structure was surrounded by people. There were kids clustered on the hillside just watching, as fire sputtered in a couple of places, and several windows were broken. The firemen were rolling their hoses up to leave.

"What are those kids on the left doing?" Robby asked.

"Throwing stones at the firemen," Evan replied. "So why are campus police just standing there watching?"

I focused my lens, trying to get a photo of the firemen climbing back onto their truck, grateful to have the powerful lens Evan had bought me. There was light spilling from windows of the dorms surrounding the upper side of the commons, and from the small fire in the ROTC building, but I wasn't sure how to adjust for the mix of light and dark. I snapped the picture and hoped it would turn out.

The fire truck turned and left the commons and a large cheer went up. A boy with a flaming rag ran to one of the broken windows of the building and tossed it in. A few minutes later, campus police began moving and headed into the crowd near the ROTC building to try to disperse them. Some of the kids ran up toward us, but most of them seemed to go in the other direction toward Main Street and downtown. Behind them the ROTC building was finally catching on fire, flames licking the walls and roof.

A large boom shook the air and a huge plume of smoke drifted off the ground near the bottom of the commons, filling the darkness with a gray shadow.

"That's tear gas," Evan said. "Let's book."

"We're far enough away." Robby said, but Evan shook his head. A fire truck with National Guardsmen hanging on the sides and sitting on top of it, their rifles silhouetted in the fire's glow, came charging onto the commons. It stopped in front of the ROTC building, which was finally engulfed in unruly flames. I focused my lens on the truck and took my shot.

"Let's split," Evan urged again, as sheriff's deputies started chasing kids up the hill toward us. We ducked behind Prentice Hall and practically ran as we retraced our steps to East Main. A small explosion shattered the air around us and I jumped.

"What was that?" Portia asked.

"Ammunition stored in the building," Evan said. "Come on, keep going."

Army trucks were roaring down East Main from the direction of Walls and heading toward Campus. Behind us, the ROTC building continued its intermittent booming. We watched the trucks roll by from behind some trees lining the sidewalk of Midway Drive and then dashed across the street when they had passed.

We went around to the back of my house and stood there catching our breath. My mom still wasn't home, but when we went inside Willa looked up from the television show she was watching.

"I keep hearing thunder," she said.

Portia and I exchanged a nervous look, but we all sat down and watched T.V. without telling Willa about the fire. It was better that she find out in the morning when it was all over.

My mom came in after a while and sent Willa to bed.

"A friend of mine called from the dorms," Portia told my mom. "The ROTC building burned tonight."

"So that's why all the sirens and booming," my mom said. We nodded noncommittally. "I hope your dad gets home soon. The news will be on in a few minutes, maybe there will be something about it."

When my dad came in, we bombarded him with questions and he put his hand up to stop us.

"Portia, get me some coffee, will you honey?" he said and she looked at me since I was closer to the kitchen than she was. When I got back, my dad was smoking, his big frame filling the armchair he was sitting in.

"So the building is completely burned out," he was saying. "It took a while, but the ammunition finally began to explode, and then the thing was really blazing. The Guard chased off the last of the onlookers, and they made sure the kids were in the dorms and staying put, even if it meant gassing and shoving them, and I saw a Guardsman hit a kid with the butt of his rifle, but I was too far away to do anything about it. There are Guardsmen in all of the buildings now, and they shut down the movies and things they had going to keep the kids busy and locked up the dorms for the night. There were a few arrests, but I don't think they caught any of the kids responsible for the fire."

My dad stopped and shook his head. "This is a bad business. It's like we're UC Berkeley or something, except our kids don't have a clue what they're doing." He shoved the end of his cigarette into the big marble ashtray on the coffee table, dabbing it out.

We talked over the fire until almost twelve-thirty. When I finally did go up to bed, I laid awake for a long time thinking about the silhouettes of the Guardsmen on the fire truck, wondering what Governor Law-And-Order would say about the whole thing. What would campus look like without the ROTC building, since it had been there for longer than I could remember? If the pictures I had taken tonight came out, it would be the perfect highlight to my photo essay. I just needed shots of what the building looked like after the fire.

I woke up the next morning eager to go to campus and take some photos of the ROTC building.

"I can go, can't I?" I asked my dad over breakfast. "I mean, the curfew is only at night, right?"

"I suppose so," he said. "But take Portia or Evan with you. Or both."

I wasn't looking forward to going over to Evan's house to ask him to come, but I didn't have to. He showed up for pancakes like the neighborhood vagabond after he got back from church with his parents. My mom had saved some batter for him, just in case, and she turned the electric griddle back on when he walked in.

"There are Guardsmen everywhere," he told us, his eyes lighting up over the stack of flapjacks my mom set in front of him. I handed him the syrup and went to make him a glass of Nestlé's.

"Rachel wants to go see it," my dad said to him. "Go with her, will you? I don't want her getting herself into any trouble with those guys. They see a pretty girl and they're sure to hassle her."

My face started to burn at my dad telling Evan I was pretty, but it was wasted. Evan just said "Sure, Art," as unmoved by the idea as if my dad had asked him to pass a napkin instead.

"Did you see the press conference with Rhodes on television this morning?" Evan asked.

My dad shook his head. "What did Governor Law-and-Order have to say for himself?"

"He said 'the people who perpetrated the vandalism in Kent are the worst segment of society, worse than the brown shirts and the commies and the vigilantes,' and he's going to do whatever it takes to 'eradicate' them," Evan said, an amused look on his face as he waited for my dad's reaction.

"He's a Melvin, as you kids would say," my dad replied, snapping a lighter on and inhaling the flame into his cigarette to make it glow. "He'll say anything to look like he's in charge."

I ran upstairs to get my camera and ask Portia if she wanted to go with us. She was on the phone in my dad's study, but she nodded when I whispered to ask her if she wanted to go.

She followed me down to the kitchen a few minutes later. "My friend, Karen, lives in the dorms and she told me the cops didn't even try to stop the fire for a long time."

"They were probably happy to see it burn," my dad answered. "The ROTC has been wishing for a new building for ages. That one was only supposed to be temporary in the first place."

"Let's go," I said, eager to see the damage.

As we walked along Crain, a tank rolled slowly by us chugging toward downtown. We cut down to East Main and crossed over at Hilltop Drive. Down by the Prentice Gate, a huge army vehicle was parked in the middle of the street with armed soldiers patrolling around it, looking every bit as intimidating as they were trying to look.

"What is that?" I asked Evan.

"Armored personnel carrier," he said. He and Portia kept walking, so I did, too. I thought the soldiers might stop us and ask if we were students, or maybe tell us we weren't allowed to go on campus. But they just fixed their stares on us.

We started up Hilltop and an army helicopter flew over, its din pulsing and then receding.

"Ugh, I can still feel their eyes on me," Portia said.

"They probably still are," Evan said, laughing. "With that mini skirt and those legs, it wouldn't surprise me at all." I looked at him, but he just shrugged and gave me a look that said "well?" I wished I had worn a mini skirt, too, but I had on a stupid pair of bell bottom jeans. Portia wore a faint smile on her lips.

Two jeeps passed us going in the opposite direction, followed by a cop car with two officers in front and two in the back, shotguns pointed outward and resting on the open window frames.

"It's like we woke up in the middle of a war zone," I said.

"Not quite, Bug," Evan said. "But it sure is creepy."

I pressed my lips together. I didn't know how to dress for an invasion the way Portia did, and I didn't seem to know anything about the seriousness of the National Guard rolling into town. I was never going to be grown up enough for Evan.

We came up behind the student union, and the smoky, charred scent of the ROTC building filled the air before we could see it. There were Guardsmen everywhere it seemed, but there were kids out, too. The afternoon was really beautiful and everyone seemed to be outside just because they could be, the cold finally gone, the curfew lifted for the daytime.

As we walked around the building, our pace fell, first Portia, then me, then Evan. The burned out shell of the ROTC building looked like a skeleton cowering from the daylight. I moved the lens on my camera back and forth until the ruins and the crowd of curious people walking by it came into focus. There was a fence up around the remains of the building and soldiers were standing guard, as if there were anything more that could be done to it.

I took more pictures as we got closer. Portia veered off when she saw a group of her friends. Some of the students were talking to the soldiers. Evan and I passed a couple who stood close together talking to a Guardsman who had a lilac sprig in the barrel of his gun. I stopped and began to focus my lens as an officer walked up to them and said something to the Guardsman who pulled the flower out of his rifle and handed it to the officer. I lowered my camera, the shot lost.

The girl took the lilac from the officer. "What's the matter with peace?" she asked him, her pretty face softly challenging. "Flowers are better than bullets."

The officer gave her a disgusted look and walked away. Evan put his hand on my back to tell me to move forward.

I took a close-up of the ruins, a black char coating what little was left of the clapboard sides so that it looked like a burnt marshmallow. When the Guardsmen weren't looking, I took a couple of photos of them. I didn't want anyone asking me why I was taking photos of the Guard, even though it was for a school project. A few of the students were taking photo ops with some of the soldiers, though, like they were visiting circus people not to be missed. Two more Guardsmen joked with a young man, smiling and just hanging out, as another boy snapped their picture.

"There's going to be a rally at noon tomorrow," Portia said when she found us. "It was supposed to be about the war, but now everyone just wants to complain about the Guard. People are really mad about how they've just come on campus and started ordering everyone around. But I can't miss poly sci," she added, losing the fervor she'd had a moment before. "Midterms are coming up and I want to be ready for law school."

I started thinking about my project as we walked home. The rally would be the perfect place to get the finishing shots I needed to show the struggle going on between anti-war students and the establishment.

There was one thing standing between me and the rally, though, and that was school. I had never cut school before, but I had never had a reason to, either, let alone a reason as important as Pratt. Maybe I was just as driven as Portia in my own way.

"See you guys," Evan said when we reached home.

"See you," I said, as Portia said "bye." I slowed my pace, Evan and Portia ahead of me, each going in their different directions, my mind working out an idea. It had taken me seventeen years, but I was beginning to figure out how to make my own decisions like they did, and it felt good, in a scary, stuck-at-the-top-of-the-Ferris-wheel kind of way.

Before I went to bed that night, I stopped at the hall telephone and called Michelle.

"Can you meet me at Crain and Willow tomorrow?" I asked after we exchanged hellos.

"Sure," she said. "What's up?"

"It has to do with the bet I have with my dad about my senior art project. I'll explain tomorrow," I said, keeping my voice low. "See you then."

"Okay," she said. "See you tomorrow."

I placed the receiver in its cradle and headed upstairs to bed, glad I had splurged on three rolls of film earlier in the week. If everything went the way I planned, I would finally take some pictures my dad couldn't think were anything but dynamite.

THE AIR WAS LAYERED with spring and the smell of jet fuel as I walked down Crain to meet Michelle. Helicopters had been flying all night, their searchlights peering into our neighborhood with clocklike regularity. I had sat in my window seat imagining what it must have been like for Evan to hear them in Vietnam, knowing they were friendly. They didn't feel friendly now. They felt like something to fear, prying into our little lives like Big Brother.

A metal bird flew in low on its way to Walls as I reached Willow Street, the roar drowning out traffic on Main. The sun fell through the trees at an angle, pouring the promising day onto rooftops and streets like water from a garden hose. Michelle wasn't there, late as usual.

My dad would turn off of Crain before he reached Willow as he headed to work, but he would still be able to see me if he looked down the avenue before he turned. I walked further up Willow, just enough to be out of sight. A woman looked me over suspiciously when she came out to get her paper, probably worried I was one of the radical invasion forces coming to take over Kent.

I started to worry that Michelle had forgotten. If I didn't get an excuse to school, they would be sure to call my mom and tell her I hadn't shown up. I paced, trying to think of a new plan. I might be able to catch Robby as he walked past if he hadn't left before I did. But he'd want to know why I was skipping and he'd probably rat me out just for the fun of it.

"Hey," Michelle said from behind me.

I turned.

"I was afraid you forgot!"

"You know I'm always late," she said. "And those stupid helicopters kept me up most of the night."

"My dad and some of the other marshals took calls from students at the radio station last night. He said a helicopter searchlight was on them the whole way home and when they got to the roadblock at Crain and Luther, a Guardsman shoved his bayonet into the driver's window and demanded to know where they were going. A bunch of middle-aged college professors."

"It's crazy," Michelle said. "I heard there was a big sit in by the gate and the fuzz promised the kids that Mayor Satrom and President White would talk to them about their demands, but then no one showed and the Guard tear gassed everyone back onto campus. But you didn't ask me to meet you to exchange gossip. What's up?"

I pulled the excuse I had written from my pocket.

"Will you give this to the school receptionist for me?"

"What is it?"

"I don't think you want to know."

Michelle looked at me steadily. "What are you up to?"

"Nothing," I said. "I just can't go to school today."

"Why?" she asked, holding the word before releasing it like a balloon.

"There's going to be a rally at noon on campus, and I have to be there to take pictures. I have to finish my photo essay and it has to be perfect. It has to be so great my dad won't be able to say no to Pratt."

"So you forged your mom's name to an excuse?"

"Yes."

"Rachel Morelli, that's the first bad thing you've done since second grade when you stuck chewed up gum on Dave Taylor's pencils because he said you were skinnier than Olive Oyl!"

We both laughed, but I was still nervous. Breaking the rules wasn't really my thing.

"So you'll do it for me?"

"Of course. Just don't get caught or we'll both be in trouble," she said, but her tone told me she wasn't really worried. Michelle wasn't the type to mind an occasional detention if she thought she was doing the right thing when she got it. But I was risking a lot more. If my dad found out before he saw my project, there was no way he would let me go to Pratt.

We started walking back down to Crain. "If you see any cute Guardsmen, give them my phone number," she said.

"I don't think the Guard guys are your type."

"You're right," she agreed. "Unless you find one that's *really* cute."

"Okay."

"I'll call you later. Be careful, huh? I'd rather not get in trouble with summer coming up."

"I will. And thanks. I owe you big time."

She smiled and waved as she rounded the corner. I waved back and then headed down to East Main. Crossing the street, I watched for my dad's car, but I had missed him. I walked through Prentice Gate past the Guardsmen with their long stares, and headed for Rockwell Hall. It was my favorite building on campus, with its Grecian inspired limestone exterior and long, beautiful windows.

The high ceilings always made me feel peaceful, like a tranquil church. It was quiet in the early morning, and I tucked myself away in the literature section trying to keep my attention fixed on an old volume of *Adam Bede*. But my thoughts kept roaming like an undisciplined toddler. I wished I had brought my pencils and drawing pad to sketch the main room, to try and capture the way it smelled of old books and the scraping sound the heavy wood chairs made when you pushed them back from the tables. The new library would be finished soon, and it was supposed to be great, but it made me sad to think that Rockwell wouldn't be the library anymore. I liked the feel of old buildings, and how pretty they were. I didn't know what they would do with Rockwell. Not that it mattered. With the pictures I would take at the rally, I was heading to Pratt, and, someday, when my dad saw my drawings in some important gallery showing, he'd admit to me that I'd been right all along.

As long as he didn't catch me before I could convince him, because if he did, he'd never let me go. My pictures had to be perfect. I put *Adam Bede* back on the shelf and quietly paced the aisle between the stacks, counting down the minutes until 11:10, when I thought it would be safe to head to the commons. There had to be enough people there that I could blend in and see my dad before he ever had a chance to see me. If he even came. There was always the chance he'd stay in his office through the whole thing.

I slipped out of Rockwell, a fugitive from one school so that I could go to another. My stomach tightened and I kept my gaze moving, afraid of seeing anyone who might recognize me and tell my dad I'd been on campus. But the day was warm and bright and I began to relax as I got near the commons.

There seemed to be enough people that I could slip into the crowd if I had to, and I dodged some of Portia's friends easily.

Kids were clustered near the fence surrounding what was left of the ROTC building and up near the Hub. There weren't as many people as I had expected, though. Maybe the rally was just going to fizzle and I had risked everything for nothing. I needed the rally to be big enough to show how important this was to my generation.

I weaved into a group of students outside the Hub. "My professor cancelled our class 'cause only a few of us showed up," one boy said.

"Mine, too," another replied.

We hung out waiting for something to happen, for someone to start making a speech. Those who were carrying books held them loose by their hips as if they were almost forgotten.

The sky over the commons was shockingly blue, and the smell of blooming dogwoods drifted across campus with the occasional cool breeze. Trees in bud with soft greens dotted the lawns, everything fresh and new. It was the kind of day that made me wish I had been born a bird, because it almost made you feel like you could fly. I was still trying to figure out how to draw that feeling.

Eleven o'clock classes ended and the commons started filling up with kids walking through on their way to noon class. People were clustered around the Victory Bell, and a few were waving American flags and chanting about the war. But the kids were as mad about the Guard being on KSU ground as they were about the war, maybe even more after two nights of curfew.

"Pigs off campus, pigs off campus…" echoed over the hillside as kids encouraged one another to get louder.

"One, two, three, four, we don't want your fucking war," followed, as one group and then another took up the chant so that the sound was coming out in stereo around the hill.

The crowd swelled and what had been several hundred suddenly began to feel like a couple of thousand. It was warm and I took off the canvas jacket I was wearing and tied it around my hips. I moved more freely through the mass of kids, keeping alert for my dad or any professors who knew me. The crowd was mostly students, but there were faculty and staff now, too, as the lunch hour approached. Kids were hanging out on the terrace of Taylor and others were watching from the windows of Prentice, Johnson, and Stopher halls. There was a carnival feel to the day, everyone soaking up the sunshine and warm breezes. Music drifted from stereos in the dorms.

I stood between Johnson and Taylor taking photos of the kids who were chanting down by the bell. An army Jeep drove onto the commons and began circling some of the crowd, while a campus policeman with a bullhorn told them to disperse, but everyone just stood there watching. Someone threw a croquet ball at the jeep. I twisted my lens and took a shot, but I wasn't sure how well it would come out since the jeep was moving. Then it drove off, back to the area where the Guard was clustered near the ruins of the ROTC building.

A bang rang out from somewhere behind the Guard, the same noise that had made me jump on Saturday night. A sudden arc of smoke flew over me, streaming above Taylor Hall. The bang came again and again, as the sky filled with tear gas on both sides of Taylor, but most of it seemed to be on the back side of the building, near the bell. I followed the scrambling throng past the pagoda toward Prentice, away from the Guard, trying to get clear of the smoke. The acrid air made my nose a little runny, but most of the gas was being carried away on the shifting breeze. The bell was ringing even though I couldn't see it from where I was. I coughed, the skin around my eyes stinging just a little.

I had just reached the safety of the Prentice parking lot, where the gas didn't reach, when someone grabbed my arm. "Aren't you supposed to be in school right now?"

I wheeled, but I already knew it was Evan.

"What are you doing here?" he asked a disapproving look on his face.

"I came to get pictures. What are you doing here?"

"I was curious," he said, "but I'm not cutting school to get my look. You shouldn't be here."

Everything inside of me raised like hackles on a dog. "Since when did you become the truant officer?" I asked. I'd been prepared to face my dad angry with me, but not Evan. He was the one encouraging me to go to Pratt. If he was so eager to get rid of me, then why should he care if I cut school to do it? It had been his idea to give myself only one shot to convince my dad.

"Look, Bug, I get it, you want pictures for your project. But this isn't a good place for you. These guys are a bunch of yahoos, and there's no telling what's gonna go down. I don't want you getting hurt. Especially since they're the ones with the bayonets."

"I promise not to rush them," I said, my anger fueled by knowing that I wasn't supposed to be on campus but stuck in the cafeteria at Roosevelt High instead, still too young, always too young to be with him.

"I'm serious, Bug. Don't get too close. They bayoneted some girl last night and sent her to the hospital. This is getting serious. I don't like it. I don't like you being here."

"I won't get too close," I said. "I'm not a total idiot, you know."

"I didn't call you an idiot," he said. "Why didn't you tell me you were coming here?"

"I didn't want my parents to blame you if I got caught." I left out the part about needing to learn to do things on my own, because whether I was in New York or stuck in Kent, he wasn't going to be around to help me. Pratt was finally in my reach and I couldn't lose it and Evan, too.

"I don't care about that. You should have told me."

"I am capable of managing on my own sometimes," I said. He didn't have the right to worry about me, standing there like I was some little kid. He didn't have the right to worry about me when it was so easy for him to let me go. It was hard enough for me to defy my dad without him treating me like a baby for it.

"Bug, they bayoneted a girl. A girl. These guys are out of control."

"I know how to be careful. Who do you think is going to babysit me in New York anyway? I'm not the stupid child you and Portia think I am. I'm perfectly capable of taking care of myself."

All the frustration of loving him without being loved back suddenly came pouring over me, choking me. All of the waiting and pointlessly hoping was crashing down on me until I had to struggle just to breathe. I fought back the urge to shove him. My hands were fists, aching to punch at him and push him to the ground.

He gave me a hard look. It came from that part of him that was always angry and I was touching it off like a match. He wasn't used to me fighting back like this, straight at him. He was used to me taking the low road. The few fights we ever had were quiet battles, like the day he'd attacked that kid at the Hub.

"What's wrong with you?"

"Nothing," I said, shaking my head at him. "Look, I'm sorry you didn't take your chance to go to Berklee, I really am, but I'm taking mine to go to Pratt. I'm not ending up—"

I stopped suddenly as I realized what I had almost said. My eyes stung, but it wasn't from the tear gas.

"Like me."

"That's not what I was going to say," I replied, but I didn't know how to tell him that what I had almost said was "stuck here without you." I couldn't tell him how desperately I needed to not be left behind.

"Yeah, I really screwed up my life, Bug. I get that," he said, the bitterness in his voice whipping me. "I thought you were the one person I could trust not to throw that in my face."

He turned his head and started to move away.

"Evan, wait," I said and he swiveled back. But I couldn't tell him that I couldn't bear the thought of being in Kent without him any more than I could let him think I was judging him. I stared at him open mouthed, unable to think of something to say to fix what I had done. "I didn't mean that the way it sounded," I said at last, my eyes blurry.

"You're missing your shots," he said, and he nodded toward the scene behind me.

I turned away so he wouldn't see the tears in my eyes. His angry sarcasm was like a burn to my skin. I raised my camera and took a snapshot of the plumes of tear gas drifting through the air, trying to clear my vision. While Evan and I had been fighting, the Guard had marched across either side of Taylor, standing there aimlessly as if they were trying to decide what to do. It was too windy for the gas to have any real effect, and most kids seemed content to stay and watch as a small group of demonstrators ran through the crowd heckling the Guard, calling them pigs and giving them the finger.

Evan had walked off of the parking lot onto the grassy slope below. He was watching the Guard move across Blanket Hill, the students parting to let them march down toward the practice field. They had their rifles on their shoulders, bayonets glinting in the sunlight. Their gas masks made them look like creatures from a Lon Chaney movie and they were almost comical in a grotesque kind of way. No one around me seemed to share Evan's concern as everyone stood by watching. A few kids followed the Guardsmen down the hill, calling them "fascist bastards" and other names I couldn't make out over the crowd noise, and some were throwing rocks or empty tear gas canisters. I rushed to focus my lens as a Guardsman exchanged an empty canister with a student, each of them putting everything they had into their toss like they were in some track and field competition.

Evan was gliding further down the hill, away from me. The letting go stabbed at me and I took a picture of his back.

The Guard reached the fence at the edge of the practice field and stopped. I didn't understand why they had marched down there in the first place, but they seemed surprised to find the fence blocking their way. A student stood in front of them, taunting them as he waived a giant American flag and gestured at them, but the Guardsmen stood like a wall. I tried to shake Evan out of my thoughts. I needed to concentrate on Pratt. I moved forward in the parking lot and knelt to get a better view and snapped a picture. I was sure this photo would be the one to convince my dad to let me go, the juxtaposition of the long haired student in his headband and hippie clothes waiving a flag and the uniformed Guard staring him down, their gas masks expressionless, bayoneted guns resting on their shoulders.

A Jeep came driving out onto the hill, while a Guardsman yelled from a bullhorn. "Students of Kent State, we have you surrounded."

A roar of laughter surged through the crowd since the Guard stood pinned between the fence and the students. From an open window in Dunbar, I could hear someone's HiFi playing the Guess Who's *American Woman,* and I looked toward where I had last seen Evan but he had melted into the crowd. Maybe it was better if he was angry at me. Maybe it was better if there was a bridge of no return. But that didn't stop the ache in the pit of my stomach.

Some of the Guardsmen down on the practice field huddled together like football players planning their next play. Then they broke apart and a bunch of them got down on one knee and lowered their rifles into firing position, aiming them up the hill toward Taylor and the parking lot where I was. The guy with the giant flag was still in front of them. I watched the barrels of their M-1's slowly fall until they were level with their shoulders and I began clicking snapshots quickly. My breath constricted and the noise of the crowd seemed to get further away. It felt as if their weapons were pointed right at me, as if the eyes behind the masks bore down on me. They stayed like that, their big black cicada eyes staring at us.

"They're just trying to scare everyone," a boy near me said.

"They don't carry bullets, do they?" a girl asked, and another boy answered "no" while the first boy said "just rubber ones."

Then the Guard rested their rifles to their shoulders and stood. They began coming back up Blanket Hill, slowly, in the inverted "v" shape of a flock of geese. Most of the kids on the hill were running ahead of them, out of their way, but a few were still taunting them and throwing stones or giving them the finger.

The kids near me seemed to relax as we watched the Guard advance up the hill. Someone behind me said "Watch out, they have us surrounded." I laughed a little, but then thought about how hot it had to be in those hideous masks and almost felt sorry for the Guardsmen. I looked around me. Everyone seemed to be wearing the same curiously amused face.

A chill crept through me, though, watching the Guardsmen lumber up Blanket Hill and head toward the far side of Taylor, their rifles clicking against their shoulders as they struggled up the rise. The day no longer felt like a carnival and I was ready for the whole thing to peter out and the Guard to leave campus for good. There weren't going to be any better photos than what I already had, and I just wanted Kent to go back to being Kent again. I couldn't see Evan, the crowd obscuring my last view of him, regret steamrolling through me. All I really wanted was the one thing that was impossible. All I really wanted was to tell him how much I loved him and have him love me back.

31

THE GUARDSMEN KEPT RETREATING up the hill. I took a picture of their backs.

It was over. I released the heavy breath pressing on me and tried to figure out what I should do. I could go to school, saying I was feeling better. But I wasn't as strong as Elinor. I had to find Evan first and make things right between us. Somehow.

I scanned the crowd and found him about twenty-five yards to my left staring at the Guardsmen as if he didn't dare turn his back to them, as intent as a cat near a birdfeeder. Some of the kids who had stopped to watch started moving again heading to class. Others were milling around chatting to each other. A cute boy with a buzz cut, the kind the ROTC students wore, stood near me and watched the retreat, a half smile on his face.

The Guard had almost reached the Pagoda at the top of the hill, their backs to all of us. In another moment they'd be over the hill and out of our sight, crossing the commons down toward their base by the ROTC building. A few kids were still taunting them, throwing rocks in their direction and gesturing, but most kids were too far away now. The demonstration was over.

As I started to turn toward Evan, the Guard suddenly stopped and wheeled around, all of them moving in the same way at the same time like choreographed dancers. They drew the barrels of their rifles down level from their shoulders, and one man in front stretched his arm out with a pistol in his hand. They were aiming toward the Prentice parking lot where I was standing, trying to scare the kids one last time, so I raised my camera to return their aim. As I worked to focus the lens, smoke exploded from one of the rifles followed immediately by a thunderous crack. And then another and another. Everyone started running and screaming as something warm hit against my right side.

Everyone around me exploded into action. Before I could look to see why my shirt was wet, a boy running toward me fell hard to the ground, his face a molten scream on his way down. People ran past me, shrieking. Glass from car windows shattered in sharp bursts around me. Bullets. Real bullets. So much noise. A razor of fear cut through me as turning and running flashed through my mind in feelings rather than words. Kids crouched behind cars, but I was still in the open, a bullseye with nowhere to go. Someone ran into me hard from my left, leveling into my shoulder, snapping my head toward the sky, buckling my knees and making me fall. My camera tumbled from my grasp. Arms wrapped around me, gripping me. I put my hands out to brace myself, thudding to the asphalt as the person who ran into me fell on top of me, covering me, smothering me. Above me rang the *pop pop pop* of the rifles over and over again. Glass shards pelted my hair. Hands came over my head, enveloping it, shoving it down against the ground as if they were trying to push my face into a hole that didn't exist, and I felt the missing fingers before I saw their emptiness stretching to shield me. Around us, kids were still screaming, running, tripping. The tang of bullets hitting metal cars in the parking lot echoed behind the crack of the bullets leaving their guns. I could see a strip of sky and grass and people whirling past, but Evan was blanketing me. We lay there, my arms pinned underneath me, Evan's legs tilted toward the shooters to cover mine. His warm breath blew across my cheek, making me know the pavement underneath the other side of my face was sun drenched and rough. And still the *pop pop popping* was raging through the air like it would never stop, as if it would shatter our bodies like glass.

Silence. Suddenly. Boring into my ears to the very core of my brain, making me think I would never hear anything again. So much silence it made me think of a conch shell, roaring and inexplicably taunting.

Then sound exploded all around us as sharply as the gunfire had, as though someone had turned on a blaring stereo. Wailing. Crying. Cursing. Desperate calls for help.

"Rachel? Rachel, are you okay? Rachel, are you hit?" Evan was rolling me over frantically searching for something. I stared at him, unable to form any words in my head, let alone send them to my mouth. Why was he calling me Rachel?

Evan yanked my shirt up to see my ribs, running his hand against my skin, his face filled with disbelief.

Rachel!" Evan said, fixing his gaze on me so I had no choice but to concentrate. "Rachel, you're not hit, right? It's not your blood? Answer me!"

"No, I'm not hit," I said. "I'm okay, I think." I didn't understand what he meant about the blood, but my shirt was covered in it.

Evan let out a breath and then looked up the hill to where the Guard had opened fire. I was up on my elbows now, but my legs felt too weak to stand. Scrapes from the pavement streaked my palms and my right knee burned from the impact with the ground. A small throb echoed through my shoulder. Evan was on his hands and knees over me, staring at the hill where the Guard had disappeared, making sure they weren't coming back. Then he looked around us, but I was still staring at him, framed by a blinding sky.

"Come on, people need help," he said, standing and putting his hand out to help me up. I rolled slightly to my side and stood, catching sight of the cute boy I'd seen right before the shooting began. He was lying on his stomach, his eyes staring vacantly. His jacket was soaked in blood. He'd been shot in the back as he tried to run away from the Guard.

I turned to tell Evan they had killed the boy and almost tripped over a girl lying just behind me but Evan pulled me back toward him. Her face was the gray color of a dolphin. Her eyes were glass. Her head lay in a swamp of blood, soaking the strands of her short dark hair where they touched the pavement of the parking lot. The blood spilled out from all around her, her neck a gaping mass of tissue and broken bone. The books she'd been carrying to class lay scattered around her like a halo, her purse still clung to her arm. A boy was leaning over her, desperately trying to get her to respond, begging her to answer him as Evan had begged me while others were running over to help. The wetness against my side was cold. 'It's not your blood?' rang in my head. I looked down at my shirt. The blood soaked and splattered on my clothes had come from her. So much blood. Evan moved in close to me. I held my shirt out to see it, my hands shaking. He put his right hand against my stomach, standing close so his voice fell into my ear, soft and straight.

"Don't think about it now. There are people who need us. We'll come back for her. We can't help her now." *Marines always come back for their dead, Bug.* Now I understood what Evan meant, standing there looking into this girl's unseeing eyes, why it was so important that you'd risk your own life for it. A minute before, she had been standing beside me and I hadn't even noticed her in the crowd. Now she was soaking into me and I was supposed to leave her behind.

But all around us people were calling for help, yelling and crying, and Evan pulled me forward. Further down the hill, three or four students were bent over a body lying on the ground, trying to stop the bleeding that was pouring from his back as they shouted for an ambulance over and over. A girl who was standing by watching them suddenly fell against someone beside her, fainting. Another girl was bent over the grass, heaving the contents of her stomach. A boy in a camouflage jacket was running through the crowd yelling "where are the ambulances? Why aren't the ambulances coming?"

Jagged teardrops of glass littered the parking lot, and the sinkholes of bullets dented cars. My gaze swept Prentice, some of its windows blown out, and I thought about the girls who had been hanging from those windows only a few minutes before. I turned toward Dunbar at the bottom of the hill, peppered with more bullet holes and broken windows. Even that far away, kids could be lying dead.

Evan took my hand and dragged me into the grass where several people were wounded. He let go of me, dropping to his knees beside a student who was bleeding from his abdomen.

"Can you help him?" asked a girl who was kneeling beside the boy, crying.

Evan pulled his t-shirt off and shoved it into the gushing wound, pushing down to try to stop the bleeding. The skin along Evan's left chest was stamped with scars, dominated by a long line across his ribs. More of the branding Vietnam had left on him.

"Corpsman! I need a corpsman!" he yelled, scanning the area around us. I looked helplessly at him, but he had already realized his mistake and a soft "damn" fell from his lips.

"Rach," he said, "lay your jacket over him. We can't let him go into shock."

I undid the knot in the sleeves of my blood splattered jacket and pulled it from my hips to lay over the boy.

"No, wait!" Evan said, grabbing the jacket from me with his bloody hand. "You press on the wound, you have two good hands you'll stop more blood."

I knelt beside Evan and looked at the t-shirt and then at him.

"Can you do this? He doesn't have time for you not to be sure."

I nodded, catching a breath and pressing my hands into the already wet t-shirt. I started to push, watching the boy's face, hoping I wasn't hurting him more. He was staring at me, his eyes begging for more help than I could give. Evan laid my jacket over him and bent down to whisper in my ear.

"Tell him he's going to be okay, Rach, and keep telling him. He'll believe you, he wants to believe you. Tell him. Tell him he'll be okay. No matter what, keep saying it."

I looked up at Evan, his eyes even deeper than the cerulean sky behind him, pushing me, sending me into the unknown with complete faith in me. I turned to the boy's dark eyes.

"You're going to be fine," I said with conviction I didn't feel. "The ambulances are coming any minute. Just hold on, okay?"

"They shot me," he whispered, as though he still couldn't believe it, his hand flopping trying to grab my arm.

"I know. But you're going to be fine. Just lie still. I hear sirens!" His blood was squishing between my fingers, sticky and hot and the smell of iron hung heavy. Some kids ran over to us, forming a protective circle around us with the girl who had been there first, as though they thought the Guard might come back to finish the job, as if they could stop the Guard if they did come. Through the gaps between their legs, I caught a glimpse of a white station wagon appearing from behind Taylor.

The kids around us started calling for help, their voices filling the air. I fought the tears pulsing from my eyes as I wiped my face against my shoulder. I couldn't look at the boy again. I was afraid he'd be dead with more fear than I'd ever felt in my whole life. "You'll be okay," I kept saying, as I watched two men run toward us with their litter.

"Jesus Christ!" one of them said as they reached us, the circle of kids opening like a book for them.

"Look out, Miss," the other said, pushing into me and pulling Evan's t-shirt off to check the wound. I stood and brushed the hair out of my eyes, blood dribbling down my arms and face. My hands were caked in the gumminess of the boy. I had lost Evan in the crowd, which spread and clustered in dizzying movement, the sun forcing me to squint. I swept my gaze back and forth, panic roiling up like vomit, finally seeing him further down the hill helping a girl who was crying hysterically.

"You'll be okay, kid," the man said to the boy, pulling bandages from a small black medical bag and throwing them on the wounds, pressing them as I had pressed the t-shirt. His words meant the boy was still alive and I looked down to find his face, forcing a smile as he kept his eyes fixed on me while they moved him onto the litter.

"You'll be okay," I said one last time as they lifted him and started running for the ambulance. I followed and winced as the door slammed shut, my legs trembling. The ambulance lurched forward and faded from sight, the red dome light on top swirling like a glass mug of blood being stirred. I turned and another ambulance was leaving. Two more were just arriving and by the lettering on their sides they were from Stow and Ravenna. Kent's one ambulance wasn't enough for today.

People were still on the terrace of Taylor Hall and had returned to hang out of the windows of Prentice, staring over the hill and the parking lot like it was a movie playing out before their eyes. Everyone seemed dazed, unsure of what to do next.

Cold rippled through me and my mouth swam in saliva. I swallowed hard to keep from getting sick. The crowd had become an elusive butterfly, shifting and changing before I could see its colors and I couldn't find Evan. I started walking aimlessly in search of him.

Some of the protesters had started to gather together, heading for the bell. Their fear was changing, growing, undergoing a metamorphosis. I felt it before I saw it. I couldn't identify it at first. It was like a change in wind direction, subtle and different.

But as I stood there getting my bearings it became stronger, clearer. It was anger. Pure, uncensored anger. Swelling like a wave looking for someplace to crash down. It rose inside of me, too, like an unfamiliar geyser burning from somewhere near the core of me. There was a power to it that was palpable, an electricity humming through all of us gathered there. I followed the growing crowd past another boy lying face down near his spilled blood, his arms helpless at his sides, his palms facing upwards. He'd been shot through the head, his skull broken apart like a walnut shell. Another student held an American flag upside down in protest, its tip soaked in the boy's rusting blood that had pooled in a giant puddle on the pavement. A living boy and a dead boy. The living boy waived his flag, crying and screaming, hoarsely calling the Guard "motherfucker killers" over and over and over. I walked past them to the back side of Taylor as kids gathered at the Victory Bell. The crowd was yelling about the Guard.

"Murderers!"

"Fascist Pigs!"

"Killers!"

Angry voices tolled the hillside in a sporadic, growing cadence.

Someone behind me slipped hands around my waist and I turned to look up at Evan.

"I was looking for you," I said, the words falling from me like a plane spiraling out of the sky.

He nodded. "I need to get you out of here." His voice was quiet and firm. "It's not safe."

"We can't let this happen," someone in the crowd yelled and immediately there was a swell of voices crying out for justice against the Guard, as unarmed boys began to shout about making the Guardsmen pay for what they had done.

We were suspended, caught at the top of the hill between the parking lot and the Victory Bell below us, Taylor Hall standing guard at our backs. Time had frozen somehow and all that mattered was the anger pulsing through the crowd as if we were one person, trapped in a wake of helplessness. Dr. Frank came running over and rushed down the hill. He looked out of place in his crisp dark suit and wire rimmed glasses. He crashed through the kids gathered on the hill, his face filled with panic.

"He's been talking to the Guard," Evan whispered and I followed the line he had traced with his eyes connecting Dr. Frank to where the Guard was gathered watching us. Professor Lewis and Professor Baron, both faculty marshals, were moving through the crowd from the same place trying to talk to kids as they followed.

Dr. Frank got most of the kids to sit down and he was standing before them begging them to understand that the Guard would attack us again if we didn't disperse immediately. His high pitched voice rose out over the commons, his words swelling with terror.

"I don't care whether you've never listened to anyone before in your lives! I am begging you right now, if you don't disperse right now, they're going to move in and there can only be a slaughter! Would you please listen to me?" His arms were out and he was gesturing and begging as he paced before the students who had grown quiet as they sat on the hill. His desperation reverberated through the word slaughter, sinking into us the knowledge that gestures and stones were no match for bullets.

"Jesus Christ! I don't want to be a part of this!" he screamed, and his anguish filled the farthest corners of the commons. Defeat moved through the crowd like a single note, vibrating forward and backward, pushing the sound out horizontally, an inescapable physical law.

The kids who had been sitting down rose and slowly began to walk away, some holding onto each other, some crying, some pulling reluctant friends along, some like lonely lost souls moving in a daze. Faculty marshals moved through the remaining crowd making sure they reached any nonbelievers, begging them to leave. Down by the ROTC building, the Guard was standing, ready.

"Come on," Evan said to me, his arm on my back to turn me toward the west side of Prentice Hall away from the Guard and the carnage. My gaze swept back toward the parking lot where a Guardsman was throwing tear gas at the body of the boy who'd been shot in the head and I swallowed the sickening wail rising inside of me.

"Rachel!"

My dad's voice came from behind me and I turned.

He was mad. Really mad. His face was red and he was out of breath from running from his office or wherever he'd been.

"What the hell—" he stopped, his face morphing as he realized the state of my clothes and hands and arms, even my face and hair. "My God, you've been shot?" He grabbed me, his eyes searching for the source of all the blood.

"No, I'm okay, Dad."

"You're covered in blood!"

"I was close to a girl," I said, the words trembling slowly.

"But you're not hurt?" His voice was incredulous, and I realized from what I could see of me that I looked like something out of a horror picture.

"She's not hurt, Art. It's not her blood," Evan said.

"For the love of Christ! Why are you here? Why aren't you in school?" My dad's concern vacillated with his anger.

"It's my fault, Art," Evan said.

My dad turned to Evan, his dark eyes intense, and it was the first time I had ever seen my dad really mad at Evan.

"What's she doing here?" he yelled. "What in Heaven's name were you thinking?"

"It's not Evan's fault!" I said grasping my dad's forearm to make him look at me. "I cut school to take pictures of the protest. Evan just happened to be here. He didn't even know I was coming!" I looked down at my shirt. "I'd be dead if it wasn't for Evan. He kept me from getting shot."

My dad's gaze searched him, but Evan was silent.

"Evan's the reason I'm alive."

My dad nodded slowly, unwilling to admit his error, pushing the strip of hair he combed over his bald spot roughly into place. He grabbed me and hugged me tightly before pushing me away, his eyes misty. "Get her off campus. They're threatening to open up again if we don't get the kids out of here right now. Those SOBs could start shooting again at any moment. You've got to take her home. I have to stay and get these kids out of here before this erupts again."

"I'll take care of her, Art. I promise."

"You'd better. And don't let her mother see her like that!"

Evan just nodded and put his hand on my elbow, pushing me toward Prentice as my dad turned and disappeared into the crowd. But I stopped after a few steps.

"My camera!"

"Leave it," Evan said. "It's probably in a million pieces."

"Please, we have to get it," I said. Evan had given it to me with his disability money. Abandoning it felt wrong. "And what about the girl? We have to go back for her." We were only yards from the parking lot, but the hill was shading us from a full view of it. I didn't want to pass the boy who had been shot in the head again, but I couldn't leave. Evan looked hesitantly toward the parking lot and let out a sharp breath.

"Wait here."

He ran back to the Prentice lot. I could only see parts of him as he reached the pavement, the hill and the curve of Taylor and cars blocking my view. He swerved suddenly to avoid one of the bodies, but I didn't know who or even how many there had been. Then he ducked and I couldn't see him, but when he came into view a few seconds later he was coming back.

He jogged toward me, my camera cradled in his good hand, the bloodied strap hanging down, swinging gently from side to side. He handed it to me.

It was dented and scratched all over. The lens was broken, with big chunks of glass missing and the rim was bent. The back cover was buckled. My film was lost. I started to cry.

"Not here, Rachel." He put his hand on my arm.

"What about the girl?"

"They're getting ready to take her. There's an ambulance for her. She's not alone."

Evan slipped his hand over mine and steered me down the hill. He looked back for the Guard but they were still down by the burnt out shell of the ROTC building. We walked past Prentice and onto Midway Drive. We began to pass people looking at us with curious, shocked stares as if we had risen from the apocalypse to a world that hadn't known it had come. They gaped at us, Evan shirtless, his hands stained a ruddy brown, and me, my hair matted from blood, my clothes and hands and arms covered in it, looking at the world with the flickering eyes of a rabbit. The blood, dry and cracking, stretched over the sides of my face where I had pushed my hair from it. Evan put his arm around my shoulder and stared back at the curious until they looked away. I clutched my camera and tried to keep in step with him, but his legs were so much longer than mine that I began to run out of breath. Police cars and army Jeeps raced past while behind us I heard people calling to one another, "what's happened?" and "There's been a shooting," and "Oh, my God!"

When we got to Theatre Drive, Evan pushed me to the right. "Let's go behind Music and Speech," he said. "They'll be less people, less Guard."

He slowed our pace for me as we neared East Main Street.

There was a small group of soldiers standing at the corner their weapons pointed at anyone and anything, including us, as we approached.

"Don't point your rifles at her," Evan said. "Can't you see we aren't armed?" He looked one of the younger ones in the eye. "This isn't your Nam."

The boy looked at him a moment and then lowered the muzzle of his rifle. My pulse surged, afraid of what the rest of them would do, their faces trapped between anger and fear. They must have heard the gunshots and Evan and I stood before them as bloody witnesses. Slowly they lowered their rifles one by one.

"What the hell happened?" one of them asked.

"Your buddies just shot a bunch of unarmed college kids," Evan replied, his voice as hard as the pavement where the dead lay. "And people call me a baby killer."

They looked uneasily at each other, but Evan just shook his head and pulled me into the street and we left behind the campus I had grown up on and could no longer recognize as mine.

32

I TOOK A DEEP BREATH when we reached the other side of East Main, but Evan kept pulling me toward home. An ambulance wailed past us, its siren a bow being raked across a violin. The whole town seemed to be punctuated with the sound of sirens and a helicopter buzzed over us coming from the direction of Walls. We cut through side streets and came up to Evan's house from the back through a neighbor's yard, hugging trees and garages so no one would see us. We reached the edge of his yard and he stopped. He dropped my hand.

"It's Monday. My mother will be at bridge. You'd better come to my house and get a shower. Rita will freak if she sees you like this. You can put something of my mom's on."

"It won't fit," I said. His mother was five inches taller than I was.

Evan measured me with his eyes like he'd never noticed how small I was before. He nodded. "Come on."

We slipped into his house and he paused, listening to make sure no one else was home. Then he led me up to his room.

I laid my camera on his dresser and stared at its broken, mangled corpse. I closed my eyes a moment to shut the image out, but the girl was in my mind waiting for me and I opened them quickly to see the reality surrounding me. Evan came in from the hall with a towel, his hands still damp from having been washed. He pulled a couple of t-shirts from his dresser, putting one on top of the towel.

"Go take a shower," he said. "I'll get you some clothes from your house. I'll try not to let your mom know yet." He pulled the other t-shirt over his head, and it cascaded over him like a waterfall.

I slipped my keys from my pocket. "Just in case."

He tucked them into his good hand. I caught a glimpse of myself in his mirror and a small sound of shock flew from my mouth. Evan laughed. "You look worse than I did when they blew my fingers away," he said. We stared at each other a minute. "Soap and everything's in there." He stopped at his desk and scribbled a note for my mom to tell her I was with him and safe.

I followed him to the door and watched him disappear along the hall and down the steps. The Olesson's bathroom was the original with a claw foot tub with a wrap around shower curtain. I took my shoes and socks off and stepped onto the cool white and black mosaic tile floor. I dropped my clothes in a pile, my skin tight under the sticky dryness of the blood covering me. Clumps of my hair fused together by blood fell against my face as I bent to turn on the faucet. I pushed them back and plunged my hand into the stream, waiting for it to get hot, careful to keep the red droplets of water falling over the tub.

The warm water cascaded over me, eroding the dried blood, making it give way to the living flesh beneath. I shuddered and pressed my lips tight against the flow, not wanting to taste it, making sure it was rinsed clean from me before I opened my mouth.

I poured shampoo on my head and lathered it into a sopping mass of suds. The water ran over me until there were no bubbles, until it had to be clean. I scrubbed every inch of my skin, rubbing my hand over and over my side where Evan thought I had been hit. The memory of his hand running over my ribs made my breath catch. The gray faced girl swam before my eyes. I grabbed at the edge of the tub feeling light headed and sat down. I was still sitting there, the water pouring over me, crying, when someone knocked softly at the door.

"Are you okay?" Evan asked, his voice rising through the steam.

"Yes." I turned off the water and grabbed the towel, drying myself, wringing my long hair with my hands, blotting it with the towel. I slid my underwear on. Except for my socks, it was the only piece of clothing that didn't have blood on it. I pulled Evan's t-shirt over my head, so soft and warm and blue like his eyes that I let the feel of it soak into me, and I didn't ever want to take it off.

Evan's shirt barely covered my underwear. He looked away when I opened the door, holding out a small pile of clothes awkwardly. "I hope this is okay," he said. "I just grabbed stuff before your mom could catch me. I heard her down in the basement banging the washing machine door or something. She must not know yet. I left her the note."

My hands were trembling. "Thanks," I said, ducking back into the bathroom. He had brought me everything I needed, a pair of jeans and a blouse he must have grabbed from my closet, with a bra tucked into it. He must have seen the blood soaked into my bra like it was a paper towel when he pulled my shirt up. I flushed, the heat burning slowly through my face as I put the jeans on. But I didn't take his shirt off. I just slipped my arms out of the sleeves and hooked my bra together backwards and then flipped it up and on. I ran my hands over the softness of the worn, safe cotton of his shirt before opening the door.

My clothes were still in a pile on the floor, but I didn't want to touch them. Evan had a paper bag and he walked past me. "You can wash them later, if you want," he said.

I shook my head. "Do you want me to toss it?" he asked. I nodded. He was kneeling, placing my clothes in the bag and I knew I had been wrong when I told Willa that what I loved most about him was the way he got life. What I loved most about him was his tenderness and his strength, all mixed together so that you didn't know where one started and the other left off.

He crumpled the top of the bag and took it downstairs. I carried my shoes and shirt to his room and combed my hair, rubbing it dry with the towel. I looked at it in the mirror to make sure I had gotten all of the blood out. It still seemed like there could be some, somewhere. Small speckles of blood were rusting on my canvas sneakers.

Evan came in and handed me a cup of tea, closing the door behind him. It was too hot and I pulled it away from my burnt lips.

"Sorry," he said. I shook my head but started crying again. Evan took the mug from me and put it on his dresser. He slipped his hand around mine and pulled me over to his bed.

I rested my head on his chest, tears and drool and damp hair soaking his t-shirt. He stroked my hair. I stopped crying then, sinking into him, my breath rolling slowly from small, shuddering gasps to a shallow kind of labor. A still numbness settled over me as I concentrated on the pulse of Evan's heartbeat against my ear. I tried to imagine us in the hammock.

"I thought they shot you," he said, almost in a whisper. There was something in his voice that reminded me of the night he told my dad about the Vietnamese woman who had almost been raped in front of him. It was fear.

"They would have," I said, and the gravity of that thought pressed against me until I had to resist it. "If you hadn't knocked me to the pavement. I think you gave me a concussion."

He rattled with a small laugh. "Well, you gave me a heart attack, standing there like an idiotic deer in the headlights, so I guess we're even." He was smiling. I couldn't see his face nestled as I was against him, the top of my head touching his chin, but I knew. He squeezed me to him.

"You did a great job with that kid," he said. "He was lucky, to have you there."

I thought about Evan, lying in the jungle, his fingers blown off, and wished someone had been there for him. "What if he doesn't live?"

"You did your best, Rach. That has to be enough." His lips brushed the top of my hairline and I pressed my eyes closed, shutting out everything but the feel of him against me.

We laid like that for a long time, Evan's heartbeat keeping my thoughts at bay, as shock turned to weariness. I sank down into the safety of him. I didn't want to think anymore. I didn't want to be anywhere but in this haze with Evan. His heartbeat and his breath filled my ears, and half formed visions played in my mind of the two of us sitting on the hood of the Mustang up at the Twins. Far away, I heard a doorbell and opened my eyes. Evan's room was draped in the hues of rich afternoon.

"Hey," he said, smiling down at me as he pushed me up a little. He brushed my hair off of my face. "We'd better get you home before my mother realizes you're here. I think she's been home for a little while."

I sat up. I was in Evan's room, in his t-shirt, on his bed, wrapped in his arms. But the Guard was there too, and the girl. The girl with the gray face.

"You okay?"

I nodded, but I had no idea, really. We stood up and Evan took my hand. He opened his door and listened. His mother was talking to someone downstairs in the living room. "Mrs. Cole," Evan said softly. She lived on the other side of his house. They were talking about the Guard and the shootings and how shocking everything was. In the background, the television droned. The news had broken. He went over to his desk and scribbled a note on a piece of paper with his right hand.

Next door, be home late.

"I'm getting better, don't you think?" he whispered tilting his head toward the paper, and I nodded and smiled even though it was barely legible. Evan pulled me into the hall and down the stairs, both of us creeping like fugitives. He hugged the wall, his mother's voice so clear and close I was sure she would see us. We slipped into the kitchen and he set the note on the counter and we hurried out the back door.

We crossed his yard into mine, but when we got to my kitchen door he stopped. "Oh oh," he whispered.

"What?"

"You've still got my shirt on."

I looked down and shook my head. My mom would understand, once she knew.

We stepped into the kitchen. My mom was at the sink but she dropped the dish she was washing and ran over to me, grasping me, hugging me, checking me over. I felt her trembling and looked away from the glistening of her eyes.

"I'm all right, mom, I promise."

"Are you sure? Your father sent Portia home with the news. The phones are all shut down. You can't call anywhere. But I didn't know why you weren't home yet. I mean, I knew you had to be safe because of Evan's note, but I just needed to see you for myself!"

Evan was holding my hand again. He squeezed it.

"Rachel, what happened? What on earth were you doing there?" my mom asked.

"I was taking pictures," I said. "I thought it would be an amazing chance to take photographs of something that mattered. I never thought they would shoot at us. I thought—" my voice choked. Evan slipped his hand around the back of my neck.

"Oh, Rachel, if you had been shot—" my mom said starting to cry and I hugged her.

Portia and Willa came running in from the living room.

"Bug, are you okay?" Portia asked. "Dad said you were at the commons today. I tried to go to his office after I heard what happened, but the Guard wouldn't let me in the building and that's when Dad got there and told me. Kids were streaming off campus faster than the last day of the term. It was so chaotic."

"Is dad okay?" I asked.

"Yeah, he's fine. It was all over by the time he found me. We heard the shots in my classroom, but we didn't know what had happened at first and my professor told us to stay there until we knew what was going on. Then a policeman came through the building saying there'd been a shooting and school was closed down."

She came over and stood beside my mom, her face surprised as she realized I had Evan's shirt on. It hadn't even occurred to my mom yet.

"Where are your clothes?" she asked.

"I threw my shirt away," I said, my voice carrying more of an edge than I intended.

"Rachel was standing close to a girl who was killed," Evan said. "Her shirt was splattered with blood. I actually thought she'd been hit when I first saw her." Portia's eyebrows rose as Evan said my name. I still couldn't believe I was hearing him say it.

My mom shuddered. "Are you sure you're okay?"

"Yes," I answered, "it was just really awful." My mom wrapped me in her arms, telling me over and over that it was all going to be okay, brushing away my tears. Evan went to the stove and put the tea kettle on, but not before he told Portia in a low voice "Back off. Your sister could have died today."

Evan brought the kettle over and Portia got cups and sugar and tea and spoons. We sat at the table, Evan pulling his chair up beside me, while he and I pieced together our stories to make one. It was mostly him talking, I had gone numb again, willing myself to forget the glass eyed boy, and the gray-faced girl, and the boy with the bloody hole in him that felt like quicksand to my hands, and the screaming and the uncontrollable anger, and the flag draped in blood, and the boy with half of his skull blown away. But Evan left out the part about saving me.

"But you could have been shot," my mother said.

"Evan protected me," I said.

Portia looked from me to Evan and back. She could see that something had changed between us. I was sure of it. As sure as I was that something had changed. Evan had never been this protective of me, he had never held me, or caressed me. Never even called me Rachel before. It had to mean that he loved me. Not just as his friend or the girl next door. He had to love me the way I loved him.

I wanted so much to convince myself, I was even willing to take Portia's look as confirmation.

"Evan saved me," I said.

33

"I DON'T UNDERSTAND," my mom said. The look on her face made me realize how much pain I would have put her through if I had been hit.

"He pushed me down and covered me," I told her. "He made sure they didn't shoot me. They were pointing their guns right at me." I pulled in a breath to steady myself. "Some of them might have been targeting protestors, but most of them were just shooting. No one was armed but them, they were shooting at us and no one in the crowd had a gun. They didn't care if they shot unarmed people. They just shot. I was standing in between two of the kids they killed, and both of them had just been standing there, watching, like I was."

Willa came over and sat on my lap, linking her thin arms around my neck, tears on her cheeks. I squeezed her tight.

"Oh, Evan," my mom's voice was hoarse, "how can we ever repay you?"

"It's not a big deal," he said, giving my mom a look that begged her to let it go. "I'm hungry," he said. "Rachel, are you hungry?"

I shook my head no but my mother was already up. "I have some wedding soup still in the freezer, luckily," she said. It was the same cure all to my mom as tea was to Evan's mother. Evan smiled at me. He loved my mom's wedding soup almost as much as he loved her pie and he had succeeded in changing the subject.

We ate soup and my mom made the rest of them grilled cheese sandwiches. It was all I could do to get enough of her elixir down to satisfy her. Everything had the iron taste of blood to me, as though it had seeped into my lips forever.

We watched the evening news. The shootings were the lead story but they treated it like the same campus unrest stories that had been rolling over our screens since last year. They made it sound like the kids had left the Guard with no choice.

"The local news this afternoon said two Guardsmen had been killed," my mom said, as Walter Cronkite moved on to the next story, about how President Nixon said he was really sorry about the dead students, but that tragedy is invited when dissent turns to violence. I wanted to hit him, to make him hurt the way we had been hurt today. I wanted him to have to stand there while the Guard mowed down his daughters, while their blood soaked into his skin.

Evan spit out a bitter laugh. "If any Guardsmen had been shot, it would've been by the other yahoos in their unit. They weren't ever in danger."

"Why would they shoot unarmed students?" Willa asked, as Dan Rather told us about more student protests at the University of Maryland and Stanford, and how the National Student Association was calling for a nationwide strike to protest the 'appalling use of force' against the students at Kent State. She put her hands under her thighs and rocked back and forth.

Evan was sitting on the sofa beside me and all I wanted was to climb back into his arms and have him hold me like before. But he didn't hold my hand or put his arm around me and I began to wonder if I had imagined how loving he had been with me. I closed my eyes and concentrated. "I thought they shot you," skipped in my mind like a record, his voice filled with fear. But we'd grown up together. We were friends. Really good friends. Maybe that's all it was for him after all.

"I don't know, Willa, my guess is that one or two of them had had enough and started shooting, and that made the rest follow," he said.

"But they're soldiers," she said. "They shouldn't shoot their own people. Why would they do that?"

"For the same reason those soldiers shot unarmed civilians in My Lai. Because they had the power and they were sick of things." Evan took a deep breath. "Willa, most of these guys are tired, scared kids. They just came off of that truckers' strike where they'd been shot at. They probably haven't slept much, and it was hot, and the kids were swearing at them and throwing tear gas canisters and rocks at them. It would've only taken one to snap. Maybe it was even one of the older guys who thought the students deserved it."

Evan stopped and stared at the floor. When he spoke, his voice broke the silence like a razor cutting through tissue paper. "One time when I was here and you guys had company, I remember someone asking your dad about the war and he talked about how there's a psycho in every unit. You know, a guy who gets off on the whole thing. Not just gung ho to do his job and protect his country, but really eager to hurt someone. And he was right. I saw it in Nam. Every unit I was in pretty much had a guy who was just plain scary. A guy who got high on the adrenalin. I guess the same is true for the Guard."

"People hate the students," I said. "They hate them for questioning the war, and civil rights, and what we're doing to the environment. Questions scare them. Even after they had killed people, they were ready to start again if we didn't leave."

"It only takes a little hate for some guys," Evan said. "Mix in some fear and power, and it doesn't much matter if it's My Lai or Kent or any other place on the planet. Innocent people become expendable."

We sat like zombies, watching whatever news we could get until my dad staggered in, the exhaustion visible on his face. "Like nothing I've seen since the Pacific," he said to my mom who got up to reheat the soup and make him a sandwich. She sent Willa to bed, despite her protests.

Evan stayed close to me as we listened to the latest news from campus. The school had been shut down, everyone told to get off campus, and the town was probably going to be under martial law by morning. My dad had only been allowed to stay because he was a faculty marshal and a WWII vet who knew how to talk to the Guard. He had gone around with the police making sure buildings were empty and locked, and then had gone back to his office to get as many of his papers as he could.

"Traffic out of town was crazy," he said. "Kids scrambling for rides. They couldn't even call home to tell their folks to come get them. A lot of them were trying to hitchhike."

"How long do you think it will be like this?" Portia asked.

"There's no telling," he said, flicking the flame on his lighter to life and pressing it to his cigarette. "I don't know if they'll let us finish the trimester. Hell, we may not be a school at all come the fall." He blew out a long puff of smoke and for the first time he seemed old to me. I noticed the yellowness of his fingernails from the tobacco, and the lines forming around his eyes.

"How will I graduate?" Portia asked.

"We're trying to work something out," my dad told her. "We talked amongst ourselves, to the extent we could, and some professors are already talking about holding classes in their homes if we have to, if we can't get back on campus. If it weren't midterms, we could probably just give everyone the grade they were carrying. It's too far away from the end of the trimester, though. But we'll work something out. Maybe some of the churches will let us hold classes there."

"It will all work out," my mom said.

"So," my dad said, slowly blowing out another long stream of smoke, "you want to explain to me why you almost got your head blown off today?" He leveled his gaze at me like a rifle, making me shrink back. Evan leaned in toward me.

"She had no idea, Art, none of us did. One minute it was this comical scene with a bunch of Beatle Baileys trying to restore order while kids made fun of them and the next it was freaking My Lai. If it's anyone's fault, it's mine. I felt something was off and I didn't get her out of there." The image of Evan looking at the Guard so intently just before they fired came to me.

"You were supposed to be in school," my dad said. He lifted his cigarette to his mouth and stared at me.

"I skipped school to go to the rally," I said, taking courage from Evan's nearness and his willingness to defend me. "I thought—" I hesitated a moment. None of it seemed to make any difference now. "I thought that if I could take some great photos of the rally, then you would see that I belong at Pratt and let me go. I thought that it was my last chance to convince you."

I finished barely above a whisper, staring at the old oriental carpet, resting my case and waiting for the judge to pronounce my sentence for skipping school for something that had been pointless all along.

From the kitchen, the big wall clock ticked with its usual determination. Evan put his hand on the back of my neck and I blinked back the tears swelling.

"Well, it's done," my dad said, stomping out his cigarette in the ashtray on the coffee table before lighting another. The smell of fresh tobacco floated into the air as he tapped the cigarette down before lighting it.

"It's done," I echoed in a raspy voice.

My mom started clearing my dad's plate, a pall settling over us so that you would have thought we had just buried a family member. We watched the late news, but four kids were still dead and at least a dozen more injured and the country was still divided.

"I'm beat," my dad said finally, standing up.

"I'm going to go to bed, too," Portia said. She had to be worrying about Case Western taking back their law school offer if she didn't graduate properly.

"I should go," Evan said, rising. I had to bite my lip to keep "no" from crying out of me.

"Night, Evan," my dad said as he reached the stairs. He bobbed his head, as if he had already said something, and then forced out a rough "Thanks."

"Night, Art," Evan said. Then he nodded toward the kitchen to tell me to walk him out.

"I'll lock up," I said and my mom smiled just a little and wished Evan good night, giving him a kiss on the cheek and another thank you for protecting me.

I followed Evan to the kitchen and he took my hand as we entered the room. Blood pulsed through my chest as his touch flooded me. He pulled the sliding glass door open and we stepped outside and he slid the door closed. The night was cool and still. The sky was clouded now, the searchlights of the helicopters making a strange shifting glow all around. The sound of their engines throbbed in between the crickets singing. Everything else, even the neighborhood dogs and cats, seemed hushed by the day's violence. The smell of helicopter fuel pressed the air like poisonous incense.

"Rach," Evan said, his voice low and soft. I couldn't look up at him, but turned and stood motionless, facing him. My name on his voice was as sweet and silky as caramel, and I enjoyed every drop of the sound as it slipped from his lips. He still had my right hand in his left, and I felt a tremble, not sure which of us it was.

"Rach," he said again, and for the first time I heard the edge in his voice. It made the sweetness evaporate and his tone told me what he wanted to say, what he was struggling to find a way to tell me. He had trembled, not me, but now it was my turn. I leapt, suddenly, recklessly, before I had time to let myself feel the pain that was coming, hoping to get through the worst of it before my heart caught up to my mouth and he knew how much he was hurting me.

"It's okay," I choked out. "I know you don't love me the way I love you. I know you would have done the same for Portia or Willa or any girl, really. I get that it doesn't mean anything else to you, that I'm only your friend. I don't expect anything, honestly—" and as the last words fell from my lips he slipped his right hand through the back of my hair, which fell between his fingers as he sealed them, resting his fist full against the nape of my neck, holding me gently and tightly. I tilted my face up to his. He dropped his head, his lips catching on mine. His left arm pulled me to him, pressing on the small of my back. He kissed me. The kind of kiss you give the girl you love, full of hunger and release. The kind of kiss I'd dreamed of, his tongue warm on mine, gentle and asking. The kind of kiss I had been aching to find in him and thought impossible a moment before. I didn't know if my heart was still beating or if my lungs were still pulling air, only that his lips were soft and his evening shadow was prickly and his hand in my hair was an anchor drawing me to sanctuary.

He pulled away a little, resting his forehead against mine, the tips of our noses colliding softly, his knees bent to reach me, and we stayed like that a moment and I needed the time to believe this was real.

"I didn't do anything heroic today," he said in a hoarse whisper. He slid his hand around my wrist and pulled me over to a lounge chair. I sat on his lap sideways, his arms wrapped around my hips. My face was almost level with his this way and it seemed a little strange not to be looking up at him.

"Yes, you did," I insisted, and I slipped my arms around his neck.

He shook his head. "If it had been some other girl, then yes," he said, "it would've been heroic, I guess. But not you. You I couldn't live without."

His voice was so quiet I could barely hear it. I pulled his words in thirstily, as if they could quench the ache for him that had lived inside me for so long.

"Covering you came from the same instinct that kept me alive all those months in Nam. It was self preservation. When I thought you were hit, Rachel, I've never been so scared in my life. Not even in Nam. Not even when I saw the blood all over me and wasn't sure where it had all come from." He paused a moment looking out over the yard, lit by a dim glow of far off helicopter search lights. "Nam taught me a lot of things, but mostly it taught me what I can and can't live without."

Tears dropped onto my cheeks, one and then the other and Evan pulled me into him, pressing my head against his neck, my eyelashes wetting his skin as we collided. My head ached from all the tears I had cried, but my heart was throbbing.

"That girl today—" he said, stopping as he stroked my hair, his voice tight.

"The one with the gray face."

"No," he said. "The other girl who died, she wasn't far away. I didn't know if you saw her."

I rocked my head just a little to say no.

"Well," he said, "she was laying there, blood spilling out from underneath her, and there was a guy there, her boyfriend, I'm sure. The couple we saw yesterday with the Guardsman with the flower in his M-1. Remember?"

I sat up and shook my head at him. "No, it couldn't have been her," I said as if I could change what he was telling me if I refused to believe him. "She just wanted peace. It couldn't have been her."

"It was her, Rachel. And he was cradling her and she was talking to him, and she was dying. I could tell from the look on her face. I'd seen it so many times in Nam. The same look Tom had. The same look they all had when there was just enough time for them to wonder if it were real. I knew she was dying, Rach, but he didn't. It was all over his face, this impossible belief that help was coming and somehow this wasn't real and he wasn't losing her."

His words were like a heartbeat inside me, proving we were alive while others lay dead, and it didn't make any sense.

"I didn't do anything heroic today," Evan whispered. "I just couldn't be him."

A small sob choked me. I pulled myself off, just a little, and looked at him, his beautiful eyes an oasis in the endless desert of sadness. I leaned in and kissed him, sinking my hands into the short bristles of his hair, moving them upward until it became luxuriant tufts between my fingers, knowing even with my eyes closed that I was wrapping myself in its tender amber color. Salt flavored our tear stained lips.

The noise of a helicopter began to move in and Evan jumped up aqnd pulled me back against the wall of the house faster than I had time to understand. A searchlight swept the yard, the beam of light hitting the spot where we'd been sitting a moment before like a shotgun blast. I pressed against him and he wrapped his arms around me. The helicopter moved away and the noise faded as quickly as it had risen.

"You'd better go in now," Evan said, but he held me just as tightly as he had the moment before.

"Evan, today, when you got angry with me—"

"It doesn't matter now," he interrupted.

"Yes it does. I wasn't afraid of ending up like you, that wasn't what I was going to say. I was afraid of being stuck in Kent without you. I've been dreading you leaving for school. Leaving me."

He laughed, surprise on his face, and wiped tears from my cheek.

"Will you be all right?"

"I'll try," I promised, knowing the gray-faced girl was waiting for me somewhere in the dark of my room.

He ran his fingers along my forearms as he brought his hands down to put them into mine. We stayed like that, neither of us pulling away, and then he kissed the top of my head and walked me to the door. He bent and pressed his face against the side of mine. "If you need me, you know where to find me."

I didn't look up at him. I would have started crying, helplessly and forever. I squeezed his hands and slipped inside, locking the door behind me.

I crept upstairs and brushed my teeth with a methodical intensity. I padded past the other bedrooms.

"Rachel, are you all right?" my mom called from the dark as I passed her open door.

"Yes, Mom."

I stepped into my room without turning the light on. Kicking off my shoes, I dropped my jeans and socks in a pile. I slipped my bra off from underneath Evan's t-shirt. I tried to smell him in the soft cotton of his shirt, but only lavender soap filled my nose. I looked around the dark room. The gray-faced girl was everywhere, staring at me with her hollow eyes, angry at my happiness.

I'm so sorry.

I climbed into bed and pulled the covers up to my chin, trying to concentrate on Evan. I laid there for a long time, the things he had said filling my mind. But my thoughts always circled around to the dead, and the Guard, and the girl with the flower who just wanted peace, and the boy in the ambulance, and the blood on the flag, and the gray-faced girl. The elation of Evan being mine was weighted down with pain and weariness like a sinking boat, and I let myself fall into to it, drifting into a half sleep on the opposing currents.

I woke sometime toward morning, suddenly. My heart was pounding faster than the volley of bullets on Blanket Hill and my skin was sweaty and cold. My dream had been about the Guard. Pointing their rifles at me, the glass eyes of their gas masks turning them into glinting, faceless monsters shimmering in the sunlight. But, this time I had seen Evan running toward me, so lifelike it was as if it had happened that way and I had been seized by terror that they would hit him as I woke.

I threw the covers off and jumped out of bed, rushing to the window. Evan was swinging softly in the hammock, wrapped in his military jacket. I wasn't sure if he could see me in the darkness. I slipped on my jeans and a bra and a different pair of sneakers than the blood speckled ones, grabbing a sweatshirt from my closet. The house was dark and quiet, the yard still.

"Hey," he said quietly.

He pulled me down from the cold night air, wrapping me inside his coat. He put his arm around me as I laid my head in the crook of his shoulder. The smell of his skin was soft and earthy and I snuggled deeper into him.

The next time I woke, the sun was cresting the treetops, helicopters landing down by Memorial Stadium. Evan opened his eyes when I raised my head to see if he was awake and we lay there quietly, watching the sun moving in toward us.

He pushed my hair back from my face as he rolled to look down at me.

I reached up and stroked the side of his face. The shadow of his beard glistened with golden highlights in the sunrise

"I feel so guilty," I said.

"I know. It's the hardest part to get used to."

"It's not ever going to go away, is it?"

"I don't know. I doubt it. But I think, maybe, if you live in a way that's true and right, maybe you become a living memorial to them. Maybe then you are a bit of light coming out of their darkness." He looked out over the yard, his face reflecting the weight of the struggle to appreciate the gift of being alive. "Or maybe that's just some nonsense Miss Dictionary says that sounds good and makes us feel better. I don't know."

I laughed. "Miss Dictionary is very wise."

He grinned. "She is. Much smarter than Raskolnikov. I'll bet you five bucks my mom's got her face pressed to the window right now, having a cow."

"I hope so," I said, picking my head up and kissing his cheek. I rolled from underneath him and jumped off the hammock and pulled him along behind me to my house and breakfast.

34

MY MOTHER WAS SITTING at the table with a mug of coffee cradled between her hands. She looked up at us with a startled expression.

"Rachel, when did you go outside?" she asked. "I checked on you at three and you were asleep."

"I woke up around five, I think," I said. "I had a nightmare, so I went out to the hammock with Evan and watched the sun come up. And why were you checking on me at three in the morning?"

"I couldn't sleep," she said. "I kept thinking it could have been you." I fell on my knees beside her chair. She hugged me and kissed the top of my head. "Let me make you some breakfast," she said. Evan sat in the chair she left and as I followed her with my eyes, I saw her look over at us. I smiled at her, just a little hint of a smile, an inside joke of confirmation, and she smiled back.

My mom made us pancakes. Portia and Willa came down not long after the smell of bacon frying began to fill the house. Willa pulled her chair in between Evan and me. The skin under her eyes was purple and raw as she turned to look at me and then him.

"Excuse you," Evan said, nudging her with his elbow, "that's my girlfriend you're squeezing out."

"Really?" Willa asked, her face lighting up in a smile.

"Really," I said and she clapped her hands together.

"Oh, thank God," Portia said. "I didn't think anything could make you two figure it out."

"Stop teasing your sister," my mom said from across the kitchen.

Evan chuckled and picked up the Plain Dealer, but I didn't want to see it. Portia dug into a different section. Both of the girls who were killed were in the honors college with her, so she knew them. She hadn't been close to either, but she'd been friendly with them. She picked up on every bit of news voraciously, as if knowing more would somehow make it better. I wished I knew less.

"Where's dad?" I asked.

"Upstairs on the phone," Portia answered from behind the paper, "trying to figure out where he can hold classes."

Someone knocked on the back door and I looked up to see Michelle standing there. I waved her in and she came over and hugged me.

"I was so worried about you," she said. "I've been calling, but your phone's been busy."

"My dad," I told her, "Trying to get the latest on what's going to happen with the remainder of the trimester."

"Are you okay?" she asked. My mom brought a plate over and set it down in front of her. "Thanks Mrs. M.," she said to my mom, who stroked Michelle's head before going back to flipping pancakes.

"I'm okay."

"What happened? You weren't there when it happened, were you?"

I took a deep breath. It was better to get it over with. Once I had told Michelle, I didn't plan on ever talking about it again. The girl with the gray face was pressing on me, hovering in my thoughts relentlessly and I needed to make it stop. It felt wrong to talk about her, as if telling someone what the Guard had done to her was violating her all over again. I gave Michelle the highlights, with random interjections from Willa and, occasionally, Evan.

"Wow," Michelle said when I had finished. She shook her head. "I shouldn't have let you go. I had no idea."

"None of us did," I said. I glanced at Evan, because he was the only one who had known something was really off, but even that couldn't change what had happened. It only kept me from getting killed. And even Evan had almost been too late. The gray-faced girl's bullet could have struck me instead. I felt sick and pushed my plate away.

Evan was watching me and he put his arm behind Willa and slipped his hand onto the back of my neck to steady me again.

"Are you sure you're okay?" Michelle repeated, moving her gaze from Evan to me.

I nodded, and then I smiled.

"She's perfect," Portia said. "The love birds have finally figured it out. Only took them eleven years and a near death experience."

Michelle giggled, but she didn't say anything to tease me, she only made a stupid face that I was glad Evan didn't see because his attention was back on the paper.

We sat quietly. I didn't want to talk about what had happened anymore, but every other subject seemed to have lost its meaning or shifted out of its orbit so it no longer was recognizable. Willa went to watch television and Portia to get a shower. The doorbell rang and I got up to answer it.

Two men in dark suits and crisp haircuts were standing there, flashing badges at me. "We're looking for Professor Art Morelli," the taller one said to me.

"He's upstairs," I said. "Won't you come in?"

They stepped into the hall. "I'll get him for you," I said, turning and walking up the steps.

My dad was in his study on the phone. "Dad," I hissed, "the FBI is downstairs. They want to talk to you."

He didn't seem that surprised. "Tell them I'll be down in a minute."

I nodded and went back downstairs. The men were standing where I had left them, but their gazes were traveling all over the house.

"He'll be right down,"

"Thank you, Miss," the younger one said.

"You're welcome," I said and we stood there awkwardly until my dad came lumbering down the stairs.

"Gentlemen, I am Art Morelli. How can I help you?"

"Agent Cummings," the older man said, shaking my dad's hand. "This is agent Howell. We'd like to talk to you if you have a few minutes."

My dad gestured to the living room and I turned and went back to the kitchen.

"Who's here?" Evan asked when I walked in.

"FBI," I whispered.

"What do they want?" my mom asked.

"I don't know," I said, sitting back down. "They just said they wanted to talk to dad."

"Probably trying to get information on students," Evan said.

We all fell quiet and my mom brought another round of pancakes over to the table.

"These pancakes are really good, Mrs. M.," Michelle said.

"Thank you, darling. Do you want some more?"

"No, thanks, I should be getting home. My dad was freaking out about me coming at all. He was afraid the Guard would be hassling anyone who went outdoors. We aren't supposed to go outside today, but I snuck over. I had to check on Rachel." She took her plate to the sink.

"Maybe I should walk you back to your house," Evan said.

"Thanks, but I'll be fine," Michelle said. "The Guard's mostly down on campus, and I cut through some yards. I'll just play dumb if they stop me."

"Thanks for checking on me," I said, slipping out of my chair and walking her to the door. "I'll call you later."

"You'd better," she said, her smile letting me know I wasn't off the hook for Evan details.

She gave me a hug before leaving. I sat down at the table. Evan was deep in the paper again, but he looked up at me after a moment or two.

"You okay?"

I couldn't slow the growing need to start drawing. It was a scream inside of me that had to come out. "I'm all right."

"I think I'll go home and get a shower and a shave," he said, "if you're sure."

"It's okay. I want to draw, anyway."

"Sounds good. I've got some things I want to take care of, too. I'll check on you later." He slipped his hand into mine as he stood up, his touch holding the kiss he didn't want to give me in front of my mom. I squeezed his hand before I let it go.

My dad walked in. "Well, it didn't take long for the Feds to show up."

"Were they looking for information on students?" Evan asked.

"They wanted to know which students were there whom I recognized." He gave me a hard stare.

"I didn't do anything wrong," I said. "Well, I mean other than cutting school. All I did was take some pictures." I was glad now that my camera was ruined. I didn't want the FBI using my film against the students. But then I thought maybe my pictures could have shown how unprovoked the attack was and I was sorry all over again.

My mom came over and put her arm around me, staring at my dad. "She had my permission to miss school, if they ask, to work on her art project."

I looked up, surprised.

"I'm not having her get in trouble over this, Art. She didn't do anything wrong," she said, her voice like cold metal.

"They're not interested in Rachel," my dad replied. "They wanted to know about the kids who died and were injured, and they had some names of SDS kids. They wanted to know who else I knew who might have been part of the demonstration and the fire the other night."

"What'd you tell them?" Evan asked.

My dad laughed. "Not much," he said, walking over to pour himself a cup of coffee.

"I'll be back later," Evan said.

"Yes, we know," my dad said.

Evan smiled and gave me a two finger salute as he closed the sliding glass door behind him. I cleared the table for my mom before heading upstairs. I took a quick shower and brushed my teeth, but I didn't even dry my hair, only brushing it out. My desk was a magnet pulling me with the full weight of its force field. I took a sheet of my favorite drawing paper, with just enough linen in it to create a subtle texture, and began to draw the gray-faced girl. I drew her as I first saw her, her head nearly severed from her, her eyes frozen, her hair laced in the thick dark pool that had once been the blood carrying oxygen through her. I worked slowly, pressing each detail I could still see in my mind onto the paper, away from me, outside of me.

I stopped to find a book on marine biology in my dad's study, searching out the picture I wanted. Following the lines with my eyes, I studied it and then went back to drawing. Everything else in the room fell from my sight, only the paper and the pencils warm in my hand and the memory bursting out of me was left. Hours were going by, but I kept pushing the image out of me, further and further. From the body of the gray-faced girl, a dolphin was rising as if it were jumping clear of a wave. I was doing my best to set both of us free.

A soft knock tapped on my open door. Willa wore her serious face. "Mom wants to know why you aren't coming down for dinner, and Evan's been waiting for you for over an hour."

"He has? Why didn't anyone call me?"

"We did," Willa said, shaking her head at me.

I let the pencil fall from my cramped hand. "I'll be right down," I said, grabbing my eye shadow.

"Evan's seen you without makeup before, just come down. He thinks you're beautiful. He told me."

"He did?"

"Yeah, he did. Just come down. He's worried about you."

I followed Willa downstairs. Evan pushed his chair back from the table and stood when he saw me. "You okay?"

I nodded, but my gaze was on my dad who was looking at us like we were birds who had accidentally flown into the house, creatures he could only recognize as he'd always known them when they were outside.

I slipped into the chair beside Evan with everyone staring at us. Evan looked around the table and smiled. "We're not going to turn purple or grow antlers."

Everyone laughed and the tension broke, suddenly, like an ice jam breaking apart.

"How's your drawing coming?" he asked me.

"It's coming," I said. My parents were both watching me, the wild bird they didn't want to startle.

We shuffled through dinner. My dad gave us an update on the progress the teachers had made. They had spent the day finding places to hold classes and calling their students to tell them. Some were letting kids who lived farther away finish by sending their assignments in by mail.

We congregated in front of the television afterward, my dad eager to hear the day's news. They interviewed people who weren't there, who knew nothing about what had happened, but who were sure they were authorities on the rally and how the students deserved to be shot and I turned my head as a woman told a reporter "they should have shot all of them."

"Turn it off," my mom said.

"You can't stop ignorance just by tuning it out," my dad said, rather gently for him.

"I don't care," my mom replied. "I won't have that kind of filthy, ignorant hate uttered in my house." She got up and went back to the kitchen.

"My friend Mary's dad said the same thing to her when she got home yesterday," Portia said. "She was crying when she told me. He didn't even care that his own daughter could have been one of the students killed."

"It's probably what John Davis' dad is saying, too." My voice was small and sounded far away. "'Tragedy is invited when dissent turns to violence,'" I added, quoting the president. I followed my mom to the kitchen.

She was sitting at the table, a cup of tea resting aimlessly before her.

"I don't know what hope there is for your generation," she said, "when there is such ignorance and intolerance and injustice in the world. And when it is perpetrated by our own government, and sanctioned by people like that woman. She is the masses." She shuddered. "I wanted so much more from the world for you girls."

I reached across the table and took her hand. I felt Evan behind me before I heard him.

"There is hope as long as people are willing to ask questions," I said. "And I don't think my generation is going to stop asking questions, even after yesterday."

Evan slid his hands onto my shoulders.

"I have a question," he said. "When's the last time you made chocolate chip cookies?"

My mom and I smiled. "I guess that's a hint," I said, getting up and going to the fridge to get some butter out.

"I was just wondering, that's all," Evan said, "but, I mean, I'll eat them, if you're making them anyway."

"I was just about to make them, anyway."

Willa came in a few minutes later and then Portia and they all sat around the table while the cookies baked. Evan called Robby because there was nowhere to go with martial law in effect and he snuck over, since you weren't even allowed on your porch after five o'clock. We moved like spinning tops between joy and sorrow, and, for me, guilt, as I tried to pretend for a while that the gray-faced girl wasn't in my room, asking me why she was dead and I wasn't. Now I knew what Evan meant when he'd told me he felt guilty for being alive when Tom Foley was dead.

A little after ten o'clock, Evan and Robby decided to go home. Robby and I had to go back to school the next day. I walked them to the door, Evan cradling my hand in what was left of his.

"Maybe you should stay home another day," he said.

"It's better to get it over with."

"I'll pick you up after school." He pulled me to him and kissed me.

"What about me?" Robby quipped.

"You can walk."

I squeezed Evan's hand before letting it go and closed the door behind them. I went upstairs and brushed my teeth and slipped Evan's t-shirt on for a nightgown and then I went straight to my desk. I studied what I had done so far, making sure it looked the way it should, picking up my pencils to make a few changes before I started drawing again.

"Rachel," my dad said, poking his head in the doorway. "I don't want you staying up too late."

"All right, Dad, I just want to work on this a little more." He walked on down the hall and I immersed myself in the lines that were speaking for me. The more the dolphin came to life, the more peaceful I felt. The ocean of the sky promised her something. Freedom or peace or happiness. I wasn't sure what, but it was something filled with release as she left behind the broken heaviness anchoring her human body to the pavement, her blood like glue. But the dolphin rose above it, sailed over it, and turned toward the clear blue.

It was almost two-thirty when I had the essence of it complete. There were still details to add and the surrounding shift to make between the land and the sea-sky, but you could see what it would be. I set my pencils down, turned off the light, and climbed into bed. I hoped the gray faced girl could feel it, somehow, and I hoped she'd be happy with it if she could.

35

I WOKE EARLY the next morning, but not in the panic of a nightmare. My mind was filling in the details of my drawing and my fingers came from their rest strong and eager.

The early dawn light was not yet enough to work by properly, but I was moving as much on instinct as I was by sight, the image coming from inside so that it scarcely needed my eyes to guide it onto the paper. The gray of morning blended softly with the colors I pressed onto the page, the pencils gliding over the surface as I linked earth and sky, water and asphalt, until they were a seamless story.

I jumped when my alarm went off at 6:45 and swiveled from my desk to shut it off. I set my pencil down and went to take a shower. As I slipped Evan's shirt off, I brushed it against my face, the old cotton as soft as his voice when he had said he loved me.

Portia was usually pounding on the door by the time I finished with the bathroom, but today there was silence, my sister suddenly without morning classes pressing on her. I peeked into her room as I walked back to mine. She was still sleeping soundly, so I closed her door to let her sleep. I combed and dried my hair, brushing it smooth. Then I put on my makeup and sat back down at my desk, rolling my pencils through my fingers, falling back into my drawing. I could hear Willa and my parents starting their day, but I wasn't hungry. I just wanted to finish and I was beginning to get close enough that I could see it.

"Rachel," my dad said, his voice breaking into the quiet of my room so that he startled me.

"Yes?"

"Are you going to go to school? It's time." He was looking at me tenderly, almost like he was afraid of what the answer might be.

"Yes," I said, "I was just working on something." I pushed my chair back from my desk and stood to stretch. He walked over and looked at my drawing, staring at it.

"You drew this yourself?"

I laughed, because it was what he used to say to me when I was little and would bring him drawings as presents. "Of course, who else would have drawn it?"

"I mean the design. It's yours?"

"Of course."

He slipped the paper into his hand and studied it for a long moment. I wanted him to like it. I wanted him to understand everything that had poured out of me onto that paper. I wanted him to think that Pratt would have been lucky to have me, even though he wasn't going to let me go. I wanted him to believe in me, because there was no line of separation between my art and the rest of me.

"I've been wrong," he said. "All this time. I've been wrong. I'm sorry."

I looked at him, my mouth dropping open. My dad never apologized. "About what?"

"Pratt," he said, as if I must be dense not to understand. "I was wrong about Pratt."

It took a moment for the words to sink in. "You're letting me go?"

"This is an incredible piece of art, Rachel."

"But our deal, I don't have any pictures. My film was ruined yesterday. I don't even have a senior project now."

"Oh, I think you do," he said. "But whether this is it or not, this shows me that you belong at the best art school you can get into. And if that's Pratt, then that's where you should go."

I leaned against my desk.

"Now, don't start crying," he said. "I guess I just never let myself see how good you are. You belong at Pratt. It can't be any less safe than here. We'll find a way to pay for it," he added, as if I had started to argue with him that we couldn't afford it.

I slipped my arms around him and he hugged me. He let me cry a minute and then he patted my back. "Come on now. If you're going to school, you'd better get going."

I pulled away and wiped my face with a tissue. "I love you, Dad."

"I know that," he said, turning away without looking at me. "I love you, too," he added, his back to me as he headed down the hall.

Michelle was waiting for me on the corner when I reached Crain. We walked to school together like we always did, but neither of us said anything about Monday and I wasn't ready to tell her about Pratt. It felt like if I told anyone, my dad might change his mind. In every class, kids talked about where they had been when they found out about the shootings since school had only told them there was an emergency on the KSU campus when they were dismissed early.

I sat quietly as kids debated endlessly about what they had heard or seen, some of them angry at the Guard, some of them angry at the students. There was so many times someone said something that wasn't true, but I couldn't bring myself to defend the truth. I wasn't ready to tell anyone I had been there. Maybe I never would be. Every class was painful and I sat there thinking about Evan and Pratt and wondering how happy I should be. When the final bell rang, I raced to my locker. I grabbed my things and ran out of school, weaving through the exiting crowd.

Evan was leaning against the Mustang, parked across the street. I dodged traffic, the smile on his face making me think he knew already.

"Can you believe it?" I asked, my breath coming hard.

"Believe what?"

"You don't know? He says I can go," I told him. "He says I can go!"

Evan's jaw dropped. "What made him change his mind?"

"My drawing."

He smiled and then laughed before he picked me up and swung me around. But when he put me down, I wasn't smiling. He pulled back and gave me a quizzical look.

"It's what you want, right? I mean, Pratt is all you've wanted for as long as I can remember," he said. "Why aren't you happy?"

"What about us?" I asked him. "I know you've been applying to schools, but you haven't told me anything. What about us?"

"Let's go to the lake," he said, walking me over to the passenger door and opening it.

Evan headed up Mantua, pulling my hand over to him and resting it on his jeans. "I haven't said anything because I didn't want to influence you," he said. "Especially after what happened. I wasn't sure if you'd still want to go away. Or if maybe you'd want to go away because of it. I don't want you to say yes or no to Pratt based on me. Your decision should only be about you. The rest of it we'll make work. So the question is, do you want to go to Pratt?"

He looked over, searching my eyes, and I turned that search in on myself. It was everything I had always wanted and now I could have it, if I still wanted it.

"Yes," I said after a moment. And then I smiled and even laughed a little. "Yes, I want to go to Pratt. More than anything else I've ever wanted. Except us."

"Good," he said, turning onto the gravel road that led to the lake. He parked the car and we sat there a moment, looking over the calming blue water as it reflected the trees like a painting. "Now that we've got that settled, I have something to show you." He pulled a folded piece of paper from his back pocket and handed it to me.

I opened it, letting my eyes skim over the words of a letter. An acceptance letter from Columbia University.

"Columbia's in New York," I said, making him laugh.

"Yes, I know. It's only about a half hour away from Pratt."

There were tears stinging my eyes.

"What, not ivy league enough for the sister of Portia?"

"I just don't want you to pick a school because of me any more than you wanted me to decide on Pratt because of you. I want you to be happy."

"I'll be happy," Evan said, leaning in to kiss me. "They have a very good music program."

He pulled back, taking my hand in his. "I've been thinking," he said, and then stopped in that way people do when they want to prepare you for something they are going to tell you.

"That's a good thing."

"Ah, Miss Dictionary's now a comedienne. I've been thinking of taking a duel major. One in music and one in political science. I could go to law school and become a civil rights lawyer. Or maybe even a human rights lawyer. What do you think?"

"I think you'd be an amazing human rights lawyer."

"I don't think they make very much money," he said. "You wouldn't mind?"

His words were warm going down, and sweeter than the hot chocolate at Brady's. "I won't mind."

"I guess you'll have to become famous before you die and make all the money for us," he said, his shoulders suddenly relaxing.

"I guess so." He leaned over and kissed me, soft and true so that it rang in the farthest reaches of my heart, filling up the crevices until I thought they would burst.

"Come on," he said, when he pulled away from me. "I have something I want to show you at home."

I bit my lip, refusing to ask what it was and he laughed just like he had the day we went to buy the Mustang. "We both know it's killing you not to ask," he said.

I snuggled down in my seat. Evan slowed when we got to the roadblock at Mantua and Crain, making my pulse surge, but Evan knew how to handle the Guard. Their faces eased as they looked at his short hair and the laid-back way he flashed his disabled military I.D. card at them.

"You live here?" one of them asked. He was in his late twenties with reddish brown eyebrows beneath his helmet.

Another Guardsman leaned into the window. "I remember you, you came by to pick up your girl from school earlier," he said. He turned his smile on me. "He said you were gorgeous." He slapped Evan on the sleeve in agreement.

I felt the flush run up my neck and face, but my eyes didn't leave his hands, wrapped around his M-1.

"Thanks," Evan said, and the two Guardsmen pulled back, waving him on.

Evan rolled his head toward me and smiled, but my heart was trembling, wondering how long the Guard would stay, prying at us, and if Kent would ever be Kent again.

Evan didn't say anything else until he turned the car into his driveway. "When I got hurt and called for you, I never thought we were really possible," he said. Before I could form any words to ask him what he meant, he had pulled the keys out and was closing the door behind him.

"I'm going to get my guitar," he said, opening my door. "Meet me on your porch."

I went into the house, dropping my backpack in the hall on my way to the kitchen. I got us a couple of Cokes and took them outside. Evan was just coming over. He settled down on a chair and took the guitar from its case, tuning it slowly until I recognized the melody he'd been playing the day we talked about the Beatles breaking up.

"Do you remember this?" he asked.

"You said it was a work in progress. Did you finish it?"

"I think so, yesterday, while you were drawing." His smile was missing its usual confidence. "You tell me," he said, as he started to hum and then sing.

Rachel I've been waiting so long
Just to start breathing
You look at me with honest eyes

And my heart starts believing
In things unseen
Unspoken dreams
Raining down on me
Cause, Rachel I've been waiting so long

Rachel, I was lost and spinning
Searching for a reason
Waking from those dreams they sold me
Empty and deceiving

Turned around
Caught upside down
Silence haunting me
'Cause, Rachel, I was lost and spinning

Rachel, all these shattered chords
Swirled inside my head
Losing sense, losing sound
Sinking down like lead
You caught the notes
You drew them in --
Constellations I could follow
'Cause, Rachel, I was lost and spinning

And Rachel I've been waiting so long
Just to start breathing
You look at me with honest eyes
And my heart starts believing
In things unseen
Unspoken dreams

Raining down on me

Rachel, how my heart is beating

The last note faded and he set the guitar down. "Well?"

I smiled at him. For the first time I understood why we had always been special to each other, because each of us spoke with our hands more than with words. "It's incredible."

"Miss Dictionary needs to expand her vocabulary," he said with a grin. He pulled me over to the hammock. We sat like we always did when we were little, crosswise, my right side falling against his left. But now he laced his lone finger through mine.

"I understand, now," I told him. "That day at the Hub. When you scared me. Now I understand. I feel like finding those Guardsmen and slamming them into a wall, beating their faces till they beg for mercy, and Nixon, too, for saying it was justified. I didn't know I was capable of so much anger. I'm sorry I didn't understand before."

"I wish you didn't."

"I wish I were like the protesters. I want to make a difference, but I'm just not cut out for demonstrating and tear gas and bayonets. Or bullets."

"You are demonstrating, in your own way."

"What do you mean?"

"That drawing. It's a statement of truth against the Guard and the news media and the people who don't understand. You're fighting back in your own way, and when people see your art and they realize its truth, that's a protest."

I bit my lip, but then I nodded as I brushed my cheek into his shoulder. Evan and I always saw the truth of ourselves best through the other one's eyes.

"What did you mean earlier when you said you called for me when you got hurt?"

I felt the pause in his breath as he stared at the sky.

"When guys get hit they cry out, sometimes. Most times," he said. "Nobody's like John Wayne when they get hit. The toughest guy will cry like a baby for his mother when he's bleeding to death. Some of them cry for their wives, but mostly they call for their mamas."

"But you called for me?"

He rattled with suppressed laughter. "Can you picture me calling for my mom?"

I smiled, but I wished he'd be serious.

He pulled his arm up and slipped it under my shoulders, bringing his hand back to rest on my head. "I guess I did. I only remember that, when they were putting me on the chopper, my buddy Spidey—we called him that after Spiderman because he didn't mind the spiders and leeches over there—he said to me 'who's Rachel? You were callin' for her. You been holdin' out on us all this time?' I can still see his face, hanging over me as the corpsman told him 'he needs to go,' and Spidey said 'yeah, yeah, he's goin' home on the A train, you gonna be okay, Strings.' That's how I knew it was bad. Then they shoved my litter into the chopper and that was the last I ever saw of him. And that was the last time anyone ever called me 'Strings.'"

Evan ran his finger and thumb through my hair as I listened to his breathing. "Why are you so quiet?" he asked.

"I don't know."

"Yes, you do."

"I guess it's just that, you called for me, and you called me Rachel and not Bug, and you don't even remember it."

"I can still call you Bug, can't I?" He tilted his head to look at me.

"You can still call me Bug. Sometimes."

He smiled and settled back down. "I don't even remember getting hit," he said. "I remember before that. We were walking through some heavy brush, and it was raining. Not hard, but steady. Sarge was complaining because they had us scheduled to be in the bush for three weeks straight and we were only a few days out. He said 'I bet it's gonna rain til the day we get back in. That's what it's gonna do. It's gonna rain til the day we get God damn back in.' And Lt. Weston said, 'it probably will, especially if you keep tellin' it to,' and I started laughing a little, cause the lieutenant, he always tried to make everybody happier no matter how miserable things were. I was ahead of him, on his left. I heard his voice from behind me. And the leaves were all shiny, dark green, and the wood was a dark, soaked color. And there were birds calling to each other, and I heard a snap like I had stepped on a twig. And then I don't remember anything else. I don't remember the explosion, just a flash, like the purest lightning you could ever imagine. And then, nothing, until I was at the LZ waiting for the dust off."

"Dust off?"

"That's what it's called when a chopper gets sent in for the wounded. I guess Riley and Spidey had carried me there. I don't remember. I just remember lying on the ground at the LZ, and the rain, and the sound of the chopper coming in, and this terrible, burning pain all up my arm and on my side. There was a hole below my ribs you could've put your fist through and I saw my fingers gone but I just couldn't process it. It was like I was watching someone else's blood pouring into a puddle in Vietnam."

Evan rocked the hammock like a talisman, a place where the world was far enough away that it couldn't hurt either of us.

"But when Spidey said that, when he asked me who you were, I started to realize. The other day, when I told you to tell that kid he'd be okay, I was jealous of him, lying there with you to comfort him. Stupid, huh?"

"No. No, it's not stupid."

"My fourth day in the hospital, the mail found me. They sent my stuff from our camp and there was a letter from you. I just held it, staring at it for a long time. Finally this nurse came over and asked me if I wanted her to open it for me. And I had to say yes, because I couldn't have opened it by myself without ripping it with my teeth. She asked me as she was tearing the envelope was it from my girl, and I lied and said yes."

"It wasn't a lie. I've always been your girl, even when you didn't know it."

Evan laughed. "When did you decide you were my girl?"

"Well, I'm not exactly sure," I said. "It may have been the day you moved in. Or it may have been a day a two later. I can't remember. I was six after all." I tilted my head and he rewarded me with his delicious smile.

"I didn't know how much I loved you until you were standing there, waiting to welcome me home and I didn't have anything left to offer you."

"You have everything I need."

"I tried to push you away. But you're so stinking loyal. Like a dog."

"Thanks."

"A really beautiful dog."

"Well, now I feel better."

Willa poked her head out of the back door. "Hey lovebirds, dinner's ready."

"Okay," Evan called. "We'll be right there."

We jumped off of the hammock and crossed into my yard. Evan took my hand and tugged me behind the old Willow tree halfway to the house. I laughed as he slipped his arms around me.

"You're the best thing that's ever happened to me," he whispered.

I pulled back and shook my head. "I'm stubborn."

He smiled and nodded. "I know."

"And I'm willful."

"I know."

"And I try to fix everything."

"Yes."

"Even things that can't be fixed."

"When you do that, I'll tell you to kiss my backside and then I'll scrape up your non-stick pans," he said, still smiling. He pulled me just a little closer, his hands pressed against the small of my back. My heart lifted, just a little more.

I searched his beautiful eyes. "But you won't stop loving me?"

"No," he said, shaking his head slightly, his face suddenly serious. "I won't ever stop loving you."

I slipped my arms around his neck, complete in knowing he was about to kiss me. "I can live with that."

The End

Acknowledgements

The idea of even having an acknowledgment to write fills me with gratitude for so many people that I'm a little overwhelmed by the task. I send very special thanks to George Valentic for generously sharing his Marine Corps experience in Vietnam and his reintegration home with me, and for taking me to visit Allison's grave. I had lived almost across the street from her tiny graveyard when I was in law school without ever knowing it was there.

Thank you to my Wednesday writers' group members who have given me unflagging love and support for so very long, especially our fearless leader, Patricia Harrison Easton. We have shared more than just words on pages in this arduous passion for writing, and I am so very grateful for your encouragement and support, even if you do spoil me with your biased critiques.

Heartfelt thank you love goes out to my peers and mentors at my quirky, amazing, totally surprising alma mater, Lesley University, especially Tony Abbott, Pat Lowery Collins, Chris Lynch, and Steven Cramer. Thank you to my friend and companion in dreams, Cynthia Platt, for reading the whole manuscript when it was still not ready for prime time. Thank you to the Inner Posse for giving me laughs and love and for sharing tears. Thank you to my classmates who read parts of this.

I am very grateful to the librarians and curators of the history of the Kent State shootings, both at Kent State University and at the Kent Historical Society. Without their tireless efforts, I couldn't have understood the world Rachel

More books from
Harvard Square Editions:

lived in so intimately. Thanks to Cara Armstrong for her insights on life in Kent in the 1970s.

Thank you to my mother, Rita T. Fedel, for being my unwavering champion, for believing in me when I didn't believe in myself, and for telling me to write. Thank you also to my dad, Art Fedel, who told me not to write for all the right reasons but who would have been proud of this book anyway. I didn't win my college argument with him, but I have my revenge in Rachel's win.

Thank you to my husband, Ed, for helping me with information related to the Marine Corps and weapons, and for always supporting my writing and my Masters (except when he whined about me being away for nine days at a time) even when I should have been getting a real job.

Special thanks goes out to my daughter, who makes every day a blessing and who always cares about my projects and wants to read them. And thanks to my boys who don't care much about my writing, but who would be mad if they weren't included in the acknowledgments (although they did come with me on one of my many long day trips to Kent and they lived through my nine day absences for my MFA even when it meant there was nothing to eat in the house but Subway or ham and eggs).

Thank you to Harvard Square Editions for believing in this story as I believe in it. And many thanks to those of you who have stayed around long enough to read these acknowledgements. I hope that you have loved reading Rachel and Evan's story as much as I have loved writing it.